AS WRITTEN

IMAGINE THE POSSIBILITIES OF A LIFE LIVED...

LISA COLODNY

Copyright

As Written is a work of fiction. All names, characters, locations, and incidents are the products of the author's imagination or are used fictitiously. Any resemblance to actual events, locales, or persons, living or dead, is entirely coincidental.

AS WRITTEN: A NOVEL
Copyright © 2022 by Lisa Colodny

All rights reserved.

Editing by Pure Grammar Editorial Services
- www.puregrammar.com
Formatting & Cover Design by KP Designs
- www.kpdesignshop.com
Published by Kingston Publishing Company
- www.kingstonpublishing.com

The uploading, scanning, and distribution of this book in any form or by any means—including but not limited to electronic, mechanical, photocopying, recording, or otherwise—without the permission of the copyright holder is illegal and punishable by law. Please purchase only authorized editions of this work, and do not participate in or encourage electronic piracy of copyrighted materials. Your support of the author's rights is appreciated.

Table of Contents

Copyright..3
Table of Contents..5
Dedication..7
Chapter One 9
Chapter Two 21
Chapter Three 28
Chapter Four 37
Chapter Five 49
Chapter Six 62
Chapter Seven 69
Chapter Eight 80
Chapter Nine 91
Chapter Ten...105
Chapter Eleven..120
Chapter Twelve...134
Chapter Thirteen...148
Chapter Fourteen..160
Chapter Fifteen 174
Chapter Sixteen...190
Chapter Seventeen..201
Chapter Eighteen 211
Chapter Nineteen..225
Chapter Twenty 237
Chapter Twenty-One 255
Chapter Twenty-Two...261
In Loving Memory..265

Lisa Colodny

Acknowledgements	266
Extras	267
About the Author	273
Also by the Author	274
About the Publisher	275

As Written

Dedication

To Ray & Blanche Phillips (Pap & Ma)

So much love - so little time.

Chapter One

February 1968 – Taylor County, KY
Saturday Morning

The ground was soft under the sole of his worn boots, and he felt himself sink under the weight before contacting the remnants of rain and ice from last night's storm. His feet danced in quick, successive steps as if moving of their own volition and he slid a foot or so along the slippery path. He fought against gravity's force to stay on his feet before righting himself and continuing on his journey.

Winter was unpredictable within the Bluegrass state. He remembered many white Christmases of his youth and just as many that came and went without even a flake of snow. More often than not, Christmas had been wet, not white. This year was no exception and the worn path towards the barn was saturated like the riverbed just over the ridge.

It was probably an exaggeration, he thought. True, the path was soaked but not as sloppy as the mud that framed the riverbank of the Green River where it zagged through the woods behind his family's house. He wiggled his foot inside his work boots and smiled as if the cold, thick mud might somehow penetrate the old leather and seep in between his toes. It reminded him of being young and playing at the river with his siblings and cousins. It was a different time, devoid of adult responsibilities and stressors. He missed the simplicity of that life.

Alton made his way closer towards the old barn, pausing only long enough to steal a glance behind him and make sure he had latched the kitchen door after leaving the house. Up ahead, the old barn was easily visible with its long, weathered boards that cried out for several coats of paint. There were cracks between the planks. Others were nailed together with spacious gaps, leaving enough space between them so that the outline of a worn, old tractor was visible. It sat idle as if waiting out the winter in anticipation of spring plowing and planting.

The house behind him was small, too small it seemed when he was a boy growing up within its walls. There were times when it felt as if his only time alone was the time he spent in the outhouse. And even then, there were frequent interruptions by someone in desperate need who could not wait their turn outside any longer. He smiled at the recollection and looked quickly at the small wooden structure behind the house. Not much had changed in his parent's station of life. Although, the houses he and his brothers and sister presently called home enjoyed indoor plumbing, the outhouse was still a constant at his parent's home.

Truth be told, they did not seem to mind. No doubt, they had made the accommodation early in their life and accepted it as it was. It was a trait that he admired. Yet, it annoyed him at the same time. When he was able, he would see to it that the house was renovated with a bathroom and a big front porch for his momma. She spoke often of having a big porch with a chair or two where she and Daddy could watch the wind blow and listen to the songs of the red birds and blue jays. And aluminum siding for the exterior of the house, maybe white with black shutters like the big, fancy houses that lined the road towards Lebanon. All those houses had big porches; one day he hoped to give that to his momma. She deserved no less.

The wind kicked up, transforming the chill into an icy breeze that left his eyes watery and his nose drippy. He turned and checked the house again, to make sure the screen door was not flapping against the wind. It would be best if the cold morning air remained outside. Perhaps then the firewood stacked inside by the stove might last throughout the weekend. He and his brother, Wilbur, had spent several hours last week at Daddy's chopping wood. One entire wall of the barn was occupied by firewood. Alton hoped it might be enough to last his parents through the winter. Although Daddy was in good health, he should not be outside in the winter weather cutting firewood; not with three grown sons a stone's throw away.

Besides, the noise of the door slapping against the house would surely wake up its inhabitants. No doubt, everyone would welcome the rest. Most of the family had been up well into the early hours of the new day. There had been much to discuss as one chapter of Alton's life was closing and another was set to begin. His family was anxious to hear the details. Momma and Daddy sat, perched on the edge of the worn, wooden kitchen chairs, holding onto his every word as though they might be his last. Deep in the corner of his mind, in a place seldom mentioned, he wondered if they were thinking the same thing. What factor might fate play in his life moving forward? Would they be gathered here together next year or the year after that?

The sun yawned before peeking out from behind the clouds as if to ensure someone was finally up and about for the day. The coffee in his cup had cooled already. Its thin, ceramic bowl was little match for the briskness of the morning air. He watched as the last of its heat rose like magic and disappeared into the air. Drinking it was little more than an exercise to still his thoughts. It was tasteless, unsatisfying, as it traveled over his lips and mixed with the stomach acid that bubbled up as if in protest.

His mind raced to keep up the pace with his eyes as his gaze fluttered across the field and fixated once again, upon the structure of the old barn. His body warmed from the inside out with the thought of the many afternoons he sought comfort from the storms or hid from his brothers and sister as they sought him out. Could he retreat inside once again and find some sanctuary, even if briefly? Could he hide and wait for fate to seek him out and deliver him to his destiny? Probably not, he reconciled his thoughts. He was comforted by the contradiction of his beating heart against the stillness in his chest.

The weather was warmer for February, but it was still cold. Most of the snow had melted away, leaving the pathway to the barn wet and squishy so that the ground was so saturated it squeaked in protest at the intrusion. There was but a little breeze in the air carrying with it remnants of snow flurries that melted as soon as they engaged the ground. He loved the snow, always had. It was hard to believe he and his family had celebrated Christmas only a month ago, oblivious to the change that was about to happen upon their lives. Would they have celebrated any differently if they had known what the next chapter had to offer them? Speculating was not productive. He believed this with every fiber of his being. Yet, there was no harm in wondering.

He pushed his hands deeper into his pockets and made a fist, partly for the warmth but mostly in response to still his thoughts. His head was spinning, and he needed the counterweight to stay on his feet. His attention was drawn to the wind as it danced and twisted through the naked branches of the trees as if they were desperate to make an escape. It was a feeling he could relate to especially after the draft notification had arrived in the old, worn mailbox that sometimes swayed with the traffic as the vehicles passed by.

His daddy's hands shook as he dropped the letter into Alton's palm and stepped away as if the growing distance between them might make the news more palatable. It was a formal, cold-looking envelope and was noticeably missing a signature of receipt. No doubt the mailman, Travis', intentions were good. Perhaps, if the draft notification was missing a signature, the inevitable might be delayed and someone else might be deployed to war in Alton's place? That had been weeks earlier, it felt like a lifetime ago and he had accepted the path his life was about to take as a part of God's plan for him. Hence, the return to his childhood house, a place he had called home for the first eighteen years of his life.

"I thought I saw you walk out," her words behind his back were warm and comforting. She was close enough that he could hear the rise and fall of her chest as her breaths rushed in and out of her lungs, smell the residual fragrance of shampoo that clung to her hair, and practically taste the coffee that spilled over her fingers as she juggled the mug from one hand to another before coming to rest beside him.

He knew she was behind him before he heard her speak. It was a comfort he lacked the words to comprehend, but like the sanctuary of the barn, he accepted it. They were the same, him and her. "It's too cold for that old worn robe," he did not bother to look over at her. There was no need to. He knew she was wearing it; she always did. "You should have put on a coat or something." He turned briefly to look back to the house she had emerged from, but it was little more than an interruption. He knew her husband was still asleep, in a bed with a handmade maple headboard and buried beneath several old, handmade quilts that had been passed down from her grandmother. And the children were no doubt sound asleep in the upstairs bedrooms waiting for the wood stove to be ignited and the room enveloped by the sweet scent of cherry as the heat radiated throughout the house.

"I was in a hurry to catch you before you went back inside or someone else came out." Her words were understated as if she had asked for him to pass the butter or open the door for her. She moved closer to him as if he, like the old wood stove, might redistribute some heat from his body to hers.

"I'm in no rush," he sighed, his attention drawn to the pond that took up a fair amount of space behind the barn. Last month it had frozen over, but not enough so that it was safe to skate upon. Her son, Allen, had begged to go skating before Alton's borrowed 53 Chevy had come to a stop near his daddy's house. Louisville was only a few hours away, and with his momma's failing health, the trip home was one he made often. "You remember that time Garnet fell through and damn near froze before Delmore could pull him out?"

"I was young, you were barely out of diapers," his sister pointed out. "I doubt you recollect it. More than likely, you remember hearing one of us telling the story."

"No," he shook his head in a juvenile manner to emphasize his point. "I remember it on my own." Alton shrugged himself off the wooden fence and took several steps to the barn's entrance before yanking the door open. It groaned and protested as if it were securing the opening of a fancy bank vault in a big city and stopped short of the pocked wall whose boards did not quite meet from end to end. As a result, slivers of the dark branches of trees from beside the barn were visible between the slants and the wind funneled through with renewed force.

He motioned for her to enter first and pulled the door closed behind them, watching as she made her way towards the back of the barn to the last stall. Delmore and Wilbur had torn the wall between the last two stalls away so that it was bigger than all the others. Additionally, the stall had been stripped of everything to accommodate the mangled, twisted body of an automobile, its charred and broken bones hardly recognizable as such.

Their forward motion ceased simultaneously while they stood silently as if in prayer and stared upon the remnant of their eldest brother's car. The interior had been burned away so that only the metal frames of the car seats remained. What had been the dashboard was reduced to burned metal fragments held together by rusty filaments and brackets. The spine of the car was bent around portions of the radiator and motor. Only one wheel was distinguishable, the others were little more than melted blankets of rubber that clung to the rims like gloves.

"Why do you think they keep it?" Alton's question hung in the air between them before he added, "It must be hard to look upon it every day." He moved closer, near enough to lay hands upon the cold, hard frame of the car's roof, but did not make contact. Instead, his hand hovered a few inches away as if he feared the engagement might burn his skin even though he knew there was no danger. The fire that consumed the car, ceased to burn over ten years earlier, his brother's headstone in the family cemetery marked the moment it was extinguished.

"Momma hasn't been in here in years." Sis poured the leftover coffee to the ground. "And Daddy steers clear of this stall." She sighed a long breath as if the act of exhaling were painful and she sought an alternative method of breathing. "Delmore and Wilbur used to talk about rebuilding it."

"Garnet died in this car," his eyes were sad. "Neither of them would ever want to drive it. Most they could hope for is to sell it." He paused, his blue eyes fluttering back and forth as if he were having a seizure. "Daddy would never let that happen."

"Neither Delmore nor Wilbur would actually be able to sell it. It's not in their nature."

"What about you, Sis?" his eyes sought out hers. "Would you hold onto it? Sometimes I think we should have had it towed to the junk yard for scrap." His sister was an enigma at times, he knew this to be true. She was the only girl, and given his momma's failing health, she often met his and his brother's maternal needs when circumstances prevented his momma from assuming her responsibilities. Sometimes, she was wise beyond her years—more out of necessity than a desire to be so.

"I think they feel as if they've held onto a piece of him. Maybe there's a hair or fragment of his boot, something attached to the car. I think having it here makes them feel closer to him."

"Anything in the car burned up during the fire," the rational part of his brain argued, although his heart sometimes argued the opposing perspective.

"I know this, and they do too, but we're talking about their child. When you have kids, you'll understand better. It isn't natural for parents to outlive their children." She paused, her words deep, yet faint. "Momma and Daddy have already buried three of their children. The burden, no doubt weighs heavy on their hearts. And yes," her eyes held onto his. "I would hold onto it if it belonged to someone I loved and lost."

"I barely remember him, you know. Every day its harder for me to recall anything about him. For a while, I could hear his laughter in my head, but I haven't heard it for a long time."

"You were what, eight years old when he died?" She patted his hand, "little more than a baby, yourself."

He cringed, his body drooping as if his chest had been pierced and his body deflated like a balloon. "Don't start with that baby stuff again," he warned. "I'm an adult now, drafted to serve in a war beginning next week."

"You'll always be the baby, Alton." She pulled him into her arms and held on as if she were drowning and he was the buoy keeping her head above the water. "Promise me you'll come back to us safe and sound."

"You're being silly, Sis," he answered across her shoulder. His eyes closed voluntarily as if the moment was too painful to look upon. Even though he could not see her face, he knew she was crying, knew her face was disfigured with wrinkles of concern and worry.

"Promise me," she said again, her request more demanding and her embrace more secure. Next to his daddy, his sister was the strongest person he had ever known. As they stood there, arms wrapped around one another, she seemed almost fragile. It was a sensation he had never felt before when he thought of his sister. He hoped the feeling would never come again. He did not like it at all.

"I promise," he whispered, and prayed silently it was a pledge he could keep.

****

A Day Earlier

Momma's kitchen was by far the biggest room in the small house that claimed a portion of land on Elkhorn Hill. Although not a rare occasion, seating was a challenge when the entire family gathered for holiday meals, especially now that Delmore and Phyllis' family was growing. With the new baby, they were a family of five now. Even though Sis and her family lived next door, the four of them were frequently present for family gatherings. Once Wilbur and Alton were seated at the table, it was literally elbow to elbow with no unused spaces at the table. The table, like the rest of the house, was full, standing room only at times. Yet, any inconvenience was outweighed by the indescribable comfort of being a part of something so big and knowing the love ran deep. They were bound, one to the other, like the waves of the river and layered rings of the old trees that inhabited the woods around it. It was written in the stars that littered the night sky and the sun's rays that kissed the individual blades of grass until they grew one over the other and blanketed the hills for as far as the eye could see.

Growing up, Garnet, Delmore, and Wilbur had shared the two tiny bedrooms upstairs, while Marguerite, the only girl, laid claim to the second bedroom downstairs. Alton's crib found a home in the corner of his parent's bedroom until he outgrew the crib. Then, as a toddler, he roamed from room to room, depending on his mood, cohabitating upstairs with one of his brothers or downstairs with Sis.

It was not until Garnet's death that Alton was afforded the opportunity to sleep unabated in a half bed, alone. However, most times Garnet's bed under the window in the corner remained made and unused as Alton slid into bed next to Delmore or Wilbur. Sleep came easier for him with the sounds of his brothers snoring, echoing across the room like white noise. Luckily, as an adult, his room at Delmore's house was close enough to Wilbur's bedroom so that sleep still came easily.

"Baby?" his momma's frail voice from the family room was a wake-up call that he had been daydreaming, remembering a time long ago when his brothers and sister lived within the confines of his parent's house. The scuffing sound his momma's house slippers made against the linoleum floor alerted him that she had vacated her place on the ragged, brown sofa and was headed towards the kitchen.

"What is it, Momma?" he yanked his head from the space inside the refrigerator and waited for her to appear on the other side of the icebox. He was not a fan of the nickname given to him as a child. He was a grown man, heading off to fight a war. He was no one's "baby" any longer. Nonetheless, he bit his tongue and waited for her to stop at his side. "Are you hungry?" He could predict her response; she was seldom hungry. She ate so little, less than a bird might need to keep itself a flight. She was thin and frail, little more than skin stretched across her frame. Yet, as she finger-combed her hair behind her ears so that it lay straight against her neck and kissed the tip of her shoulders, he had never thought her more beautiful.

"No," she toyed with the small clear buttons that lined the front of her flowery, faded frock. "You want to take that jam cake out of the freezer?" She coughed into the palm of her hand and indicated to where a large pot was cooking on the stove. "Ray put on a pot of beans before he left for work." She paused to catch her breath, the sheer effort of getting from the couch to the kitchen had tired her out. "I'm going to try and put some cornbread on and fry up some chicken for dinner."

"I wouldn't go to much trouble, Momma," he pushed the refrigerator door closed. "Delmore and Phyllis won't get here till late. More than likely, they will have fed the kids before making the trip." He paused and bent at the waist so that he could look out the kitchen window to his sister's house across the field. "Sis and the kids will probably come down after dinner and wait for Delmore."

He stretched across the counter and grabbed the nearly full loaf of bread. "Wilbur, Daddy, and I can make do with bread with the beans." He took her thin arm and led her into a chair at the table. "Unless you feel up to eating some chicken?" His eyes lit up, his face hopeful that she might feel like eating something more substantial than bread and beans.

"No," she shook her head for effect and ran her skinny hand through her hair, pushing it back behind her ears, again. "I may eat a cupful of beans and a few bites of bread." She indicated to the refrigerator. "You want to pull that jam cake out and let it thaw? The children might like that with some milk for a snack tonight."

He smiled, hoping to hide his skepticism from her. Every Christmas, his momma made a jam cake and a fruit cake for each family and presented it as a gift along with the presents opened Christmas morning. Most days, she was barely able to stay on her feet for long periods of time and the effort it took for her to make the cakes was pretty much what she allotted for the entire week, or month even. As such, it was not unusual that one or both cakes tended to be a tad overdone. It was not that much of an issue with the fruit cake, but the jam cake was another matter altogether. As evident by its name, one of its main ingredients was jam and she had a tendency to burn the cakes while she napped or rested in between tasks. For days, the house would reek of burnt, coagulated sugar and jam, further exaggerated by the fact there was no ventilation in the house and the cold weather did not permit the windows be opened to better ventilate and exhaust the odors. The occupants had little choice but to wait for the unpleasant smell to work its way outside of the house on its own.

Additionally, the cakes were seldom edible. More than likely, Delmore and Sis had simply discarded theirs once they had returned to their respective homes and were away from Momma's eyes. Alton and his daddy pretended to devour the cake, emptying the thick slices into the pig trough at every opportunity. It was no secret, hogs would eat anything, including burnt jam and fruit cake. More than likely, the one in the freezer was Wilbur's. No doubt, he had jumped at the opportunity to see it placed safely in cold storage.

"Did I burn them again?" she asked, her words childish, jovial even. She waited, reading his eyes and body language. No doubt, she knew the answer prior to asking the question. Still, she waited, waiting for his response.

"No, Momma," he knelt and kissed the soft skin of her cheek, comforted by the residual scent of Luden's cherry cough drops that saturated her skin. "The cakes were perfect like always. I'm just thinking the kids might prefer a bite or two of chocolate, instead." He patted his back pocket where he carried his wallet. "I'll run up the hill to Minor's market and get a cake or something for them."

"You're gonna need your money," abruptly, she pushed her body to her feet and drug herself back towards the couch where her purse sat on the floor nearby. "I've got a few dollars."

"It's okay, Momma," he followed behind her, fearful she might tumble over in her haste to get to her purse. "I was able to cash out when I left work last week. And the guys at Ford Motor Company took up a collection for me." His smile took up his whole face as if he had told a joke. "Cigarette money for the trip."

"Baby," she pulled him as close against her as she could. "You take care of yourself and promise me you won't do nothing stupid." She swallowed to fight back the tears that collected in her eyes. "I don't care if you're brave or not. I want you to come home to me."

"I will, Momma. God has a plan for us all." He guided her to the couch and knelt on his knees in front of her, holding both her tiny hands in his. "You taught me that. My chapter's already been written. I just have to see it through."

Lisa Colodny

"You try and get a safe job, Baby. Let someone else fight that battle. It doesn't have to be you." She struggled to get the words out, her lips getting in the way as they tumbled from her mouth.

"I'll do whatever I have to do to serve my country and come back safely." He pulled her gently into his arms. "I plan to do both. I'll make you proud."

"I've always been proud of you," she held his gaze and his hands. "I always will be."

"I love you, Momma." With his thumb, he wiped her tears away and pushed himself to his feet. Somewhere deep inside he wanted to pull her into his arms and apologize for making her sad, tell her it was all a mistake, and he was not going to fight a war. Instead, he would return to Louisville, plead for his old job back, and reclaim the small bedroom upstairs at Delmore's house.

Left to right: Phyllis, Delmore (Robin between them), Daddy (Allen in front of him), Momma (Gail in front of her), Wilbur, Alton, Sis, and Kenneth.

Chapter Two

Alton had built a good life since graduating high school. Initially, he and his cousin, Bobby, had found work at the Phillip Morris plant in Indiana while Delmore finagled jobs for him and Wilbur at Ford Motor company in Louisville. Although the money at Phillip Morris was good, working at Ford was something he really wanted to do. He loved cars, all types of vehicles. For as long as he could recall, his brothers and cousins had immersed themselves in building and fixing up old cars. It was in their blood; he could see a life built around Ford Motor Company with a wife someday and children. His compensation at Ford was well above minimum wage. With his recent raise, he was making two dollars and forty cents an hour when he left. It was good money and living with Delmore afforded both he and Wilbur an opportunity to put some funds aside in anticipation of chasing their own dreams. He only prayed the job at Ford would wait for him after he finished his tour of service. God's plan for him had not changed, not really. It had simply taken an unexpected turn. Once he returned home, he would pick up right where he left off. He believed what he had told his momma, his chapter was already written. He simply needed to shuffle the pages and set the bookmark to where he had left off.

****

It was well into the night by the before the coffee cups and dessert plates were washed and put away. As expected, most arrived too late for dinner, but Delmore enjoyed a bowl of his momma's beans and a slab of bread to sop up the broth. He and Phyllis had pulled into the driveway and headed straight up the stairs to put the children down for the night. Phyllis carted Curtis, the baby, in her arms, a blonde-haired eighteen-month-old little boy with her mother-in-law's crystal blue eyes. Delmore carried Robin tucked upon his shoulder and navigated the narrow steps with crossed fingers that the child remained asleep in his arms.

At five years old, she was fair-haired like her brother, but her eyes were hazel, replicas of her father's. She was three days younger than Sis' son, Allen. No doubt, the two of them would be great friends as they grew older. In his mind's eye, he could see them running and playing in the fields behind the house and dropping from the grapevines that hung from the big trees into the Green River. Delmore's oldest daughter, Misty, at the ripe age of eight walked through the kitchen on her own accord but only barely. It was obvious, she had been asleep for the biggest portion of the drive from Louisville. She rubbed her eyes with one hand and clung tightly to a stuffed bear in the other as she followed her father to the awaiting bed upstairs.

Delmore reappeared minutes later sans Phyllis or the children and made a beeline for the pot on the stove. Even without removing the lid, he knew there was a ham bone mixed within the beans. It was his favorite. And the hearty aroma that saturated the bottom floor of the house was a mixture of dinner and cherry firewood that burned in the wood stove. "Sis, coming down?" he asked pausing long enough to scoop another spoonful in his mouth.

"She went to put Allen down for the night," Alton smiled. "He wanted to wait up for Robin, but it was obvious he wasn't gonna make it. He's been crying and cranky for the better part of an hour."

"Had an issue at work," Delmore explained. "We got a later start than I planned." He dropped the empty bowl in the sink and took several steps into the living room to address his parents. "You feelin' alright Momma?"

He offered his hand to his daddy. "Did you get the new road toward Lebanon done?"

"Working on it," his daddy answered as he hooked his thumbs into the stirrups of his Duck Head overalls and leaned as far against the couch as he could. "This new grater ain't like my old one and it's taking me a while to get adjusted to it." He paused as if he needed to collect his thoughts. "If I'd been on my old grater, I'd be finished by now, but you know how the government is. What they do and say don't always make a lot of sense." He looked out the window as if there was a distraction. "Wilbur behind you?"

Delmore shook his head. "I'm sure he's on his way. He had to make a stop first." Delmore traded a knowing glance with Alton. "He helped me move Misty and Robin into the upstairs room Alton just vacated before we headed out this way."

Alton fought to conceal a laugh. Delmore and Phyllis had successfully set up Wilbur and her cousin, Jewel, on a date several months ago. The couple had been nearly inseparable since the introduction. No doubt, Wilbur had stopped by her house in town prior to making the trip home to Elkhorn Hill.

"Make sure the kids know I'm gonna be wanting my room back when I come home." Alton offered, hoping to change the subject. Alton was fond of Phyllis. There was no doubt he would grow to love Jewel, too, as soon as he got the opportunity.

As if on que, the tires of Wilbur's vehicle spit and spun against the gravel of the driveway before making its appearance at the back of the house and jerking to a stop. He came through the door as if he were on a mission and stopped short at the entrance. "Hand me the flashlight. I need to visit the outhouse." He waited as Alton yanked a metal flashlight from a small shelf near the doorway and followed his brother out the door as if there were a fire and he had the water.

"Where's the chamber pots?" Delmore moved from his momma's side towards the stairs. "I'll need to put one upstairs for the kids. They won't go outside in the cold."

"I put three upstairs already," his daddy offered, "cleaned and ready for the young'uns."

"Thanks, Daddy." Delmore pulled an open pack of Marlboro cigarettes from his pocket and disappeared through the doorway his brothers had previously exited through. "I'll be right back."

The old man watched as the door closed behind his son and knew it would be a while before any of them returned inside. Just as well, he thought. Alton was scheduled to report on Sunday to Fort Campbell for basic training. It would be many months before they would all be together again. The weekend was all they would have for a while. They should make the most of it.

****

It was standing room only in the small family room and as such, most of the kitchen chairs had been pulled from the kitchen and lined side by side in the area. Phyllis finally made an appearance downstairs once the children were asleep and tucked in the beds for the night. She and Delmore sat as close to his parents as the old couch would allow. Nearby, Sis moved the kitchen chair away from the exhaust of the wood stove so that catching her breath was less intrusive. Wilbur and Alton occupied the other two chairs, pushing themselves as close against the wall as they could so that the walkway to the kitchen was accessible.

"Seems like living with Delmore and Phyllis has been a growing experience for you both?" Daddy said to Wilbur and Alton, offering the statement in between bouts of laughter that echoed throughout the house.

"If Phyllis just didn't wax those damned steps," Wilbur pointed out, laughing so hard, his eyes closed against his cheeks. He went on without giving Alton an opportunity to respond. "Those old wood steps are slick enough in stocking feet." Wilbur looked quickly to Alton for a consensus. "After she waxes them to the wood's grain, it's worse than walking on ice."

The room swathed in laughter in response. Everyone, including Phyllis, nodded in agreement. She sipped delicately from a ceramic coffee cup with pink flowers. "I'm not going to apologize for keeping the house clean. Besides, every time you fall you blame it on the kids and their toys." She paused and took another drink, "even if there aren't any toys stacked on the stairs."

"Sometimes, there are," Alton laughed, looking to Delmore for support.

Delmore laughed, his eyes squinting against his cheeks. "You're on your own, brother."

"If you aren't careful, Robin's going to grow up to hate you," Phyllis laughed, her accusations only half said in gest. "The way you tease her with those cookies," Phyllis shook her head and waited for Alton to respond.

"Don't I give her an entire bag?" Alton explained, looking awkwardly past Delmore and Phyllis to his Momma. Her look of confusion was not lost on him, and he wanted an opportunity to clarify.

Before he could explain, Phyllis added, "There's a cookie warehouse on the other side of the railroad tracks in Louisville. Alton buys an entire bag of broken cookies for a nickel and sits outside on the front step of the house with a quart of milk and eats the cookies in front of her."

"You know how shy she is," he laughed, "she won't ask for a cookie. She sits on the step and cries."

"He goes on and on about how great the cookies are and makes her cry." Phyllis waved her hand at him. "She'll remember when she's older."

"I'll make it up to her, I promise," Alton laughed, his amusement echoed through the first floor. "Allen and Gail will set her straight." He folded his arms as if he were posing for a picture. "They love me."

"I hate to break up the party, but I think I'm calling it a night," Momma explained as she steadied herself on her feet and headed towards the bedroom using the furniture and walls for support. "Are we doing anything special tomorrow?" She stopped at the threshold to the bedroom and waited for a response. Alton knew posing the question had taken her last reserve of energy. She was empty as she awaited a response, any response would do. Sunday was his last day at home. He would be away from his home and the people who loved him for a long time. There was much unknown about his journey ahead and the people in his life who would assume the role of caring for him. Her question was a valid one. What were they going to do tomorrow and the day after?

"No Momma," Wilbur explained. "I think we are all hanging close by the house." He looked across the room to Phyllis. "Jewel may come by for dinner with the kids."

"Willard Lee and Winfrey are coming over to say goodbye before I head out on Sunday." Alton rubbed his chin, feeling pleased his cousins were able to visit before he deployed. "Maybe Buck, too." His friend was in the same boat, drafted like Alton. But unlike Alton, Buck was without a scheduled date to report. "Is everyone going with me to Fort Campbell?" It was a question that had been on the tip of his tongue all night. Although, a portion of his heart wanted the entire family to trek along and say goodbye at the steps of basic training camp. A more rational part realized it would make the event harder, especially for his momma.

"No," Daddy said before anyone else could respond. "We'll say our goodbyes here on Sunday when Delmore and Wilbur head home to Louisville." His eyes were teary as he went on. "There's no point in dragging it out and making it harder than it already is. Wilbur and Delmore can escort you to Fort Campbell."

Daddy swallowed, his lips quivering in response to the silence that followed. "Once you get a schedule and know when you get a leave, your momma and I will make the trip to see you as many times as we can." Daddy joined Momma at the door and waited to see if there were any inquiries. "Night everyone, remember to say a prayer tonight before bed. Ask the Lord to watch over our baby as he embarks on this new chapter in his life and to find comfort within the pages God has already written."

"Night, Daddy," the boys and Sis said in unison. "Night, Momma."

The door behind them seem to close in slow motion and Alton half expected to see one or both of his parents race back through the door before it closed and offer an option to the one Daddy had presented. Alton knew his daddy was right, there was no need for the entire Phillips clan to convoy to Fort Campbell. It would be a waste of time and money. And Momma was not able to make the trip, he did not want her to sit at home alone while everyone else accompanied him to his destination. Yes, he nodded to no one in particular. Daddy was right. It would be less painful for everyone if only Wilbur and Delmore made the trip with him. Basic training would pass quickly, and he would be on to the next chapter. The only way to get finished was to get started. Like heaven and hell, one could not exist without the other. The thought was both comforting and terrifying at the same time.

Delmore, Wilbur, and Alton in the backyard of Momma and Daddy's house.

Chapter Three

For as warm as yesterday had been, the complete opposite could be said of the weather on Saturday. Sis had not loitered at the barn for long. Once she had Alton's promise he would return home safely, she had made a beeline back to the house and her own family. Alton knew she was fighting to hold back her tears as she made her retreat. And he knew by the way her body sagged as she approached the back door of her own home, that she had not been successful. No doubt, once inside, the uncertainty of their time together sank in, and her body wept from the worry of it all.

****

Alton shivered and wrapped his arms across his chest as if the act might ward off the cold. But he knew it was little more than an exercise. The rush of cold uncertainty that enveloped his body had little to do with the inclement weather. In any event, Daddy had the old wood stove in the barn working double time to keep the immediate area where Alton and his cousins were gathered warm and toasty for the impromptu farewell party. Willard Lee was the oldest of the well-wishers. He was tall and thin with short dark hair that he combed to one side of his head. His brother, Winfrey, was not as tall or as lean and his hair was a shade lighter and curlier if it were ever given an opportunity to grow out. One common factor for both brothers was their eyes. They had the most incredible, piercing, ice blue eyes, of anyone else in the extended family.

Buck and Alton had been best friends since middle school. One seldom ventured far from the other, all throughout high school and beyond. Even the last year of living with Delmore and Phyllis in Louisville had affected their relationship only minimally. One would frequently make the trip to the other.

"Turn that up!" Willard Lee waved to where Alton sat in an old red 41 Ford truck with the windows rolled down and the driver-side door ajar. "I love this song." He jumped to his feet and offered up a toast with a glass bottle of coca cola and stomped his feet in rhythm to The Monkees, I'm a Believer.

"It ain't Hank or Elvis, brother," Winfrey added as he pulled his Levis as high on his waist as he could and popped the top off another bottle, "but it will do." He closed the distance to the truck in a few steps and offered the bottle to Alton as if it were a trophy. "You know, Cousin," he smiled and his eyes lit up as if he had flipped a bulb on somewhere in his mind. "We could load up and make a run for Canada, all of us." He patted Alton's shoulder. "Uncle Sam's already got his claws in you and Buck. No doubt, Willard Lee and me is on a list somewhere, too."

"How'd we get to Canada?" Buck, who had been sitting on the periphery of the discussion edged closer to the red truck. "We ain't got enough money to get out of Kentucky." Buck was shorter than the other young men with sandy blonde hair and a close-shaved beard and mustache that made his face look smaller than it probably was. It could also have been the thick, dark glasses that sat perched upon his nose. Buck was a quiet, thoughtful, young man with a heart of gold. The kind of friend, Alton often thought, that would strip the shirt off his own back and hand it over if the need arose.

"That don't sound right," Winfrey added. "If we sold everything we owned, we might have enough," Alton laughed, "but it ain't like Canada is going to just open the door for us. Don't we need a passport or something?"

"Not to get into Canada," Willard explained, "just a birth certificate or driver's license." He paused, "lots of city people who don't support the war run away there for sanctuary."

"They'll have to wait till the war is over and see if they can come back home." Buck explained, moving his fingers anxiously against his hands. "Some get locked up once they return home. Don't seem like either of those choices is a good one." He finished off his soda and dropped the empty glass bottle in the wooden crate Daddy kept near the front door of the barn. "I'd miss my family too much to even consider something like that."

"I couldn't run away if I knew there was a chance I wouldn't see my momma or daddy again." Alton's words were sobering as the barn grew quiet with only Bobby Goldsboro's song, Honey, echoing on the old truck radio. "Besides what kind of men would we be if we ran away." He shook his head. "No sir, my daddy didn't raise me to run and hide when things get scary. He expects me to face my fears and stand my ground."

He swallowed the last drop of soda from the glass bottle, holding its thick bottom to the sky as if he were posing for a picture. "Whatever fate God has planned for me has already been written. Ain't nothing I can do to affect it."

"What do you want to do tonight?" Buck asked, his eyes wide as his stare followed Alton's body moving into the threshold of the big barn door. Alton stood silently looking across the frozen landscape of the yard until his gaze perched upon his parent's house. He folded his arms as if he were frozen, stuck in time and place, not a muscle moved as he took it all in.

There was a stillness in the day as the cool breeze blew frigid air through the branches of the big maple trees and framed the back of the house. The tiny porch looked smaller than it was with the wood and kindling overflowing from the firebox and onto the floor. Daddy's chair was there too. Pushed as flush against the wall as it could go as if aware it would not be occupied until the green buds of spring infested the tree branches. It made him sad to consider he would not be home for the rebirth of spring or summer. He would be lucky if he made it home next year for Thanksgiving or Christmas.

Although he much appreciated that Uncle Sam had given the reprieve of ignorance during the holidays last month, deep inside the confines of his heart he wished he had known. How much sweeter might his momma's jam cake tasted, had he known? Might he had made a point to be home earlier on Christmas eve, before the kids were put down for the night? The children were always so excited, unable to contain their enthusiasm through dinner, especially the older ones, Gail and Misty. True, the younger ones were not as engaged. Allen and Robin were barely five and at the age where Santa pictures at the five and dime store were not an option. Santa was a still a scary stranger to them. The thought of him sneaking around the house during the night as everyone else slept was not an appealing experience. Still, now Alton wished he had been a part of their evening. If he had known he would be away from them for the next two or more years, he would have made sure he was home with them then.

"What are you doing?" Willard joined him at the door and followed Alton's eyes to the old house. "Someone here?"

"No," Alton shook his head. "I wish I'd brought Daddy's camera up here. There's only a little bit of snow on the ground but I think it makes a pretty picture."

"Boy," Winfrey joined his brother at the barn entrance and pushed at Alton's arm. "Ain't nothing there but your old house and we've seen in hundreds of times." Winfrey did not try to hide his confusion.

"But I'm seeing it in a different light now. It's my home and when I leave here tonight, I'm not sure how it might look when I see it again." He paused and looked away as if looking at the house was painful. "Or if I will?"

"You will," Buck jumped to his feet as if he had springs on his shoes. "You can't think any differently." He shook Alton's arms so that his entire body shook and moved in tandem. "You're coming home, and I don't want to ever hear you say any different." Buck wiped tears that flowed down his cheeks. "You hear me?"

"Yes," Alton swallowed, not meeting Buck's eyes. They had known each other all their lives. Yet, Alton could only recall a time or two he had seen Buck angry or brought to tears. It was painful to consider he was his friend's source of pain. Alton regretted letting the words escape from his lips.

"Let's go to the movies?" Willard Lee bent to the ground to snatch an old, deflated football from the dirt floor of the barn and tossed it to Buck as if he had pressed rewind on a cassette player and wanted to revise the play list and redo the last moments.

"Tickets done gone up to a dollar and a half," Alton explained shaking his head. "I won't get paid much until I get finished with basic training. I've got to watch my money."

"It's on me," Winfrey offered, his hands shaking as if he were in the midst of a seizure.

"And I'll pick up the tab for dinner at the Dairy Queen," Willard Lee patted his back pocket where his wallet made an outline like a grave against the pocket of his denim jeans. "Couple of chili dogs, fries, and peanut butter bar?" His words were like a song, "Will be a while before you get another chance."

"I think I'll just spend my last evening at home with my family." Alton's words were prayer-like as if he were in church and recited the prayer alongside the preacher.

"We could cruise up and down main street for a while?" Buck offered, moving as close alongside of Alton as he could without making bodily contact. "Might run into that Joann girl from school."

"Gas is thirty cents a gallon, better hold onto your cash, boys," Alton smiled shyly. "And she was just a friend. I barely knew her."

"You really want to spend the evening here with your family?" Winfrey asked.

"Yeah, Delmore and Wilbur are heading back to Louisville tomorrow. I guess, we'll drop off Phyllis and the kids at home and then, head to Fort Campbell. Sis won't be going with us. Tonight's the last night to spend with Momma, Daddy, Sis and the kids," he smiled. "And Daddy wants me to ride with him to the garage and see the new grater he's driving."

"Saw him on it heading towards the new road towards Knifely," Buck offered before tossing the flattened ball behind a stack of rotting lumber. "Sure is bigger than his older one." His laughter echoed throughout the barn. "Lot of machine for any man."

"Uncle Ray can handle it," Willard Lee announced as if he were on a stage. "You should see him mow down those trees on highway eighty-eight towards Greensburg. It looked like a bomb exploded. Tree trunks were everywhere."

"I'll get him to ride by there on the way back and let me see the new road," Alton promised before reaching through the window and flipping the radio off. He slammed the door closed, not paying much attention to the cloud of dust that jumped from the floor and covered the truck deck like a storm. There was little need for any action. Most likely, the truck would sit idle until his return, no one would be bothered by the dust. Once he returned home, he would make a point to make sure it received a good cleaning. It would be a single task left undone on purpose, his beacon in the darkness of the night. His daddy's old red truck would be imprinted on his heart until he was able to find his way safely home.

"What about Delmore's old 53 Chevy you've been driving since high school?" Winfrey asked as his eyes traveled the short distance to the driveway where a black car sat idle as if waiting for its driver. The morning sun reflected off its back metal bumper to such extent, Winfrey used his hand to block the sun's ray and took his time to appreciate the car. Its smooth exterior and sleek design was extraordinary. There was not an imperfection anywhere on the car's body. Delmore and Wilbur had spent countless hours at Jimmy Cable's automobile garage, sanding the frame in preparation for the new coats of paint when the opportunity presented itself and they could afford it.

It was a labor of love for the brothers, one that consumed every spare dime and hour they had put together over the last few years. Money was tight, there was seldom anything left over to indulge their fondness for old cars. Which is why they usually purchased the cheapest vehicle in need of the most reconstruction, knowing it would take many years before the rebuild could be completed. It was only over the last few years

Alton had been old enough to be of assistance for anything other than cleaning up the barn or discarding the trash. Winfrey smiled as his eyes traveled to the elegant cursive writing on the side of the car, between the driver's door and the fender. *Misty Lee*, it read in thin, white letters consistent with the name, *Rockin' Robin* written on the passenger's side.

No way could Delmore or Wilbur have penned the names of Delmore's daughters on the car. Neither of their hands were steady enough. And Alton's handwriting was horrible. It always had been. Not to mention, he was a terrible speller. Winfrey could see in his mind's eye, years earlier, as Willard Lee's fixed hand painted the names using a handmade stencil while the others watched in awe.

"I'll park it in the empty stall next to Garnet's." Alton looked behind to the barn as if he could see through the structure and see the wrecked heap that was his brother's car. "You guys can wash it up for me a time or two until I get home."

"We can do that," Buck chimed in before anyone could offer a contradiction. "Be happy to." He motioned for Alton to lead the way and watched as Willard Lee and Winfrey followed behind him. The single file line that trailed through the snow looked like the pied piper with a handful of rats following the music. Unlike the piper who knew exactly where he was guiding the rats to, Alton was more like the blind mice, marching towards a new destination and wondering how the remnants of the chapter would be written.

****

Time flew by quickly once Alton's friends bid their farewells. True, Willard Lee and Winfrey lived only a half mile or less away, just across the top of the hill in the same house they had grown up in as children. Most summer days, the jaunt up the hill and across the road took less than twenty minutes, ten if the boys ran instead of a leisurely walk. And the Herron farm was probably no more than ten miles past the cousins, especially if you took the shorter route through Roberts Road. Still, as

Alton stood near the side of the house, in the small strip of land between the driveway and house, it felt as if they were continents away.

The same might be said for the remnant of the day as Alton sat comfortably in the old, brown leather armchair stationed close enough for its occupants to take full advantage of the heat radiating from the wood burning stove, but not so close as to scorch the material of the worn chair. Along the other wall, with the front door between, the matching sofa was filled to capacity as Sis, Momma, and Daddy, sat attentive as if attending a sermon at church.

On the linoleum floor, Allen lay on his stomach, pushing several toy cars back and forth as if they might go forward of their own volition if he allowed it so. He was small for his age, with a round face and light brown hair shaved as close to his scalp as the barber's talent would permit. His naked feet snaked from the legs of a faded pair of denim jeans, the soles marred black from the soot and smoke of the wood stove. Periodically, he looked up from his play as if he understood the ongoing conversation of the adults. But deep down, Alton hoped the child was not able to comprehend. It was better if Allen's attention was confined within the little house on the hill, in a place they all knew as home. He did not need to comprehend the implication of civil service in real time. Instead, let his understanding of war be among the plastic green and brown soldiers he played with frequently. Alton prayed that would be all the extent of familiarity for his nephew. He did not need to know the harsh realities. Alton wished the same might be said for himself, as well. Being drafted did not necessarily mean going to Vietnam with a rifle clutched in his hand. There were numerous other ways to honorably serve one's country. Alton hoped fate would position an alternative opportunity in his path and think no less of him for his desire to be out of harm's way.

Alton with Delmore's 1953 Chevy

As Written

Chapter Four

The two-hour drive to Louisville seemed to fly by even though Alton was not able to close his eyes and take a nap. It was as if he wanted, needed, to take it all in, memorize it as it was before the new chapter of his life began.

The way the dark, angry, smoke bellowed from the numerous metal chimneys of the factory at the edge of town and raced towards the clouds in the sky as if hoping to snag a checkered flag was burned into his brain. He had looked upon it, too many times to count. Yet, as Delmore's car raced through town, Alton could not pull his eyes away. It was as if he was seeing it for the first time.

The parking lot of the Dairy Queen was packed with pickup trucks and cars of every size, color, and model. Odd for a Sunday night, he thought. Most folks enjoyed Sunday dinner at home, especially during the long, cold nights of winter. As his vehicle grew nearer, Alton was able to pick out Willard Lee's and Winfrey's, as well as Buck's old beat up, black ford truck. If Alton squinted, his eyes, he could almost make out their images in their usual booth, the one farthest from the counter, closest to the window where they could keep an eye on their trucks. The greasy scent of meat assaulted his nose as the image of a chili dog and fries fixated upon his thoughts. Willard Lee had stated actual fact, they should have rode into town yesterday for lunch.

By the time Delmore's car made the quick trip across the county line, the fragrance of old man Martin's dairy farm was prevalent in the air and as unpleasant as it normally was, still it was familiar, and he was comforted. Time passed, seasons passed, life moved on and was different. Yet, it was not, and life stayed the same.

These were the things he wanted to pack in his suitcase and take along on the journey. The sights, the sounds, and the smells, he wanted them all, good, bad, pleasant and unpleasant, bottled up and tucked into his pocket.

****

It felt as if Alton had no more than said his goodbyes to his parents and sister before he was repeating the act again with Phyllis and the children as the car pulled into Delmore's house on Orchard Avenue in Louisville.

His sister-in-law carried the baby from the car while Delmore carted the sleeping form of their daughter, Robin. As before, the oldest child, Misty, rubbed the sleep from her tired eyes with Wilbur holding onto her hand and guiding her up the icy steps that led to the front door.

"Come in for a second," Wilbur advised holding the door open as Alton took gentle steps across the ice-frosted porch. "I need to use the bathroom before we head out to Fort Campbell." Wilbur disappeared down the unlit hallway almost as if he had been an apparition and Alton had simply imagined his brother there in the flesh.

He watched as Misty made her way cautiously up the stairs, her tiny hand using the wall for support as she climbed up the shiny, waxed wooden steps. Alton took his time to consider the interior of the house as if he were a stranger, but that was not the case. With the exception of the last week when he had opted to spend his last week at home with his parents, Alton had called Delmore's house his home for the last few months since graduating from high school. The house was more than familiar to him and to Wilbur. It felt odd to look upon it with eyes of indifference and he wondered how it might look when he returned home. Even if nothing inside the house changed, would it still feel the same upon his return?

Last year, Wilbur laid claim to one of the bedrooms upstairs while Alton homed the other more recently. Judging from the discussion Delmore was currently having with Robin and Misty, the girls had reclaimed the room Alton had vacated last week. It was comforting to eavesdrop on his brother's conversation as he coaxed his daughters into bed. It was obvious by Delmore's pleas, he was anxious to get back on the road. Fort Campbell was less than three hours away, he wanted to eat a bite and spend as much time as possible together before Alton reported to basic training.

"Do you want some sandwiches or something for the trip?" Phyllis appeared as if by magic at his side. She was a pretty woman, tall and thin, with movie star brown hair and make-up. Her nature was pleasant, and Alton knew her to be a kind and caring person. There was little doubt in his mind, most wives would not have welcomed her husband's younger brothers into her home, even displacing her own children's bedroom into what was the living room downstairs. During this time, she had cooked their meals and washed their laundry without resentment or hostility. Truth be told, he respected her a great deal. And since Wilbur was currently dating Phyllis' cousin, Jewel, perhaps his admiration was genetic and ran in his family.

"No," Alton shook his head as if recollecting she had asked him a question. "I figure Delmore will want to grab some dinner once we get closer to Fort Campbell."

"Okay," she mixed the word within a long breath that rushed from her mouth. "You take care of yourself, Alton." She pulled him into her arms before he could respond. "Come home safe?"

"Of course," he smiled, pulling away from her so that he could look into her eyes. "Probably be safer where I'm going than living here." He pointed to the stair steps as his words ceased.

"Why would you say that?" He knew by the way she asked the question, her feelings where hurt. "I've loved having you here—"

"Those damned steps," he laughed. "How many times have I fallen down them during the time I've been here?" He paused for a brief second. "I won't miss waxing day at all." He pointed to Wilbur as he made his way from the bathroom and came to a stop at the bottom of the staircase. "My brother agrees with me."

"What?" Wilbur turned as Delmore walked delicately down the steps.

"Miss falling down those slick-ass steps?" Alton laughed.

"Not for a second!" Wilbur added. He checked his watch. "We should go. I've got an early shift in the morning."

"I can take him myself, if you'd like?" Delmore asked, stepping carefully down onto the hardwood floor.

"No," Wilbur grappled with his coat and stopped near to the door. "I want to go. Just think we should head out as soon as we can."

"Be careful," Phyllis kissed her husband on the cheek and took Alton's hand. "You take care, and we'll see you the first opportunity you have for visitors."

"Kiss the kids for me," Alton asked, his throat tight as if the hand of his heart was choking the life out of him.

"I will," she waved and watched as the men gathered their coats and waited, one on the other, until everyone was wrapped safely in outerwear to ward off the cold of the night air.

The snow was falling harder now, its pace easily discernible against the lamplight of the streetlight that stood guard in front of the house. No doubt, it would accumulate quickly now that the temperature had dropped. It was a bittersweet moment, knowing the sun would rise in the morning to reveal a charismatic winter wonderland that would also mark the first day of his journey away from home.

****

"I half expected Sis to follow behind us," Alton offered as he stretched himself over the front seat and turned the radio volume down. It took several seconds before Light my Fire by the Doors faded away in the background.

"She wanted to, no doubt," Wilbur explained, toying with the radio knob so that the music was only barely audible. "But the drive home from Louisville is a long one, especially if you're driving it alone." He stole a glance at Delmore. "And I doubt she could get another day off from the factory. I read somewhere how the Fruit of the Loom companies are running all three shifts at full capacity right now."

"I imagine the need for underwear and knit shirts is at an all-time high." Delmore added as he stole intermittent glances back and forth from the road to the rearview mirror where he could barely make out the outline of Alton's reflection. "Are you bothered that she didn't come?"

"No, no," Alton shook his head to emphasize his intent. "She does so much for me. I understand." He fell against the back cushion, his image disappearing into the safety of the darkness. "I've never been away from home for more than a week or two. And when I was away, I've always known she was close by."

Seconds later, his body was positioned between his brothers, arms atop the back of the seat. "Even living in Louisville, we came home to Elkhorn Hill almost every weekend." His voice was hoarse, tired. "I can't imagine being so far away, for so long. What if something happens to Momma and today was my last day with her?"

"Momma's doing better," Wilbur explained. "And I'm sure there's a process to contact you and get you home if she were to take a bad spell and need to see you?"

"I guess," Alton's words were stronger, more confident. "At least I hope so." He motioned for Wilbur to give him a cigarette. "And Daddy couldn't seem to let go of my arm. He followed us to the car and waited in the cold until we pulled away." Alton wiped at his eyes with the hand not holding the cigarette. "He stood in front and watched us all the way up the hill. I saw him in the mirror." Alton fought back the tears. "I've never seen him look so sad." He wanted to mention his brother, Garnet, and how his death had affected his parents. Instead, he held his tongue, not wanting to draw a comparison and add further worry and concern to his brothers' plates. Their current loads were heavy, and he didn't want to add to their burden, emotional or otherwise.

"Momma said her goodbyes from the couch," he added as an afterthought, his words flat, thick with concern. He searched the memories in his mind as if one might flip through file folders, fingers strumming the tabs before coming to lite upon the desired file. He could not recall a past incidence where he had intentionally caused his mother any pain or discomfort. She was fragile and had been since his earliest recollection. There was nothing he would ever do to put her in emotional compromise, until now. And he wished with all his heart, he could return home and tell her it was a mistake, a misunderstanding. "She couldn't even see me to the car. It was just too hard."

"She wanted to be strong for you," Delmore reiterated, his words tinged with impatience. "But I think it was just too much for her."

"I hope she'll be able to see me sometime while I'm in basic training. I'll be at Fort Campbell for three months. Who knows what will happen after that?" Alton had always known his Momma was different, hanging on a thread and prayer at any given moment. However, it never felt as real as it had today. It was like an old feeling and a new one, simultaneously.

"Let's just take things one step at a time," Delmore advised. "We'll visit you as much as they will allow us to. Sis, Momma, and Daddy can drive up once you get settled and can have visitors. They can stay with us at the house in Louisville."

"Don't worry, Baby," Wilbur soothed, reaching across the back of the seat and patting Alton's hand.

Alton cringed at his brother's use of his nickname. He had hated the term of endearment for as long as he could recall. But sitting there between his big brothers as they drove through the snowy night to a destination with so many unknown variables, he was surprised to discover he found it comforting. Like the image of his daddy's red truck tucked away inside the old barn, the feeling was warm, with the familiar fragrance of a ham bone, beans, and bread. The impression reeked of burned jam and overdone fruit cakes. And he could not wait until the next time he could uncork the bottle and relive the memories again.

****

Three weeks. It had been three weeks since Delmore and Wilbur had dropped him off at Fort Campbell for basic training. Fort Campbell was located on the Kentucky – Tennessee border, between the towns of Hopkinsville, Kentucky and Clarksville, Tennessee. It was home to the Screaming Eagles, of the 101 Airborne, the Army's only Air Assault Division. The fort, itself, was huge with over one hundred thousand acres for training and residential living quarters for the army personnel. In addition to the training facilities, there were hospitals, schools, shopping facilities, and restaurants. None of these institutions were unfamiliar to Alton, these were businesses he was more than familiar with and had frequented at home on more than a single occasion.

What was a unique consideration was the realization that Fort Campbell was nearly twice as large as the entire city of Campbellsville. It was as daunting and intimidating as any experience he had encountered to date. He had a smalltown heart and mind and he was sure the rhythm of his heart was a melody of lamplights that pointed in the direction of home. Each day that passed was one day closer to being finished with his service commitment and heading home. He marked the days that passed like a tattoo upon his heart and held his breath until he could be reunited with his family and friends. And he was grateful for the companionship of the friends he made during the many weeks that passed during basic training.

Bentley Peters was a local boy. Born and raised in Hopkinsville, he was more than familiar with Fort Campbell. He and his family owned a large dairy farm in Christian County and had Bentley not been drafted, he was set to take over the family business in the Fall when his father, Paxton, retired. Bentley's life to date, was the stuff movies were written about. Prior to answering his call to service, he was captain of the football team, homecoming king, and an honor student. To hear him tell it, he had lettered in so many extracurricular activities, he needed several lettermen's jackets to pin them all upon.

Bentley had led a charmed life from the moment he was born, yet his demeanor was such, it was not obviously evident. Bentley had occupied every position within this father's company, including the mailroom and janitorial services. He knew every aspect of the family business from the ground up. He felt he had more than earned an opportunity to manage the family business. There was no doubt in his mind, he was ready for the task. The only thing standing in the way was the plain-looking draft notification that slithered into his inbox. There was a moment he considered asking his father to consider "making it go away," but he knew better. Paxton Peters believed in service, country, and God. He had served himself but in a noncombat capacity. No doubt, if and when the opportunity would present itself, Paxton Peters would see to it that his son served but in a manner that did not put the last Peters male in compromise.

For as much of a standup guy as Bentley was, he was still confident that he would find his way home to Christian County and no doubt be touted a hero upon his return. He did not live with the day-to-day uncertainties Alton and other soldiers who resided in the barracks did. Bentley was able to look past the war and see a job, wife, and children. Alton did not have the same luxuries, physical or mental. Albeit he considered frequently what his "adult" life would look like one day. Would he be like Delmore who had built a life with a wife and kids? Or would he be more like Wilbur, waiting until the perfect woman came along? Would his fulfilled life be centered around farming like his Uncle Arvin, or would he punch a timecard at Ford Motor Company for the rest of his life? For now, these thoughts would have to be put on hold. For Alton, and for Bentley Peters.

In spite of their differences, Alton liked Bentley. There was something about him that reminded him of his brother Wilbur. Both were quiet and thoughtful, more likely to be the guy who jumped in front of a punch to thwart an altercation versus throwing the punch that would cascade the event. Buck was like that, too, the thought bringing a smile.

If Bentley Peters was most likely to be the guy who stepped into a punch, Cooper Butterfield was more than likely, the guy who threw the punch in the first place. He was tall and lanky, with long arms and legs perfect for a basketball court standoff. His dark hair and eyes gave him an almost exotic appearance that found great favor with the ladies. But there was nothing exotic about Cooper. He was born and raised in Perry County, Kentucky.

The town of Hazzard was small, smaller than Campbellsville, with generations of families who scraped out a living in the coal mines of Kentucky. Cooper was quick to anger and just as eager to apologize and carry the load in apology. There was little waiting for Cooper in Hazzard, except a life in the coal mines and a certain early death once black lung set in. Cooper was anxious to get out of Hazzard and he had no intention of ever returning. To hear him tell it, any place was better than Perry County, even Vietnam.

The circumstances of Fort Campbell prompted Bentley, Cooper, and Alton to become friends quickly. Alton was grateful for their friendship and support. Perhaps, he prayed, there was a chance they might be stationed together, wherever they were going? Until then, there was much to learn about each other, about the war, and about the art of marching.

****

"Don't worry," Bentley promised as the remnants of his blonde hair that did not fall victim to the barber shook in agreement. "I'll help you with the marching. Meet me outside before lights out."

"You're trying too hard," Cooper followed behind them offering encouragement between the discussion points. "You let the TC get into your head. Kick his ass out and don't think so much on it."

Alton rubbed his ankles where bruised imprints of a boot toe were visible. "I think the training commander means well but I just can't get it," he paused. "Can't dance either." He thought of the homecoming dance his junior year and how desperately he wanted to dance with that girl in his math class. What was her name? Joann something? He had flirted and eyed her for most of the year but never worked up the courage to even look at her. Let alone, talk to her. His heart had practically jumped from his chest when Buck mentioned asking Joann to the movie several months back during his last night at home. Alton's response was not exactly accurate. It was true, she and he were just friends. Mostly because

Alton never found the courage to ask her out on a date or to dance at homecoming.

"You don't dance?" Bentley grabbed the mop handle and crooned a few lines of Groovin' by the Young Rascals as Cooper took an Elvis-like stance and moved his leg and pelvis like Alton had seen Elvis do on the Ed Sullivan show. He could not help but laugh. Cooper was certainly no Elvis and Bentley's singing was terrible, but he was grateful for their assistance and for their friendship.

"I'll see you guys after chow." Alton waved them off and disappeared out the back door of the barracks while he struggled to twist his body into his winter jacket and zip it as far as it would go. He lit a Winston cigarette and counted what was left in the pack. He needed to make the pack last till pay day and that was several days away. He walked briskly towards the kitchen, watching as the evening sky grew dark against the setting sun. If he was late for kitchen duty, the TC would tack on more time and Alton was tired of peeling potatoes. Hopefully, Bentley and Cooper could help him with marching in time and his days of kitchen duty would be behind him. And he wondered what had become of Joann?

****

Alton had always been a fan of baseball, basketball too. As a youngster, he had played both sports with his brothers, cousins, and friends who lived on or around Elkhorn Hill. In the spring, when the boys picked baseball teams, he was usually picked first. Sometimes it was because one of his cousins was picking, but most times it was a result of his skill. He was a fast base runner, probably the fastest of the kids who grew up on the hill. He was a good hitter, too, able to bring the other runners across home plate consistently and reliably. His skill set also included the ability to play both infield and outfield. Although he preferred shortstop, he was a capable and efficient first baseman as well. If his family had been able to afford the fees, no doubt he would have successfully made the high school team. How different might his life had been had he gone on to play in college? Would he be more like Bentley who was simply marking time in this place until he got to the next destination?

Basketball was another sport Alton excelled in, sort of, provided the position he was given was that of a point guard. He had an incredibly accurate arm and, like his skill in baseball, was very fast. However, given his height, he would never be a candidate to play the positions of forward or center. He was seldom a match for anyone who was taller than he was. And most everyone he knew was taller. Not that he was short, he was not. As Delmore had explained dozens of times, he was of average height as long as he did not hang out with the basketball team. Once either of them lined up beside members of the basketball team, the rationale for being of average height, diminished significantly.

Given then that he was of reasonable athletic competence, why was mastering the art of marching in time such a challenge for him? And why was everyone else able to master it so effortlessly. Bentley and Cooper had said as much when they offered to help him out.

Since Alton's arrival three weeks ago, he had attained high scores across the board in every training attribute except marching. He could not, for the life of him, keep in pace and step with the rest of his squad. His training commander, Bruce P. Titan, was a mountain of a man. There was little doubt in Alton's mind that Commander Titan had, indeed, mastered the art of basketball and was most likely a forward or center on his high school team. Although his height was indicative of a basketball player, there was little else reminiscent of a successful basketball player. Commander Titan was thick, with bulky arms and legs made more for wrestling than taking a jump shot. He seldom smiled and announced on more than one occasion that his sole goal for basic training was to ensure everyone came home safely.

His other purpose was to remind Alton every time he was out of step by kicking the ankle of the foot that was out of step, leaving thin, dark bruises every time his boot made contact with Alton's ankle. "Phillips!" Titan screamed in a manner reminiscent of television's Sergeant Carter while Gomer Pyle tried his hardest not to smile as he marched with his squad. Despite Titan's unique training technique, Alton respected him.

And when Titan's time at Fort Campbell was up, Alton knew he would miss him.

"It was unfortunate," Alton wrote to Sis. "I did not get to say goodbye to him. He was strict but really knew his stuff. He taught me well and I'm a better man after knowing him." Titan's tour of service had come its end and Titan disappeared from Alton's life just as quickly as he had entered it. And thanks to Bentley and Cooper, the kicking ceased prior to Titan's exit after Alton mastered the art of marching.

Chapter Five

It was hard to believe what was going on in the world outside of the place Alton had called "home" these last months. Alton struggled to get his thoughts onto the page. He had never been a high achiever in school. In fact, most of his grades across the board were C's and D's, with a few F's scattered about to make the point that college was not going to be in his future. But for as mundane as life at Fort Campbell was, it seemed the rest of the world, even within the United States, was spiraling out of control. He rushed to get his words on the page so that his sister would know he would not be able to make the trip home. There was no need to wait for him at the depot in town. He would not be on the bus; his three-day leave had been canceled.

The news of the Massachusetts highway patrol's massacre of two hundred black students during a civil rights protest was still prevalent around the army base. As far as Alton was concerned, a man was a man, regardless of the color of his skin, and he treated everyone with the same respect. The same was true for his fellow soldiers of color and no one was more supportive of them than Alton. And no one was more disappointed to learn that all approved leaves had been recanted as the Army scrambled to ensure none of their soldiers might fall victim to similar acts of protest or support. It was true, the soldiers were protected, in a way, by the bubble of Fort Campbell and inside its sanctuary. Factors were more controllable than outside its walls where others might influence the soldiers and their actions.

Still, he was disappointed. He was down to his last eight cigarettes, four stamps, and only enough change in his pocket for a soda or two. At least if he were home, he could bum a Marlboro from Delmore or a Salem cigarette from Sis. He was not fan of either of those brands but either was better than nothing. Maybe he could use the change to call Wilbur or Delmore and see if either of them was able to visit and bring him a few bucks for cigarettes. He was not able to leave the base, but nothing prohibited family members from visiting, especially on the weekend.

He sealed the letter and licked one of his last four stamps before donning his jacket and making his way to the base post office. Fingering the change in his pocket, he decided to swing by the mercantile first and use the phone. He could place a collect call to Delmore's house. Although he and Wilbur would still be at work, as would Sis and Daddy, Phyllis would no doubt be home with the kids.

Momma would be home too. Her health prohibited her from leaving the house for long periods of time. She usually only made short trips to Aunt Evie or Aunt Betty Jo's. If she made the trip to Delmore's, she and Daddy would plan to stay overnight so that she could rest before starting the trip home.

If she were home, she was probably resting and not able to hear the phone ringing. Plus, Momma and Daddy could not afford a private telephone line. No doubt, someone on the hill was using the party line. It was seldom free for long and if you were able to make a call, it would only be a short time before someone continually picked and hung up to determine if the line were free. Or worse case, make noise in the background to alert those using the party line that their time was up.

Anxiously, Alton dialed Delmore's phone number and waited for Phyllis to answer his frantic plea for help. Seconds past before he heard her familiar voice on the other line.

"Hey, Phyl, it's me," Alton's voice was calm, cheery as if he were down the street and asking if it was okay to drop by.

"Everything ok?" her words were anxious while she waited for him to respond. In the background, he could hear the baby babbling, voices

As Written

from the television, and the girls arguing over something he could not make out the specifics of.

"My leave got canceled because of that business in Massachusetts."

"We've been watching it on the news. It's just horrible what happened to those students," she said, her words breathy as if she was performing another task while conversing on the phone. Alton knew her well enough to know she was probably mopping or washing dishes, something like that. It would be a rare occurrence for her to simply be sitting down and talking on the phone, especially with three young children at home.

"Would you ask Delmore if he's able to come by on Saturday?" He looked round to ensure his conversation was private. "I'm low on cigarettes and short on money." Alton was a proud man from a family of even prouder men. They were not the type of people to ask for or accept the charity of strangers but believed fully that charity began at home.

"Of course," Phyllis answered quickly. "Are you sure you can make it till the weekend?"

"Yeah," he smiled into the phone as if she could see him. "I'll stretch my cigarettes out and I can eat at the mess hall."

"Does he know what kind you prefer, and he can just bring them with him?" she said in reference to her husband.

"He does. I prefer Winston but will take whatever I can get," he paused. "I'm sorry, you know?"

"For what?" she was distracted by the baby's crying as it became louder and louder.

"For drinking the cokes you had hidden in the washer and making those black marks under the table with my boots after you mopped the floor." His words were strained. "Wilbur and I were just teasing with you. Didn't mean any harm."

"I know you didn't," she said, tears thick in her mouth. "And I forgive you." She cleared her throat. "Now don't give it another moment's thought. You focus on taking care of yourself and getting home. Robin's asking for those silly cookies, and she won't take them from anyone but you."

"You tell her, I'll get her two bags when I come home next time."

"I'll tell her," Phyllis said above the baby's screams. "I have to go. We'll see you over the weekend."

"Thanks," he called out just as the receiver clicked and the line grew silent. She was a good woman, his sister-in-law. He had always known this but was grateful for the reminder. He hoped to find someone one day who would love him and his family as much as she loved Delmore and his family. Pray on it, his momma would say. And that was exactly what he intended to do as soon as he returned to the barracks.

****

The walk to the post office was a short one but making the trip against the frigid afternoon wind made it seem like a much longer journey. Gloves, he considered. He had been at basic training for a while and had yet to ask for a pair of gloves. No doubt, the army would issue him a pair, no?

If not, he would just make do without them. Rumor had it, his squad was being made combat ready in anticipation of supporting the South Vietnamese. If that were the case, he knew Vietnam was hotter than hell. The last thing he would need would be gloves and he was not wasting his money or his family's money on something to be discarded so soon after making the purchase. He would just have to make do.

The young woman behind the counter of the post office was attractive in a plain kind of way. She was young, his age, maybe a year or two older. Her hair was brown but not really that dark. It could have just as easily been blonde but the way she had it tied up in a ponytail and twisted into a sloppy bun in the back, it was hard for him to tell. Her eyes were pretty and reminded him of Willard Lee and Winfrey's, except he would not have used "pretty" to describe theirs. Her figure was slim, although he could only assess what was visible above the counter. And what was above the counter definitely was impressive. Even hidden away beneath the thick, blue sweater, he knew God had blessed her generously. Most importantly, she was flirting with him. At least, he thought she was.

As Written

Maybe not? Hell, he could never really tell. Delmore always said he was clueless about matters of the heart.

"What can I do for you today, Private?" her words were throaty as she held his gaze, her eyes locked with his as she bit her bottom lip.

"Mailing this out to my parents," he slid the letter across the counter and waited for her hand to reach across the counter and snatch it from his.

"Just the one, today?" she smiled. "Usually there's more, at least two or three."

She was right, he thought to himself. Most times, he mailed letters out at the same time to Sis, Delmore (or Wilbur), as well as Momma and Daddy. "Just the one today," he smiled. "I'm hoping for some visitors this weekend. So, I can tell them what I normally write."

"That's nice," her words were drowned out by the clank of the stamper in her hand as it tattooed the name of the army base and the date across the top of the envelope. "Did you get your orders yet?" She was making small talk, he knew, but welcomed the attention just the same.

"No, not yet," he straightened his chin and caught her gaze as if they were engaged in a dual and he needed her to break contact and look away first. "But some guys in the two-four said they got their orders." He paused and wished he had lit one of his last few cigarettes before engaging her in the stare down. The motion of exhaling the smoke between his lips would have been a good distraction. He felt his confidence waning like a deflated balloon in the pit of his stomach.

"Where are they headed?" Her eyes drifted away from his momentarily before jumping back into battle and locking on like a torpedo launched from a submarine.

"Vietnam," his answer was calm, but his mind exploded with the implication that his will was stronger than hers. She had averted her gaze first. Maybe if he had not always avoided eye contact at the school dances, his participation might have been more than just holding up the gymnasium wall. He might have enjoyed a dance or two. His mind flashed back to Joann and how it would have felt to hold her at an arms-length away and sway from one leg to the another in rhythm to the music.

Would he have been near enough to catch the Strawberry scent of cologne from her skin or shampoo from her hair? That was a chapter that would remain unwritten. He would never know the outcome.

"Maybe it will be like leapfrog?" her words cut through his recollection like a slamming door. He hoped his body had not jumped in response and he missed not having a cigarette again.

"Leapfrog?" he questioned, moving closer to the counter and resting his elbows atop the rough grain of the surface between them. He remembered playing leapfrog as a child, one player leaped over another player as they sat upon the ground. His thoughts jumped back to home and it brought a smile to his face.

"You know," she smiled to reveal perfect rows of white teeth to him. "Every other troop is deployed to Vietnam. Maybe you'll be deployed elsewhere and out of harm's way?"

"I doubt that's the case, but I like the way you think," he laughed deeply, hoping she would not see that his teeth were not as perfect or as white as hers. He was suddenly self-conscious, knowing the years of smoking had left its mark. And in his family, a visit to the dentist resulted from an acute condition of discomfort. There was no money in his household for preventative care. "What's your name?"

"You writin' a book?" She was definitely flirting with him. He did not need Delmore to confirm or deny it. There was no doubt. The only thing missing in validation was for her to flip her hair or pop a tiny bubble from the gum in her mouth.

"No," he grinned, scratching at the grain of the worktop where a tiny grain of wood had been pulled away from surface. "You live here on base?" Perhaps he considered, retreat and flank from another perspective might gain him the victory of her name, her phone number if he were lucky.

"Yes," she was being purposefully evasive, and he knew it. Maybe his talent for flirting was more inept than he had believed. Or maybe it was a side-effect of the journey. Fate was better preparing him to be comfortable in his own skin, away from the safety and security of being "Baby".

"My parents work on base," she answered before he could inquire. "My dad is an electrician, and my mom works in the mess hall." She leaned across the counter and flipped through several envelopes until her finger halted on the one she wanted. "I can live on base with them until I'm twenty-one."

"Maybe, we can grab a bite one day?" The words spilled from his mouth so quickly, he jumped in response and turned quickly to ensure the words were his and not from a stranger who might have walked up to wait in the line behind him.

"Maybe we can," she smiled before adding, "Mary." She toyed with the hair that had broken free from the bun. "My name is Mary. I work every weekday, but I'm usually done by two." She looked away shyly but there was something ingenuine about the action. It felt more scripted and contrived. Alton was even more intrigued and held onto her words as if they were like the air he needed to breathe. "We'd have to do a late lunch or dinner?"

"Either is fine with me as long as it's after the weekend," he straightened his back, as if an officer had entered the line and prompted a salute. Delmore would not be able to get to base until the weekend. Until his brother was able to visit, he was without funds for anything, cigarettes or romance.

"You got other plans for the weekend, Alton?" If the words were butter, her tongue would have sliced it effortlessly into thin bite-size pieces.

"No," he looked away, his hands finding their way anxiously into his trouser pockets. "Just low on cash until the weekend when my brother visits." It was then he realized she had used his first name. "How'd you know my name?" If he had been wearing his dress trousers and shirt his name was fully displayed, but he was wearing a thick jacket over his army fatigues. He waited nervously wondering if he had been lured into a stalker's lair.

She slid a letter across the counter to him not attempting to conceal her amusement. "It's on your letters, silly. You've told me your name every time you pick up your mail."

"Oh," his face reddened. "Right, how's Monday?" He paused only a beat before adding. "Let's grab an early dinner on Monday?"

She tapped her nails atop the counter as if she were a judge deliberating a case before her court. Moments pass like hours before she went on, "I'd like that. Which one?"

"Which one of what?"

"The boys who write letters back to you, is one of them the brother who's meeting you over the weekend?"

"Yes, Delmore," Alton admitted, feeling remnants of the stalker vibe rearing its ugly head, again. "So, Monday at 2:15? I'll meet you in front of the diner?"

"Okay," she nodded for affect. "Can I ask you another question?" She did not wait for him to respond. "Do you have a girlfriend back home?"

"No," his face flushed, and he hoped his expression did not betray him by alerting him that he had thought of Joann again. There was never anything between them. He had never worked up the courage to dance with her. Let alone, ask her to go out to a movie or for soda. He had no idea why he thought of her again.

"Who's Kathy?" her words were succinct. "Her letters are postmarked from Louisville?"

"We worked together at Ford and went out a few times, mostly breakfast after our shift ended," he explained. "She's a friend." The door behind him opened so abruptly, both Alton and Mary jumped at the intrusion. "I'll see you on Monday then?" He moved to the side to allow the newcomer space to approach the counter and made his exit through the door before it connected with the frame.

Outside the air was frigid, stinging his face and neck where the skin was exposed to the elements. He should have been uncomfortable, numb to his core as he walked back to the barracks. But he was not, his body was warmed by the heat that radiated from the firing neurons in his brain as he replayed his discussion with Mary. A date, he repeated the words over again. He had a date with a pretty woman who worked on the base. The only thing that could thwart his romantic evening would be Delmore's inability to float him some extra cash. Perhaps another phone call was called for? This time he would wait until the time when he was guaranteed to speak with Wilbur or Delmore. He doubted his sister-in-law would be a sympathetic ear.

****

The hospitality room at Fort Campbell smelled medicinal, but not in a good way. It was more like something pleasant had been sprayed in the air throughout the room in the hope of concealing something more foul. Whatever had occurred in the time between the first visiting session in the morning and the last session in the afternoon, could not be considered a success. The room reeked. It was a purulent mixture of burned wood, body odor, and the aromatic odor of meat and greasy takeout food.

Delmore and Phyllis arrived promptly on time, holding a greasy bag of burgers and fries from the McDonalds near the base in one hand and two of their three children in the other. Apologetically, Delmore pointed towards the carrier where the baby slept peacefully and watched as Phyllis eased him gently into the empty chair across from Alton. "We had to bring the kids. Jewel wasn't able to watch them today, after all."

Alton ruffled Robin's hair and slid a package of animal crackers across the table to her. She dropped her crayon atop the table and looked curiously to him as if to acknowledge she knew the cookies were not the ones he usually ate or shared with her. Eventually, her attention turned to her mother. "Open?" she asked as her thin fingers reclaimed the crayon and she adjusted herself upon her knees to allow better access to both the table and the cookies. Once the bag was opened, she smiled, pushed a broken cookie into her mouth, and turned her attention back to the coloring the animals on the page of her book.

"You're missing one?" Alton pulled the chair out and dropped himself comfortably in the seat. Misty, the oldest child was not among the last visitors of the weekend.

"Someone in her class had a birthday party. They were having Ehrler's ice cream brought in for the party. She's cried all day since we told her we were coming here, instead." Phyllis explained, watching as Robin snapped another perfectly complete cookie in half and popped it into her mouth.

"Ehrler's ice cream sure would taste good," Alton licked his lips, "especially those little candy eyes they put on the ice cream in the cones." His hand snaked across the table to accept the other half of the cookie Robin offered to him. "Thank you," he grinned, thinking again of the broken cookies he taunted her with and shared a knowing glance with Phyllis as if to say, I told you so. She doesn't hate me.

"You look good, brother," Delmore's words were anxious as if he expected Alton to look more worse for the wear. "They treating you okay?" He chewed anxiously on his fingernails, starting from left to right as if he were eating corn on a cob. From across the table, Alton could see the nails were chewed to the quick and the skin around the nail was red and angry. Now that Garnet was gone, Delmore's role within the family had expanded, and being the oldest came with great responsibility. He worried all the time, about everyone within his circle. Delmore was a good husband, father, son, and brother—he carried the bite marks on his fingernails to prove it.

"I'm good," Alton explained, watching again as Robin smashed another cookie and picked at the tiny remnants on the table as if they were seeds. Had his interactions with her resulted so that she thought crushing them was the correct way to eat them? Did she not realize it could be eaten in bites from the cookie as a whole? He made a mental note to correct that notion once he returned home. It would be a new game for them, they would only eat whole cookies.

"I thought Wilbur might come with you." Alton went on, with basic training coming to an end soon, he wanted to make sure he took every advantage of being with his family every opportunity he was given.

"Wilbur and Jewel got married this weekend," Delmore reported, dropping his hand into his lap as if the act might deter him from chewing on his nails. "They're probably headed home from Tennessee right now."

"Good for them," Alton laughed, not really surprised. He did, however, feel a tinge of jealousy, as he imagined the celebration the family would have for them and realized he would not be around to celebrate the event. Jewel had two small children, Debra and Cherida, from a previous marriage. Just like that, Wilbur was a father. He had an instant family. Alton felt it again, deep in his stomach and radiating into his lungs until he could not get his breath and his heart hurt as a side effect. He was jealous. Once again, imagining the life he could only pray he might enjoy one day.

"Any update on your orders?" Delmore asked, his words constricted as if he had read Alton's thoughts and knew his distress. Alton knew his brother was the most empathic person he had ever known. He felt things deeply and mourned the losses of others as though they were his own.

"I'm heading to recon training after I finish basic next week." He paused to allow his words to register with Delmore and Phyllis. He knew by the way his brother's eyes teared up, Delmore had put two and two together and came up with Vietnam. He knew Alton was heading to another continent to support the American troops already engaged in combat with the North Vietnamese.

"Does Daddy know? Or Sis?" he added quickly, wiping at his eyes and turning his head away.

"I just found out this morning, right after chow." Alton's words came out in one big breath as if his words had simply run dry, like the gasoline tank on his daddy's old red truck. The gauge quit working years before the truck gave out. As a result, the driver had to "guess" approximately how many miles were left on the old girl's engine. Sometimes, he got it right and arrived in the old red truck at his destination. Other times, he arrived under the steam of his own feet. It was a gamble; one Alton had learned to accept over the years.

There was relief, once the words were out of his mouth. It was evident by the manner in which Alton eased his back against the chair, exhaled, and waited for his brother to respond. It was as if the weight of knowing had traveled through the air and across the table to find a resting place within Delmore's body. And Alton was instantly sorry and felt guilty for his transgression. He longed for a simpler time and by the look in Delmore's eyes, he knew his brother did too.

Was it too much to wish that they were all together in that simpler place and time? Trouble was, would he move backward or forward? If he chose to go backwards, how far would be enough? If he chose to move forward, what might the future hold for them, for him? Could he peek inside and steal a glance before deciding? Unfortunately, it did not work that way, life was a gamble, and he was not the one holding the dice. But what if it were that simple and he was solely responsible for his own fate? Might he fast forward through the pages and pray for a favorable ending? Or was there sanctuary in not knowing, in simply living life and playing out the hand?

Alton was never an avid reader, but he did enjoy reading comic books when he was younger. True, no one in his family had money for luxuries, even little ones, but the library in town always had older issues that were free to anyone who wanted them. There had been several Saturday mornings as a boy he had left the small stone, cathedral-looking building with several tucked safely under his arm. And it was evident to him, after reading the first few pages, if the story would or would not hold his interest. If not, he had little invested, it was easy to simply discard it and move on to another one he had carried home. If only, he thought again, he could do a redo, where might he end up?

"When?" The single word was all Delmore could muster the energy to ask. His hand reached out to Phyllis who sat quietly in the chair beside him, not bothering to wipe at the tears that fell down her cheeks.

"Late summer," Alton answered. "I'll be assigned to Fort Knox so it will be easier to get leave and see Momma and Daddy for a spell." He forged a smile across his face and willed himself to look his brother in the eye. "It will be okay. Louisville is only forty-five minutes away from Fort Knox. It will be really easy to be together until I deploy."

"When are you going to tell them?" Delmore's words were dry, faint as if he were speaking from the bottom of a well.

"Was hoping you would do that for me?" Alton shrugged and accepted another cookie from Robin's tiny hand. "I don't want to tell them in a letter or on the phone." His eyes locked upon the child's face as she went on about coloring in her book, oblivious to the conversation ensuing around her or the implication. "I'll be fine, brother. I promised Momma. And I always keep my promises."

Chapter Six

It had been many years since Alton paid much attention to the changing of the seasons. In fact, other than holiday shopping at Christmas time, he had not given much thought to the significance of the turning leaves, falling snow, or rebirth of spring. However, after packing up his meager belongings and climbing aboard the bus headed to Fort Knox, his perspective was marred, and he could not help but notice how blue the sky was or how deeply the green hue of the grass reflected off the sun's rays once they pulled away and the distance from Fort Campbell grew.

The fragrant scent of mature honeysuckle was strong as it assaulted his senses across the open window of the military transport bus. He could not help but wonder behind which of the cluster of tree branches that darted out and into the road the aromatic flowers might call home. The breeze was cool against his cheeks and burned his eyes, but he did not care, he felt as if he were drunk only without the clouded vision and staggered pacing. He had never smoked anything other than a cigarette and wondered if the euphoria that had overtaken him was similar to the aftereffects of smoking something else. It was new and beautiful, yet familiar, like running into an old friend. It reminded him of home.

Fort Campbell and basic training was behind him now and he was one page closer to the end of another chapter of life, one step closer to planting his boots back in the dirt of Elkhorn Hill. And when that time came, he was never leaving the hills of Kentucky again. He had no desire to travel anywhere else or taste the culture of a faraway place. Like his brothers and sisters, he would build his home near his parents and make a life close enough to hear the birds sing and see the fireflies in flight all from his momma's front porch which he would sit upon often.

The trip from Fort Campbell to Fort Knox was only about three hours away. He could have easily slept the drive away like most of the other soldiers seated around him. A few had transistor radios glued to their ears so that their music was not a distraction to the others. Some had carted magazines or a book for the trip, their heads buried beneath the pages as if to ward off the truths they were evident to face.

Alton could afford none of those things. Instead, he flipped through the small stack of black and white photographs Sis had sent to him. He could not help but smile at the pictures, especially the ones of Allen and Gail. It was easy to picture them posing outside the old house and Sis instructing them to smile and stand still. Gently, he pulled two of the images apart, careful not to damage the photo on the bottom. He did not have too many pictures of Daddy and Momma. Everyone was so busy all the time, running about seeing to chores and making a living to put food on the table. This one was special. Momma was fixed up all nice and dainty in a new dress with light colored lace around the collar and with her hair combed perfectly into place. And Daddy was in dark trousers and a shirt instead of the Duck Head overalls he wore all the time. Alton smoothed the wrinkled paper back into place and tucked it safely into his shirt pocket. He would make sure to get a small album for the pictures, first chance he got. His reconnaissance training would take up the next few months. Sis would, no doubt, send many others between now and then. Would be nice to have a way to collect them all and keep them safe to admire.

He shuffled the pictures as if they were cards until they were aligned in perfect precision. One photo was different from the others, similar to a school photo or one dispensed from a vending machine. He smiled at the face of the young woman as if she were looking back at him through the photo. She was younger in the photo and smiling in a way he had not seen in the short time he had known her. He could not help but wonder what had happened just before the photo was snapped to make her smile like that. Had someone goosed her or told a joke? Would he ever get the chance to ask her?

They had only been out on a few dates, but he knew he would miss her and her smile. Mary left quite an impression on him in the short period of time since they met. He wished the words came as easily in real time as they did in his mind. Their goodbye had been little more than a handshake and a kiss on the cheek. And he regretted he had not asked her for more. He hoped it would not be another regret he would carry with him as the years passed. He swallowed the knot in his throat and wished again he had asked Joanne to dance.

****

There was little doubt in Alton's mind that the month of April had brought nothing to Fort Knox but rain. It was evident by the cascade of yellow and blue flowers that covered the bushes in and around the perimeter of the Fort. They bloomed well into the month of May and June. The weather, too, was as if it were out of a story book with a cool breeze that rustled the flowers just enough to agitate their fragrance across the yard. And the sun, although high in the sky, was kinder, gentler, as if saving the sun's full force for use at some later time.

His view from the window had been marred only by a thin layer of dust that covered the outside pane. And if he had a shop cloth from Jimmy Cable's daddy's garage, he might have considered washing it clean to get a better view of the Sherman tanks off in the distant field. It was only slightly better than watching golf, as the tanks moved back and forth across makeshift perimeter markers on the ground that looked more like a life-size game of chess than a battlefield. It had been many months since his arrival into Fort Knox. It felt as distant as an old memory, especially now that he was nearing the end of his training.

"Two are down again," the irritation in Cooper Butterfield's voice was evident as he paced anxiously across the barrack's threshold and dropped his knapsack atop the bunk next to Alton's.

As Written

"I saw," Alton looked back behind them and out the window to where several other Sherman tanks maneuvered around two that were disabled and partially blocking the exercise of the others. "Your team up again?"

Cooper shook his head in lieu of an answer pushing away the dark locks that fell over his eyes. "Yes, even though they canceled leave, we are still short some soldiers." He unbuttoned his shirt and stepped out of his army-issued trousers before grabbing a clean towel and bar of soap from his locker. "I'm going to grab a quick shower before heading over to see what's wrong with them."

"Those tanks are junk," Alton followed him across the room, stopping short of the shower while Cooper stepped out of his shirt and underwear. "More are broken down than on the field."

The barracks at Fort Knox were more spacious than the ones at Fort Campbell. With eight men sharing the area, it was more than roomy and the fact they only shared the bathroom with seven other soldiers was a plus. Another plus had been discovering Cooper was also stationed at Fort Knox and one of the seven soldiers in the barracks.

"It is what it is," Cooper's words were barely recognizable as he called through the flow of water from the showerhead. "I wish you were assigned to the motor pool. The way you work those cylinders and pistons, we'd never have any tanks down. Where did you learn so much about vehicles, anyway?"

"My brothers are the Picasso's of automotive reconditioning. If it has a motor and wheels, most likely they can fix it." Alton smiled, his mind's eye recollecting both Wilbur and Delmore's images nearly buried under some old car or another. It was about all they did when they were together. He wondered if Garnet had enjoyed working on cars too. Try as he might, Alton pressed his brain as hard as he could, as if the act might help him recollect but it was useless. Day after day, his memory of the oldest Phillips brother dimmed like the wick on a candle. What would happen when the thread disappeared beneath the wax?

His heart ached at the thought. "Besides, my TC said I will most likely be a scout or something, maybe learn to read the maps and use the radio."

Alton said the words with pride and felt guilty for the boastful indulgence. Then again, it was better than revealing how scared he felt or how hard it was to fall asleep every time he thought about shipping to Vietnam.

"Motor pool is a lot safer," Cooper appeared from the shower, wrapping a towel around his waist and finger combing his wet hair. "I grew up thinking the big town of Hazzard was the devil's lair, but I've decided Vietnam is."

"I'll go where they send me," Alton's words were formidable as if the discussion was over and there was nothing left to say. Cooper's wet footprints on the floor were a distraction, it reminded Alton of making angels in the snow on the field behind Daddy's barn. Garnet's angel was much bigger than the impressions left by Alton and Wilbur, while Delmore's and Sis's were somewhere in between. Did that mean the measure of a man or woman was the image they left behind? Would that be a consideration for determining the size of their grave?

Cooper pointed to a folded piece of paper and shredded envelope. "Bentley's letter is over there, if you want to read it." It took seconds for him to step into a clean pair of boxer shorts and a knit shirt.

"Ain't much for reading," Alton held his hand up as the letter might be contagious and he wanted to ensure there was a safe distance between it and him. "What did Bentley say?"

"He said it's hot as hell over there." Cooper zipped his trousers and buttoned his shirt. "And he's tired of peeling potatoes."

"At least he's not on the front line brandishing a machine gun at folks he don't even know or care to," Alton explained. "Most he'll have to worry about is burning the eggs and running out of coffee." He did not mean to sound envious, but he knew as soon as the words left his mouth, they were tinged with jealousy. Mr. Peters was a powerful man. It was no surprise to Alton that the long arm of Bentley's father had plucked Bentley off the battlefield and dropped him safely into the kitchen. Jealousy reared its ugly head again as Alton said a silent prayer that his own fate might offer similar sanctuary.

"You gonna see Kathy tonight?" Cooper stepped into his boots and folded his hat upon his head.

"Her family isn't keen on her getting out after dark since the King assassination. Seems like the city, especially Louisville, is alive with unrest. "If I can't come to her, we can't get together and I ain't going nowhere tonight." Alton smacked at the window. "TC's looking for you, you better get out there."

"All our passes have been revoked," Cooper whined, pulling his lanky body towards the door before checking himself in the mirror. "What's he going to do to me?" He pushed his bangs out of his eyes and smiled. "Ain't nothing left to take from us." He nudged his chin at the window. "You want some OT?"

"I would but I can't," Alton explained. "I waxed and buffed the barrack floors this morning," he advised. "Only thing that's left is cleaning the latrine." His mind wandered again to the outhouse at home. How the stench that irradiated from it in the summer sun could not be masked even by the lavender bushes that grew wild in the field at Mr. Benningfield's place. Alton fought back a smile, remembering how Daddy's frown was evident even under the bandana tied around his face as he tossed handful after handful of lime into the seat's opening, hoping to ward off the foul smell coming from within. Alton's heart ached at the thought, his mind racing frantically as if sheer will could transport him back to his daddy's place on Elkhorn Hill. It was a trip he would gladly make, smelly outhouse and all. It was his home and he longed for the time when he could return.

****

June 1968

Dear Sis,

Hope all is well with you, Kenneth and the kids. Haven't heard from Momma or Daddy in a week or so, sure hope Momma's okay. I can't bear the thought of something happening to her and me not able to be there. You'd know to call the Red Cross, right? If something were to happen, the Red Cross can get me home quickly. Make sure you have the representative's number so that you can reach me quickly, if you need to.

I'm nearly finished with recon, only about three weeks left. Delmore and Wilbur have been coming by about every chance they get, dropping me a few dollars here and there when they can. I feel bad asking them since they both got families of their own now to care for and feed. I know when I get out and come home, I'm gonna have a lot of repaying to do, to everyone. I will try to put back some money. Once I get out of Fort Knox, it should be easier to save some. Won't need much once I get to Vietnam, I hear Uncle Sam will take care of most everything.

Was good to see cousin, Bobby, last weekend. He didn't get to stay long because he came too late but we got to spend a few minutes together. About an hour after he left, I learned I had a four-hour furlough. If I'd known, I could have left with him and drove to Elkhorn to see Momma and come right back. My TC said I'll get leave next weekend for a few hours. So, come to Louisville and wait at Delmore's for my call. Gotta go for now, have to get in line for my check. Tell Allen and Gail to be good and I will see them soon.

Chapter Seven

Letters were his lifeline. He inhaled their words from the paper into his lungs until he was saturated from head to toe with their essence. Each letter was like a puzzle piece of the whole of him. And as much as he hated writing, his letters out were better than any session with the camp therapist. The letters were the ebb and flow of his life. It was hard to imagine life away from home without them, they were as a tentacle to home.

It was maddening how slowly the time passed. Surely, he might have lost his mind if not for the letters stamped with the Elkhorn postmark on the envelope. And the pictures that lined the wall near his bed were a godsend. Sis had made sure everyone at home, even the children, were accounted for in the photos. Although the focus of her lens had been the faces of the family, there were familiar places that warmed his heart as well. In one photo, most of the old house was visible. And in another, Daddy's old red truck partially visible through the open door of the barn, practically brought tears to his eyes. He closed his eyes, holding onto the picture in his mind for as long as he could. He steadied his breathing, as if the stillness might enhance the songs of the crickets and tree frogs that lived in the field behind the house. The scent of the honeysuckle that grew around the pond in the summertime was intoxicating and he inhaled deeply as if he could detect the fragrance across the miles that led to Elkhorn Hill.

It was true he had never had much growing up. He did not own a wardrobe of colorful shirts and jeans. And he seldom had more than one pair of shoes at any given time. Most of the meals placed on his daddy's table came from a garden or the slaughterhouse. Although he never went to bed hungry, there was many an evening he could have done with one more bowl or plateful.

Material possessions were minimal in his daddy's house but there was plenty of love and hugs, lots of smiles and laughter. And through the darkest of times, they had one another's backs. His brother's death had tested them to the extreme, but they had walked through the fire, spat at the dark clouds in the sky, and embraced the sunshine of a new day.

That was how he felt every time he looked at the pictures tacked upon the wooden wall near his bed. Some of the other soldiers had photos of their wives or girlfriends posted nearby. Others had put out pictures of scantily clad models taped at various angles around the bed and wall. Only Alton's idols were black and white photos of children, parents, family, and old cars. These were the treasures he would take with him into the jungles of Vietnam and prayed the time would come quickly when he could lay hands upon them in real time. Until then, he would simply keep his head down and focus on the task at hand.

****

The army was making him sick, mentally and physically. As July came and went, it seemed to Alton it was day after day of the same tasks. He was tired of the food, of the nondescript uniform, and of being under constant surveillance. He was little more than a number, a walking, breathing replica of all the soldiers who walked the halls before and any that might make the trek in the future.

Yet, there was something to be said for repetition. As over the last four weeks, he had become proficient at working the radio and understanding maps so that he could quickly assess and evaluate coordinates and call out for support on the ground and in the air. Good thing too, as his time at Fort Knox was coming to an end. It had not been an easy task, but he completed the test for licensing, was able to drive army issued trucks, jeeps, and half-tracks. His mind flirted back to the time when he turned sixteen and proudly displayed his driver's license to his family and friends. He had never been prouder, until now.

Now that training was over and Vietnam was as surely in his path as the sun setting in the afternoon sky, a rendezvous with his family was in order. There was little need to make the two-hour trek to Elkhorn Hill only to return the next morning to the airport for the flight out. It would be better to meet them in Louisville over the weekend and say farewells. Luckily, he would have the entire afternoon and night. They could meet for dinner and pass the time talking and smoking outside the restaurant, might even have a chance to see Kathy before he shipped out.

He hated to ask but he needed money for a haircut. His TC had been hassling him for the last few days, but Alton did not want to let the camp barber cut it again. It had taken a month to grow back out after the last time. If Daddy could spare a few bucks, Alton could get it cut by someone in town while he was in Louisville. All he could do was ask. He wanted to look good for the end of training photo that was scheduled in the morning, and he wanted to please his momma's eye.

****

It was standing room only at Bob's Big Boy just off Preston Highway in Louisville. Luckily, the room offered to Alton and his family by the manager was big enough to accommodate everyone with three big tables placed strategically around the room to afford a spacious walkway between. There were more than enough wooden chairs scattered around the tables and a half a dozen metal chairs folded against the wall. The dark paneling that covered the walls made the room darker, even though the light from the setting sun flooded into the room as if a switch had been flipped. To compensate, several electric lamps sat precariously atop wooden tables as if guarding the passage of those who entered and exited. There were framed photographs that lined the various walls. The largest, a black and white photograph of Churchill Downs, occupied the biggest wall while several other smaller photos of the Louisville Slugger warehouse on Main Street took up the other. A small black and white television tucked away in the corner and muted so that the occupants could tally the score was the focal point as a runner for the St Louis Cardinals crossed home plate.

Alton pushed his empty plate towards the center of the table and stole a glance towards his momma's which looked as if she had hardly eaten a bite. Technically, she had taken at least three bites and it appeared as if four or maybe five french fries from the plate were missing. Otherwise, her plate was pristine; it could just as easily have been a photograph on the wall.

Momma looked tired. The drive from Elkhorn had taken its toll on her. The way she ignored the hair that hung loose from the clip was a sure sign she was exhausted. No doubt, her thoughts were elsewhere, focused on her son and the journey he was about to take. As was the custom, Daddy was at her side, his plate practically licked clean. Meatloaf was not a common factor for dinner at the family table. He had made quick work of the two thick slabs and mashed potatoes.

"Delmore?" Daddy called across the table. "You want to help me finish your momma's?" he pulled the nearly full plate from the center of the table and sliced it efficiently into two portions.

"I guess," Delmore accepted the plate before turning back to Phyllis and Jewell who had taken their stations with the children at the other table. "Honey?" he said to Phyllis, "the kids want some more fries?"

It took Phyllis only seconds to assess Robin and Misty's partially empty plates. "They didn't finish what they had." She pointed to Jewel's youngest daughter, Cherida, whose plate was empty. "You want some more fries?" Cherida nodded and watched as Phyllis dropped several fries onto the plate.

"What time is your flight tomorrow?" Wilbur moved awkwardly in the chair next to Delmore and scooted as close as he could to allow Sis to slide into the empty space.

As Written

"Flight isn't till ten in the morning, but the TC said to be at the airport by eight," Alton answered and watched as Sis refilled the white, ceramic cup in front of him with coffee.

"Hard to believe you can get there from here," her words were poetic as if she had not meant to say them aloud. She cleared her throat and sat straighter in the chair. "I mean from Louisville to Vietnam, seems like a world away." Her eyes traveled across the room to the other table where her children, Gail and Allen, were arguing over something undetermined. "Gail," she warned, "just let him have it."

"But Momma," the child pouted, her lip dropping to her chin. "It's mine. You told him to bring something to play with, but he didn't."

"I forgot," the smaller child responded as if his "on" button had been activated.

"Here buddy," Alton pulled his folded hat from his pocket and offered it to the boy. "Why don't you hold on to this for me until I get back."

Proudly, Allen slid from his chair and made his way towards his uncle's table with his tiny hand outstretched. He stopped and waited as Alton poised the hat atop his tiny head. It took several attempts for the material before the hat clung to Allen's small head. "It don't fit," Allen's words were filled with disappointment.

"It will one day. I promise." Alton patted his nephew's head and watched as the child skipped back to his seat, holding the hat atop his head as if it were a delicate prize. Time seemed to come to a standstill for a moment before it moved full speed ahead so that it felt as if there was a whirlwind in the room and Alton was trapped within its magnetic arms. What might the child be like as a man? Alton hoped he would live long enough to know the answer.

"Any word from Buck or Winfrey?" Alton's words were tunneled, his thoughts outracing his mouth.

"Buck's somewhere in Vietnam," Sis answered, "But Mr. Herron isn't sure where. And Winfrey got his notice a few days ago." Her eyes focused again on her children. "Kenneth got a letter from his brother last week.

David's already on his way to Vietnam." Her brother-in law was only a year older than Alton but drafted almost at the same time.

"So, they got us all?" Alton thought of his daddy's barn and the old red truck within. His mind's eye could hear the muffled music from the old radio and taste the ice-cold soda from the refrigerator. Even with the distortion caused by the broken truck speaker, the music had never sounded sweeter. He wondered if and when he, his friend, and cousin might all be there together again. And, even if everything was exactly as they had left it, would it still feel, sound, and taste the same? Would they be the same?

"Tell me again, Baby, what you'll be doing," Momma asked, her eyes lidded with exhaustion. It was taking all her willpower to stay upright in the chair. There was little doubt that she would be asleep as soon as her head hit the pillow back at Delmore's place. Alton could only imagine where everyone was sleeping for the night. Delmore's house was not that big. It would be a challenge, yes, but no one wanted to miss out on the fanfare. Saying goodbye was an important event in his family. No one wanted the opportunity to pass without offering a last wish and a prayer for a safe return.

"You remember that show Rat Patrol?" Alton did not wait for an answer. The words spilled from his mouth as if there was a fire inside and the words needed to get out. "I'll be a scout, kind of like Jack Moffit."

"What did you need to get another license for?' Wilbur asked. "You've had yours since you were sixteen." He stole a loving glance behind him towards his new bride, Jewell, and then to Debra and Cherida, his stepchildren. Like snapping fingers, they were a family now.

"It's more like a certification than an actual license," Alton answered pulling his gaze away from Wilbur and directing the answer to his parents. "I am excited about the half-track, though."

"Half-track?" Momma repeated, rubbing her temples like she often did when she was tired.

"Kinda like a bulldozer, you know how it has its wheels that stay on a track and pull the vehicle forward?" Alton answered. "I'm not really sure of many of the details except for what I've already told you."

"It's a long trip I imagine?" Momma asked, smoothing her hair behind her ears and unwrapping a Luden's cherry cough drop from the tiny black purse she infrequently carried. Most times, she was confident Daddy had money in his wallet. More than likely, she had brought it along on the trip specially to cart the cough drops.

"I fly to California, then to Japan, and Saigon," Alton answered, thinking how these were places he had only read about in books when he was in school. Never had he dreamed he would travel to these places. The farthest he had ever been from home was to visit Daddy's brother in Chicago. They had driven from Elkhorn and spent a few days with Uncle Truman, Daddy's oldest brother. Other than that trip, Louisville was as far from home as he had even gotten.

"What happens you once get to Saigon?" Sis asked, intermittently glancing back and forth between the children at the other table and Alton.

"My understanding is we take a transport to Cu Chi Base Camp," the words still sounded foreign, even to him. He was certain his family's heads were spinning and their hearts were breaking.

"What about your friends?" Daddy asked, "the ones you've already made at training camp?"

"Bentley went to Vietnam after training at Fort Campbell. He's in the kitchen pool," Alton explained. "Cooper and I went to Fort Campbell together but I'm not sure beyond that. He's going to Vietnam, too, but I doubt its Cu Chi. And he knows, wherever he ends up, he will probably be in the motor pool."

"I think that's where David has been assigned to as well," she stole a worried glance at Allen who was admiring the image of himself donned with Alton's cap in the mirror on the wall.

"I pray you'll get assigned to something like that," Momma said, her eyes closed in prayer.

"I doubt that's the plan, Momma." Alton moved to be closer to her side. "I wouldn't need training for the radios or maps, if I wasn't going into combat."

"Baby," she pulled him as close as she could against her chest so that he could smell the cherry fragrance of the cough drops. "You remember your promise."

"I do, Momma," he dropped his forehead against hers. "I will."

"Hi!" a voice from the door drew their attention towards the hallway. The visitor waited mere moments before pulling a taupe-colored handbag higher upon her shoulder and parading into the room. She was young, blonde, pretty with blue eyes and a clear complexion dressed in jeans and a thin blue sweater.

"Kathy!" Alton jumped to his feet and met her about half the way into the room. He motioned toward the table. "You missed dinner but feel free to order something."

"I'm good," she leaned forward just enough to kiss his cheek. "I wanted to give you enough time alone with your family." She exhaled awkwardly and looked around the room as if she were expecting someone else. "You ready?"

"Yeah," Alton turned back to his parents, his words stumbling out as if he were drunk. "I wasn't sure what time we'd be done, I asked Kathy to join us," he stuttered and avoided eye contact with his momma and sister.

"Of course," Delmore broke in, his face contorting into a smile. "We're done here anyway, right?"

"Yeah," Daddy answered as he bent down to help Momma up from the table. "You go on and enjoy yourself. We'll see you when you get your first leave." He swung around to face Alton again, his hand outstretched in farewell. "You take care of yourself, Son."

"I will, Daddy," Alton shook his hand before pulling him into an embrace and waiting patiently for Momma to make her way into his arms. "I love you, Momma."

"I love you, too, Baby." She covered her mouth as if the act might thwart the flow of tears that fell down her cheek. "Come home, soon." She pulled out of his arms and stepped into Daddy's before stumbling towards the doorway just as Wilbur squeezed by them.

As Written

"I will miss you," Wilbur did not offer his hand. Instead, he wrapped his lean form around Alton's smaller one and pulled him into his arms. "You get your ass back here and help me fix that old car." It was true. Wilbur was the tallest of the family, his slender frame towered over Sis and Alton, and only slightly over Delmore. It was also a valid statement that folded within Wilbur's arms, his brother seemed smaller, more timid than he could remember seeing him.

For as many years as his brothers had protected and comforted him, it was oddly enlightening to consider how Alton was now the protector. "Don't finish it without me," Alton warned, his smile encompassing the whole of his face.

"Don't worry," Wilbur laughed as he wrapped his arm around Jewel's slender shoulder. "Now that I'm a married man, I won't have the cash for a while." He pulled Jewel as close against him as he could. "You'll be home in plenty of time to help me finish it."

"You two take care of one another," Alton smiled to her, offering his hand to hers and holding on to it until she pulled away and he turned back to Wilbur. "You better help Daddy get Momma to the car."

Sis waited until Wilbur and Jewel left with Momma and Daddy, smiling at the picture they made as the children trailed behind them like Hansel and Gretel in search of breadcrumbs. "I'm not going to say goodbye to you," she took both his hands in hers. "Because you promised me you'd come home safely, and you always keep your promises."

"I will," he swallowed, citing a silent prayer it was a pledge he could keep. "You know I'm not much at writing letters so expect to write more than you receive."

"Whenever you can manage is fine," she whispered, as the tears built in her throat. "I'll make sure to keep you updated as best as I can on Momma and Daddy."

"Remember what I said about the Red Cross," he leaned in close against her. "I couldn't stand it if I don't get to say goodbye to her." He paused, his words cracking in despair. "And I'm not saying goodbye here, now."

"Nor should you," Sis reminded him. "You're going to grow old and fat on Elkhorn Hill with my kids tormenting yours."

"I'll see you then," he kissed her cheek.

"Not if I see you first," she took his hand as if he were her lifeline and she could not let go. She called behind her to the children. "Give your uncle a hug and run get in the car with Ma and Pap." Sis watched as Gail and then Allen hugged their uncle's neck and kissed his cheek before racing off to intercept their grandparents.

She waited until the children were gone before turning to Delmore. "We'll see you back at your house? I think the kids and I will head on back to Elkhorn tonight. Momma can rest up and Daddy can bring her home in the morning."

"I thought we were all going to stay together tonight?" Delmore exchanged a quick glance with Phyllis as if to validate that the plan had not changed.

"Your house is small, brother," Sis said. "Where are you going to put all of us?"

"Momma and Daddy are taking our room downstairs, Wilbur and Jewel are sleeping in one of the bedrooms upstairs, Phyllis and I are taking the other bedroom upstairs, there's a bed set up for you in the living room and six pallets on the floor in the other room for the kids. It's all worked out." He pulled her closer so that the three of them stood in a triangular pattern. "It's important that we take this time together as a family."

Delmore rubbed his chin as if he had an itch, but Alton knew it for what it was, a nervous gesture. "You sure you don't want a ride to the airport tomorrow?"

"No," Alton's face turned a crimson red. "I thought I'd stay at Kathy's place tonight. She can drop me off in the morning." He motioned toward the back of the room where his army-issued knapsack lay against the wall. "I'm packed and ready for the flight," he shrugged. "I thought it would be easier on everyone if we said goodbye tonight, here, instead of in the morning at the airport."

"It's hard either way," Delmore admitted, his face turning pale and ashen.

"I'll see you back at the house, Delmore," Sis pulled away and looked upon Alton a final time. "I love you, be safe and come home to us." She did not wait for a response. Instead, she bolted as if the room were ablaze and she knew where the water hose was hanging.

"It's time, big brother," Alton offered his hand and waited for Delmore to take it. "You watch over them for me, okay?" Alton took a step or two towards the door before turning suddenly and falling into Delmore's arms. It was fitting that Delmore would be the last to say his goodbye, Alton thought as he cried hot tears against his brother's chest. They were the same, he and Delmore, bred of the same wild cloth, yet deeply committed to their family unit. It was easy to look into Delmore's eyes and see his own reflection mirrored back.

"I will, baby brother, Delmore's words were strained. Alton knew it was taking all of his will not to break down and cry. Since Garnet's death, Delmore had assumed his role as the eldest to heart. It was his character to absorb the hurt and take the hit for those he loved. Alton knew if Delmore could, he would have traded places and made the trip to Vietnam, himself. But that was not to be, Alton knew, as had been said before. The chapter had already been written for him; it was his journey to see through.

Chapter Eight

The flight from Kentucky to California was uneventful. Alton, along with five other soldiers from Fort Knox, were assigned to seats in close proximity to one another. Although all the soldiers were pleasant enough, one soldier was particularly chatty and Alton was grateful for the colorful stories he shared while the plane barreled through the clouds in route to California. Certainly, being seated next to Terry during the four-hour flight was an advantage, but there was value in the quiet moments of silence that afforded Alton time for reflection, as well. He slid as far down in the seat as was comfortable, grateful for the envelopes of cash his brothers and sister had slid to him at the restaurant. Without their contributions, his meals during the trip, no doubt, would have come from the vending machines.

There had been little free time between deboarding one plane and getting on to another. Certainly not enough to leave the airport and sightsee. Any opportunity to explore the culture of the state of California or country of Japan were limited to the diners and gift shops located within the airports. If he were being honest, though, Alton probably would not have ventured beyond the airport, anyway. His eyes yearned to lay sight again on the rolling hills and blue grass of home. He had little interest in any destination other than that. He had faith that once his boots touched the muddy swamps of Vietnam, he was one step closer to going home to Kentucky.

Saigon was different, though. The solider that met them at the gate was young, an aid of some sort, no doubt. He was tall, lean, and made a picture-perfect image in his freshly ironed fatigues and hand-shined boots. He motioned Alton and the other soldiers to the side of the gate and waited for the passengers to disembark and pass by before addressing the group. The rest of the trip, he advised, would be conducted within the confines of a cargo plane. One that would transport them to the final leg of the journey inside the Cu Chi Base Camp to an airstrip within.

"You can use the facilities and enjoy the restaurants here at the airport," he went on to explain. "And you've the option to venture outside of the airport, if you'd like. Just make sure you are back at the airport by twenty-one hundred for pick-up." He adjusted his hat, "rendezvous at the west side of the airport near the taxi stand under the Delta airline terminal sign."

Alton watched as the solider gathered his clipboard and wandered away from the gate at a lightening pace. He wondered if the soldier had to meet arriving soldiers at other gates. Instantly, his momma's request and his promise stormed into his mind. Was this task his only function and what was the application process? This was, no doubt, a safe job. One that might afford him the ability to serve his country and keep his promises.

****

For as mundane as the flights from Louisville to Saigon had been, the last leg to Cu Chi Base Camp was anything but. From the moment Alton stepped off the plane, visions of the war were all around him. The base camp was little more than building after building, staged in perfect lines that stood like soldiers as if at attention. Trees were sparse; there were only patches of green for several miles around the base. Miles away, far off against the horizon, the blue green outline of the jungle was visible. Other than that, it looked just like the desert, just hot sun and dry, parched dirt.

Since the terrain was so flat, his field of vision was extreme. Everything looked the same for as far as he could see. And none of it looked appealing in any way. It was as if wooden structures had literally been dropped into the pit of hell or what we imagined hell might look like. Off in the distance, smoke bellowed in plumes that looked like giant fingers. What little breeze there was, was but a vehicle for the ash from the burning fires. The smell was pungent, a sickening combination of gasoline, gunpowder, and smoke. The sounds of the war were obvious as well. He was able to make out the distant intermittent impressions of the machine guns as they expelled their rounds. The ground under his feet vibrated as mortars impacted upon the ground. He moved anxiously from one foot to the other in an attempt to still the quivering of his legs.

There was panic in his eyes as he considered how potentiated the odors and sounds would be once he was closer to the field of combat. He fought back the urge to vomit and gathered his bag before making his way towards where the others were aggregating.

Alton had grown up watching television shows about wars, but nothing could have prepared him to bear witness in real time. Fear stopped him in his tracks. It was the first time since receiving the draft notice that he fully understood what was at stake. He thought of Momma and Sis and prayed the promise he had made to them was one he could live up to. It was also the first time since he was a child that he prayed, really prayed for God to watch over him and bring him home safely. He only hoped God could hear him over the roar of the war all around.

****

Vietnam was humid and hotter than hell, but Alton assessed he was finally getting used to it, even if it had taken a few weeks. He supposed that had been the plan all along, allow the newbies time to adjust to the heat as well as the sounds and smell of the war before dumping them into the deep end of the pool without a life preserver. Just as well, he thought. He had never been a strong swimmer, although he often thought he might like to become more proficient in the water. In the back of his mind, he could not help but hope he would still get the opportunity.

The first two days had passed quickly, during which he had been assigned a platoon bunk in the barracks, incurred another government issued haircut, and met a handful of members of troop A. Given there were about 40 to 50 soldiers in each platoon, he doubted he would get to know each one intimately. He fought back a smile considering there were less students than that in his 1967 graduating class at Taylor County High School. Had it only been a year since he had walked down the halls of that old school for the last time? For sure, the protective bubble that had covered him till now had certainly burst.

The workday was long, working and training from sunup until sundown. Nothing was left to chance. Platoon leaders went over everything one might expect to encounter in the jungle, from operating the equipment to identifying North Vietnamese booby traps. Alton had been at camp for nearly two weeks before he was finally deployed into the field.

As he made his way to the Armored Personnel Carrier (APC), the knots that held his stomach hostage the night before were slowly choking the air from his lungs. He could not get his breath and he feared he might be sick. The last thing he wanted to do was vomit in full few of his platoon. It would serve him best if he could find a more private place to empty his stomach, but he did not. Instead, he held his ground and concentrated on putting one foot in front of the other. It was really all he could do, right?

"You okay, buddy?" a soldier to his left asked, pacing himself so that he could get a better look at Alton's face.

"Yeah," Alton responded, not looking him in the eye.

"First time out, huh?" the soldier smiled and adjusted his helmet tighter under his chin.

Alton nodded, finally making eye contact. "You been here long?"

"Few months," he offered his hand. "I'm Walter. Where you call home, friend?"

"Kentucky," Alton's words were strained as if the mere mention of home was painful and offered his hand, "Alton, nice to me meet you."

"Just keep your mind on the job at hand, Ky. Don't think about this morning or tonight. Just focus on this minute, right now. You'll be okay." Walter was thin, with a narrow, clean-shaven face. He was several inches shorter than Alton, but the way he carried himself made him seem much larger.

"Good advice," Alton bit his lip and waited for Walter to slide into the APC.

"You're the gunner." Walter slapped the barrel of the MP60 machine gun that was mounted to the APC. "Remember what you've learned and keep your eyes peeled. Follow orders, no matter how absurd they might seem."

"Will do," Alton climbed into the APC and took his seat, taking a moment to adjust his helmet and flak jacket. It was not that he was not accustomed to working in the heat, he had grown up cutting hay and housing tobacco. There was no kind of work harder than farming. What was foreign was the humidity and obvious lack of shade. Kentucky was known for its rolling hills and lush green forests and trees with rivers and creeks that bled through the land like a birthmark. He wondered if he kicked his boots together, might he get back home or was he destined to wait upon the next tornado.

****

The terrain changed rapidly once the caravan cleared the perimeter of Cu Chi. It more closely resembled what Alton envisioned the jungle might look like, the main supply route to Saigon was an important military card and keeping it open so that supplies could get to the base camps was Alton's platoon's primary goal. It seemed easy enough, ensure the roads were clear, but the effort exhausted by the North Vietnamese to block it was paramount. Day after day, troop A was enlightened with a new method of hindering passage either by blocking the road or destroying it altogether.

"So, we just sit here?" Alton asked Walter, wiping the dust from the road away from his eyes for what felt like the hundredth time. You should invest in a good pair of goggles, Walter had advised him, and Alton agreed.

"For now, yes. Keep surveying the countryside for movement. Watch for snipers and booby traps if you leave the APC." Walter offered him a smoke, the package was so crumbled, Alton could not tell what brand it was. Truth be told, he did not care, not really. It was filled with tobacco and would surely help to ease his nerves.

"Our platoon seen much engagement?" Alton asked, the words sneaking out as if he had not intended to ask the question.

"Yeah, we've been in the field a lot, especially lately. The Viet Cong keep coming even as we are pushing them back. They are like black ooze from one of those old movies. It just keeps pouring over the top of the beaker and eventually fills the entire room."

"Why are all the trees cut down?" Alton pointed across the way to where dozens of thick trunks lay scattered across the field. "I bet they were nice, offered lots of shade?"

"You're thinking like a country boy, Ky. Our Rome plows knocked them down so that the North Vietnamese cannot use them as cover and ambush us." He waved in the same direction as Alton had indicated. "We can ensure the area is clear and the main supply route (MSR) remains open." He motioned for Alton to be quiet and pushed the headset tighter upon his ear. "Say again?" He spoke into the receiver and paused as the message was repeated into his ear. "Copy that."

"Let's head out," he advised to Alton. "New coordinates." The forward motion of the APC jerked, rattling both their helmets against the windshield. "You're about to enjoy your first night offensive as we move into sector one and relieve troop C."

"For how long?" Alton wrapped his hand around the pistol grip and leaned his shoulder against the gun's stock assembly. The sun was brutal, its heat burning his eyes and lips. He licked his lips and closed his eyes against the sun's harsh rays. How long, he wondered, until his body would look like the others, dark and tanned from the day-to-day rays upon his exposed skin? Would his family recognize him if he sent photos? Would Kathy?

Lisa Colodny

"Remember what I said, Ky. This minute, right now is all that's important." He tossed the spent cigarette away from the APC. You want to get home, you remember that."

****

August 1968

Dear Momma and Daddy,
I am okay. Finally got to Vietnam. Really hot but getting used to it. Please don't worry. I'm in a good unit. I am not scared. Lord has a plan for me written in his books, if I get home or not. You will get a war bond this month but only one, will sign up for soldier's deposit and be worth a little something when I get out of here. Don't worry if you don't get a letter in a day or two, we work like slaves here.
Love, Alton

****

There was not as much time to send letters home. You would think that there would be more down time but really, there was not. Endless days were spent in the field, patrolling up and down the MSR and offering support for one of the other two platoons. Any time spent at base camp was usually taken up bathing, sleeping, or enjoying a drink or two at the canteen.

Alton had managed to fire off a letter to Momma and Daddy within a few days of arriving to Cu Chi but the time between missions was occupied by sleeping in a cot with a mattress, a luxury he had come to appreciate. It was true, his bed at home was not big or luxurious. No doubt, his family had expended little money on the mattress. But it was a damn site better than the cushion that lined his cot in the barracks which was only slightly more comfortable than the sleeping cot within the APC. Most times, he slept sitting upright in his seat inside the APC or on the ground under the APC if the ground was dry enough to permit it. There were only a few sleeping cots stored within the APC and those were reserved for the soldiers with more seniority than Alton.

Given the frequency of missions, he had not been able to write anyone else, even Sis or Kathy. And although, he planned to write his brothers, the correspondence would, no doubt, be an awkward conversation. What could he say except that he had arrived in good health and planned to remain so? He supposed he could ask about the kids and his sisters-in-law, maybe make idle conversation about work at Ford Motor Company or for an update on that old car they were refurbishing. None of those topics would take more than a line, maybe two if he danced it out with fancy words whose definitions he really was not sure of. And as the exchange would be one-way, it seemed like more of a chore. He knew his momma would share the letters with his brothers along with anyone else who might pop in for a visit.

He could see her in his mind's eye stationed on the left side of the couch in the living room and reading his letter over the party line to Aunt Betty Jo. Yes, he heard her words, muffled in between bouts of coughing. Alton just got a promotion to Private First Class. She would push a cough drop between her lips and go on. And you know, he had to send his camera home for safe keeping. She would shake her head and provide the details. He wrote that he has been sleeping with it under his pillow so that it did not get stolen. Can you imagine having to sleep with it tucked under a pillow? At least with Sis, the conversation would flow more easily and honestly.

****
August 1968

Dear Sis,

I'm here in this hell hole but don't worry none. Like I told Momma and Daddy, the lord has fixed his plan for me in his book. My unit the three-four is hitting some action but I think I will be okay. I am not scared yet, but I imagine I will be in the future. Don't see how anyone has time to write letters in this place. Didn't get to stay with any of my buddies. They busted us up. Met a guy from

Lisa Colodny

Louisville, his last name is Skaggs, who knows Bobby Phillips. His brother used to work with Bobby at Phillip Morris. Wilbur bought that old 41 Plymouth from his brother. Small world, huh? Will close for now, it's raining again. Tell Allen and Gail, I will see them soon.

****

Alton had never been anywhere near a train wreck or airplane accident. In fact, he had never even been on a train and his first airplane trip was the one that had brought him to Vietnam. Still, he could imagine in his mind what one might sound like as thousands of pounds of motor and metal crashed against the ground or how it might feel as the ground shook under his feet upon the impact.

But anything he might have imagined in his mind would not have been accurate, not even close. There were simply no words to describe the sounds that echoed through the wind as a cargo plane or helicopter smacked the earth at hundreds of miles per hour. There was a sense of helplessness as the air exploded from the heat of the smoke as the gasoline-fed fires burned amid the urgency of searching for survivors and pulling them from the twisted, fiery wreck before the enemy could approach.

Although his job had been to provide artillery cover for the troops providing the actual rescue and aid to the fallen soldiers in the helicopter, he felt the loss just as deeply as if he pulled the soldier form the wreckage himself. It had taken days to erase the image of the soldier's body from his mind. The young man's body was badly burned with patches of seared tissue where skin had once been. Alton couldn't help but think of Garnet. He had not seen his brother's body but knew from the condition of his car and pieces of the adult conversations he had overheard, his brother's car had burned. Whether his brother was alive or not prior to the fire, he did not know, he had never asked. And as he watched the soldiers of the other troop drag the pilot's body away from the wreckage, he was grateful for the ignorance of his youth. He did not want to know.

It was of great comfort to consider Garnet was dead upon impact with the trees, he prayed the same was true for the pilot.

"They've blown the culvert!" Walter screamed from the other side of the APC, his hands yanking and pulling at the APC's knobs and levers with such force, Alton thought a fire might have been ignited somewhere in their compartment. Walter adjusted his goggles more securely over his eyes and navigated the APC into a one eighty turn so that they were in effect heading back in the direction they had just came. He pointed with his thumb over his shoulder to where the man-made piece of land that bridged over the water had been blown and as a result the water rushed angrily upon the ground making it impassable, especially against the weight of the heavy APC and tracks.

"What do we do now?" Alton screamed back against the roar of machine gun fire and artillery blasts that smacked the ground nearby. He knew keeping the main supply route open was an important responsibility. He fired the M60 at movement in the trees to his right, thinking the ease of pulling the trigger at a faceless intruder was easy. Would he be as inept at firing if the target was living and breathing in front of him and staring back with scared, anxious eyes?

"We got to accompany the convoy to an alternate route towards Tay Ninh to reinforce the base camp there." Walter called back. "You alright, Ky?" He adjusted several knobs on the APC and stole a quick look behind him. "If you need a minute, change places with Kris."

In the back of the APC, Kris, a soldier from Ohio, straightened his posture and tightened the grip on his rifle. "We can change, Ky."

"No," Alton shook his head. "I'm good." It was partially true, he was okay, at least he thought so. He was barely accustomed to Cu Chi base camp, the idea of going to another base camp was not appealing. He had been at Cu Chi for a little over four weeks, it felt as much like home as it was going to.

Everything had happened so quickly after he stepped off the cargo plane at Cu Chi. Almost immediately, he went to school, booby school, the seasoned soldiers called it. By the next day, he was in the field with the three-four calvary. There had been no transition phase, no freshmen year to learn his bearings. Within the time it took to blink, he was brandishing a machine gun and firing at anything that moved within the tree line. Would he know if he actually hit something? Would he feel in it his gut?

"Ky?" Walter called out again. "Either fire the M60 or get in the back so that Kris can."

"Sorry," he whispered, adjusting his body more fully around the butt of the rifle and firing into the chaos of smoke that covered the road. The gun popped like super-charged firecrackers as he fired off dozens of rounds. Was there a way, he wondered, to distinguish how it would sound when a round made contact with human tissue? Would it sound different? Was there a fragrance that would be exhaled into the surrounding air when a life was expelled? Did he really want to know the answers?

Alton in front of a Sherman tank, soon after arrival to Cu Chi Army Base, Vietnam

Chapter Nine

There was nothing unique about August nineteenth. It was not Alton's birthday, nor was it anyone in his family's. He was not sure of the date of his parent's anniversary. It was not a date that meant anything to him, until now.

The morning started off as routine as any other since his arrival to Vietnam until several platoons were ambushed on highway twenty-six near the Little Rubber Plantation by battalions of North Vietnamese who lay for about a mile within the fallen trees from the Rome Plow operation. The lead tank hit a mine and was under the heaviest of fire before they regrouped, secured their wounded, and called for evacuation of the wounded with assistance from another platoon who recently arrived on the scene.

The North Vietnamese continued to pound both platoons throughout the day as the battle to fight off the ambush and obtain medical attention for the wounded continued. Finally, as Alton's platoon raced toward the scene to offer support to the other platoons currently under attack, a helicopter landed atop the road effectively blocking their journey.

"What the hell is he doing?" Alton cried out over the echo of his pounding heart. "He's one of ours!"

"It's an ambush, a kill zone set up by the NVA," Walter answered, placing his hand over his headset so that he could better hear the pilot's justification. "He's pushing us back to safety as there's an airstrike coming."

Alton watched as the sky was lit as if by an imaginary fuse whose fire burned a vertical line behind the helicopter. Smoke and ash filled the air around the APC and Alton felt the heat of the fire upon his face. It singed the tiny hairs on his hands and under his nose. He was grateful he had foregone shaving for a few days. No doubt, his pre-beard had offered some protection for his skin. "My God," he whispered, wiping his eyes in the hope the scene before him was little more than a mirage.

For a moment, there was silence. Nothing moved. No grenades thrown or shots fired. There was a stillness, like the calm before the birth of a new day or seconds after a storm. Time slowed to a halt before the fast forward button was initiated. Everything seemed to be happening at once, in real time. Then the screaming began, hordes of pleas for help, layered between cries for help and the crushing sound of death as soldiers took their last breath. It was worse than the sound the massive trees made when they gave way to the blade of the Rome Plow.

"We have to help them," the words spilled from Alton's mouth while his mind struggled to keep up. His hand moved to the belt that secured his torso against the APC's seat.

"Our orders are to establish a platoon position at the intersection of Highways 26 and 239." With a shaking hand Walter set a new course for the APC and wiped the tears that refused to fall from his eyes.

"What about the wounded?" Alton's throat was dry. He cast a quick glance to the back where Kris and Marty sat, their attention focused on the burning field behind the helicopter as it lifted off and took flight once again.

"Most aren't ours," Walter explained, not making eye contact with Alton.

"But they are still people," Alton argued. "It doesn't seem right to —"

"Keep thinking like that Ky, just a matter of time," Marty advised from the rear of the APC, clearing his throat, and pulling his rifle closer against his body. His words were thick and throaty, unable to disguise the Southern drawl that lingered in the warning.

"Till what Marty?" Alton's words were short, his actions angry but he was not sure why. Marty was a likable guy who grew up in a small town in Tennessee. He and Alton had passed many evenings over the last month reconciling how similar their individual lives were.

"Till we send you home in a body bag," Walter answered for him. "Remember what I told you the first day we met?" He did not wait for Alton to answer. Instead, Walter went on. "You focus on this minute, right now and follow the order, without consideration or question." He stole a quick glance at the road in front of him. "Our orders are to retreat and set up at the intersection." He slammed the top three levers on the APC console as far up as they would go. "And that's what we're doing. Copy?"

"Copy that," Alton whispered, sliding down as far in the seat as the belt would allow.

Later on, after the smoke cleared and the battle ended, as his troop A made their way to Dau Tieng, Alton learned eleven soldiers had sacrifice their lives including Reese Waters, a medic Alton met a few a days ago at the mess hall. Additionally, there were over fifty NVA casualties. One tank and one APC were too damaged to be towed and subsequently left on the field. Dozens more on both sides of the conflict were wounded. Men with families just like his, praying for their safe return. No doubt, there were mommas and daddies, siblings and wives, probably even children, too, praying that their loved one would be afforded a life after the battle concluded. How was God able to tell whose prayer trumped whose?

****

Yesterday's battle would be imprinted on Alton's mind until the day he died. Maybe it was because it was his first battle? Perhaps it was the smell of burning flesh that was still pungent in his nose even though the fire had long been extinguished? From his position within the APC, he had not been able to see much of the carnage but the pleading cries for help had no trouble making the distance. He was sure, he would remember the anguish in their words for as long as he lived.

When night gave way to the day, his troop was among the troops to return to the site of the ambush. The losses to the NVA were greater than initially expected. Along the way, twenty-three more bodies were recovered and another seventy-one as a result of the air strike. The abandoned tank and APC were also recovered as was the body of one of their own. Alton watched with tears in his eyes as Reese's body was draped and lowered into the back of the vehicle. There was no need to call for a dustoff. Nothing could be done for Reese, except see that he was returned to his family for a proper burial.

****

"Is it always like this?" At first Alton did not think he had asked the question aloud. Truth be told, he meant for the inquiry to stay private. He juggled his machine gun from one shoulder to the other, rubbing the area where the gun was rubbing the skin raw.

"Like what?" Kris asked from inside the APC in the seat usually occupied by Alton. At first Alton thought the TC was punishing him for questioning the orders of yesterday. The assignment today was different. It was not the same as usual. Instead, he walked alongside the APC, making sure he kept the pace and surveyed the immediate area at the same time. His feet ached, from the tips of his toes to the backs of his ankles. First chance he got, he was going to ask his family to send a few pair of those thick, green army socks, like some of the other soldiers wore. Although the thin, white ones he had packed from home kept his feet cooler, they offered little barrier against the hard, tough leather of his boot. As a result, the skin around his toes and ankle was rubbed raw.

"Cross training," TC had advised, "is a critical concept of a platoon's successfulness." As a result, Kris was manning the M60 while Alton honed his skills in the art of booby trap identification. Alton had felt his heart drop to his knees even before the TC finished speaking. Alton did not know a lot about booby traps, but he knew enough to know sometimes the only way to find them was to walk upon them. He could hear his sweet momma's voice in his head asking him to promise her he'd return to her safely. Obviously, Momma knew nothing of booby traps and he only knew slightly more.

As Written

"It's only been a week or so since the ambush," Alton responded. "We packed up Reese's belongings and loaded them into a box with his body. His bunk was reassigned before the mattress was even cold."

"You and Black ain't getting along?" Kris asked keeping his words quiet.

"That's not it at all. Charlie seems like a nice enough guy," Alton explained, looking behind the trail of soldiers to a tall, lanky young man who seemed more inept at stocking groceries at the local market instead of pseudo-marching behind an APC. "I mean, when do we get a chance to mourn?"

"You don't," Kris advised. "Get your head on straight, Ky, or we'll be mourning you, soon enough."

"Hold up," Alton called out to Kris and then to Walter who was several paces behind him.

"What is it?" Walter stepped close to Alton and looked up as Alton indicated towards about twenty mounds of dirt stretched across the road. "Stay in the APC," Walter advised to the occupants. "Ky, with me." He turned back to the convoy. "Quiet everyone and keep your eyes peeled in the woods for snipers. Could very well be another ambush."

Ambush, the words echoed in his head as the visions returned. He heard the cries for help and smelled the stench of death again. Maybe his cousin was right. Maybe they should have all high tailed it to Canada? And where the hell had Buck ended up? No one seemed to know. His plane had taken off from Louisville, headed to California, and then nothing. The Herron family had no idea where he had planted his boots. At least Alton's family knew where he was, knew the danger that was all around him. Too bad the same could not be said for Buck's. Then again, maybe it was easier, not knowing?

One thing was for sure, if Alton's time was near, he did not want to go out like that. Although he was not sure how he wanted to go, he prayed he wouldn't suffer. Whatever happened would be quick, his body failing to register he had been hit and was dying. He did not want to have time to formulate a message or say his goodbyes. He found himself subconsciously checking the tree line for reflections from the morning sun of a sniper's gun.

"Eyes on the ground, Ky." Walter barked, not even bothering to look up. "Let them do their job and let's do ours. Everyone's going home tonight, ok?"

"Copy that," Alton whispered, fighting the urge to check the tree line again. Baby steps, it was the only way Alton could describe the manner in which he and Walter made their way closer to the mounds of dirt. Step by step, each inch was inspected for any sign of a trip wire or pressure switch.

By the time they reached the first mound, there was not a dry place on Alton's shirt. Even his palms were sweating, he had never been more terrified in his life than as he dropped to his knees to finger weave the dirt away from the mound's center so that he could take a better look.

"Marty, you and Ky take this half. Charlie and I will take the other half. Everyone else is on point for snipers." Walter sounded older than his twenty-one years. And it was hard to image he only had a few more months under his belt than Alton.

"Take your time," he barked at the others as they made their way closer to the mounds of dirt. "Charlie, with me. Take that mound. I'll start on this one."

"Come on," Alton said to Marty. "I'll start here. You start over there on those. And remember, just because one mound isn't booby trapped, doesn't mean another isn't. Treat them all as if they are."

"Copy that," Marty said as he moved farther down the road to the mounds farthest away from the APC. Alton smiled to himself, thinking he was sounding more like Walter every day.

****

Two hours, it had taken over two hours to sift through all twenty mounds of dirt and pronounce them "clean" to the rest of the platoon. It would have been an easier task without the thick flak jacket and helmet, but just because the NVA was not hiding in the woods one minute did not mean they were not the next. As a result, it was against army protocol to be without the protective gear anywhere except within the confines of base camp. And even there, some soldiers preferred to remain under the protective barriers of metal jacket and bucket (helmet).

"Load up," Walter called out as he waited for everyone to take their assigned places. "Ky, you okay on foot?"

"Yeah," Alton nodded, feeling more confident about the assignment as every minute passed. Maybe he should have held onto his camera and while longer. It might have been productive to take a self-portrait and compare it to his picture before he left home. He had changed in the months he had been away; he could feel it deep in his gut. Baby was gone, killed in the line of duty perhaps? A new man had been born outside the Cu Chi Base Camp. He was like a toddler, learning to walk on his own again.

"Not again," the words were exhaled from Kris' mouth in little more than a sigh. This time however, the route was not blocked by mounds of dirt. Instead, the block consisted of palm leaves scattered across the road.

"Ky," Walter barked again, "with me. Everyone else man your post and be on the lookout for snipers." Walter was quiet as he and Alton cautiously approached. "What do you see?" Walter asked once they were closer to the leaves.

"Leaves," Alton answered, his words deliberate. "But this feels different."

"Different?" Walter paused, "how so?"

"I don't know," Alton admitted. "It just feels different."

"Let's move the leaves, stack them stem first on the left side of the road." Walter inspected the palm leaf nearest to his feet. "Make sure the area on the side is clear before you start trampling over there."

"Copy that," Alton carefully selected the fat stem of one leaf laying across the others. After a quick check for trip wires or switches, he moved the limb to the side of the road to an area he had deemed free of devices. It did not take long to clear the road of the leaves. In most cases, the cover was only a single layer deep. Once the leaves were stacked away, two deliberate mounds of dirt were visible, one was about a foot tall while the other was about two feet tall

"Like before, take your time and go slow," Walter advised bending down to the mound nearest him and sorting through the dirt.

Alton nodded and dropped to his feet, moving the dirt away from the center as gently as he could. The dirt was looser on the top, especially on the top where it peaked. But once he moved deeper into the hole, the dirt was damper and packed to the extent moving it away was strenuous.

"Nothing here," Walter called out as he came to the bottom of his pit. If he had noticed Alton jump, he did not comment. Instead, he pushed his tired bones to his feet and watched as Alton continued to clear the dirt from the second pit.

"Walter?" Alton stepped away from the edge of the hole and pointed to the bottom of the hole where a small canister was present.

"Looks like a chicom pressure mine," Walter took long strides back to the APC and reached through the open window to the radio. He reappeared seconds later back to Alton's side. "HQ's wants us to detonate it."

"Detonate it?" Alton took a step backwards as if Walter had cited he had an infectious disease. "How do we do that?"

"Take the long arm and gently pick it up. Walk it over to the field and set it down gently. Then we make sure everyone is a safe distance and we blow it." Walter's words were as if he were giving directions to a destination.

"You want me to?" Alton swallowed, remembering his promise to his mother.

"Best you learn now than when you come across one on your own. If you don't want to do it, I can." Walter motioned for Kris to bring the arm.

"I can do it," Alton advised, motioning for the long metal arm as Kris grew closer. It took minute or two to familiarize himself with the mechanics of the arm. If was like a water hose where you squeezed the nozzle to ignite the flow of water. Only in this case, squeezing the nozzle, activated the hand at the end.

"Take your time," Walter reminded him. "Walk soft and steadily and set if just off the road."

"Why can't we just blow it here?" Alton wished he could push the words back in his mouth. Once again, he had questioned an order and the look on Walter's face said it all.

"If we blow it here, the road will be impassable, the trucks can't get through with the supplies." Walter did not try to hide his frustration. "Give it to me. I'll do it myself."

"No," Alton shook his head. "I'll do it." He adjusted the fingers of the hand on the device and pushed his weapon into Walter's hand. Sweat dripped like a river as he squatted as close to the pit as he could and collected the canister between the claws of the hand. Steady, he told himself. Just steady his hand and take even, solid steps toward the side of the road. The walk seemed to take forever and by the time he came to a stop near the designated detonation area, he was not sure Walter could hear the question over the beating of Alton's heart. "Here?"

"Yeah, Ky, that's fine. Sit it down gently and walk slowly away." Walter motioned for the rest of the platoon to load up and move further down the road. Once Alton was close enough, he handed him a medium size stone with rounded edges. It looked more like a baseball than a rock. "You play sports in Kentucky, Ky?"

"Yes," Alton held his hand out for the stone. "Some. You just want me to hit it with the rock?"

"Yeah, make sure you're clear and take a few rocks with you just in case your aim ain't as good as you think." Walter took his place behind the APC and indicated for Alton to toss the rock.

Alton could not have thrown it any better if he had tried. The stone hit the canister dead in the center, a bull's eye if it had been a target taped on the wall. The area around the canister exploded, tossing dirt and grass several feet into the air. Once the dust and dirt settled, a good size crater scarred the ground.

"Good job, Ky." Walter patted Alton's shoulder as he walked by and took his place in line towards the rear of the walking convoy.

Lisa Colodny

****

Darkness came quickly once the convoy came to a stop. It was as if a switched somewhere high in the sky was flipped and the sun dropped like an anchor behind the horizon, blanketing the spaces between the trees and military vehicles in darkness until the moon climbed its way up into the night sky and illuminated some of the places like a spotlight.

Alton tossed the remnants of his dinner plate into the trash, sliding both chocolate chip cookies into a worn napkin and wrapping them securely into the pocket of his knapsack. The cookies were tasty but not as pleasing as his momma's. There was not a secret family recipe that she might one day pass to one or more of her grandchildren. Most times she minimized the time on her feet by "guesstimating" the amount of the ingredients, given it consumed most of her energy to mix up the batter. And there was little chance of a secret ingredient. There was little money for luxuries and baked goods were a luxury. Most times it was just flour, sugar, and butter with a splash of vanilla. What was unique to his momma's cookies was the addition of several handfuls of raisins in addition to the chocolate chips.

No one else cared for the combination. Most times, she rolled out about half the portion of dough onto the baking sheet, leaving the rest to be adulterated with the raisins and rolled into another baking pan. Although not written in stone, it was understood that the combination was meant for Alton. And he liked the feeling that warmed him all the way down to his core every time he opened the oven door to check on the status of his cookies. Momma had made them special for him. Even though the cookies were often burned and crisp around the edges, they were perfect. And he longed for one now.

****

"You're quiet tonight, Ky," Stanley Jarvis stepped over Alton's feet and took the empty place between Walter and Kris, nearly smacking his head against the exterior of the APC. Jarvis steadied his plate in the palm of his big, dark hand and fell hard upon his backside in a manner that made Alton think of his brother. Wilbur was the tallest member of the family and sometimes, it seemed to those in observation that he was consumed of only two very long legs. This meant as a youngster, he could run faster and jump higher than most of the other boys who lived on and around Elkhorn Hill. It also meant he had a much greater distance to "travel" when he tumbled off the tobacco wagon or fell from the barn's rafters. It seemed to Alton and Delmore, Wilbur's legs were a frequent obstacle to him staying on his feet. And being brothers, there was never a missed opportunity to remind him.

"Tired is all," Alton scanned the area in front of the APC again, watching the way the leaves moved in the moonlight and listening for the sounds of the jungle for any indication that the troop was not alone.

"No story tonight?" Jarvis stuffed one of the smaller portions of beef between his lips and wiped his mouth with the back of his sleeve. It was true the best meal of the day on the field was dinner. The kitchen unit arrived early each day and set up quickly preparing bacon, eggs, and bread for the soldiers. There was plenty of fresh fruit and even pancakes were available. Lunch was usually the only meal the soldiers ate from their rations. It was not a bad meal but feigned in comparison to the steaks and breasts of chicken that were roasted nightly on the grill. Most times, there were potatoes and vegetables, more fresh fruit, and even dessert. Uncle Sam did his best to see that no American soldier in Vietnam went hungry. Alton could not help but think of Bentley Peters. Had dinner been prepared under the hand of his handsome, blonde friend from Fort Campbell? Alton made a mental note to inquire in the morning when the food trucks delivered breakfast. Perhaps one of the soldiers who set up the meals in the field might know Bentley?

"Story?" Alton repeated, even though he had heard Jarvis quite clearly. Jarvis was a mountain of a man with thick arms, legs, and neck. His hands were huge, perfectly fitted to work the gears that steered the Rome Plows. Alton knew without looking the tips of Jarvis' fingers and his palms were calloused from the long hours of plowing down the trees in and around Hobe Woods. It would have been impossible not to have felt the scars as their hands made contact upon introductions last month.

"You always have some story to tell," Jarvis stuffed a spoonful of beans into his mouth and laughed, his dark eyes squinting into the darkness as if something had caught his eye. The distraction was fleeting, a moment regained once his attention turned back to Alton and the others. His free hand made a slapping sound against his thigh. "That one about your brother trying to get to the outhouse and your sister coming up behind him and knocking him to the ground causing him to fill his britches is priceless."

Alton's laughter was drowned out by the squeals of the other soldiers as one and then another recanted various pieces of Wilbur's event. Alton saw it all again in his mind's eye. His brother could not have been more than thirteen or so, with Delmore's hand-me-down jeans rolled up around his ankles. His pace was anxious as he took uneven steps towards the outhouse, pausing every few steps and offering a silent prayer that his stomach might settle so that he could finish the trip.

Sis had recanted the story so many times, Alton heard her words on the ledge of the night air as it passed by him and the other soldiers. "I could hear his stomach rolling," Sis had said. "Not an empty growl but a screech as if an animal had died inside of him." She laughed and added how she knew he was trying to get to the outhouse before he messed his pants. She followed him out the door and waited a few steps behind him as he danced along the back yard towards the outhouse, stopping every minute or two as if to gather the contents of his stomach and force it still.

It had only taken him a minute or two to realize she was behind him and had devised a plan. Sis laughed child-like and stalked him like an animal might her prey.

"Sis," Wilbur pleaded, his arms wrapped around his midsection as if he were pregnant with child. "Leave me be, please."

"What's wrong, little brother?" She moved closer, her hands stretched towards him and with mischief in her eyes.

"Don't touch me, Sis, please?" he added as an afterthought and his expression one of great hope.

She closed the distance between them in three successive steps and gave him a single shove once she was close enough to lay hands on him. Wilbur did not try to break his fall until the moment of impact, his hands breaking contact with his stomach just as his body made contact with the hard ground under his feet.

The odor was the first indication Wilbur had emptied his bowels, followed by a dark stain that erupted on his backside and down the inside of his legs. "Sis," he half laughed, half cried. "Just you wait." But Alton knew it was all said and done in fun. Wilbur, himself, had told the story dozens of times as an adult and always with affection. There would be no retaliation, at least, not until the next time.

"Ky?" Jarvis' voice was like a beacon pulling Alton from his recollection and back into the present day and time. "You with us?"

"Yeah," Alton laughed. "I was just thinking about my sister and brothers. I don't think Wilbur ever paid her back for the outhouse push." His thoughts danced through the memories as it they were file folders, and his mind was the finger that flipped through them one by one.

"He didn't get her back?" one of the other soldiers asked, dropping his empty plate to the ground.

"No," Alton shook his head. "At least if he did, they didn't share the story with me." His gaze drifted back to Jarvis as he pushed the last bite of steak into his mouth and wrapped his lips around a worn canteen.

Jarvis swallowed the last drop, holding the canteen's bottom to the sky. "So, no story tonight?"

Alton shook his head. "Not tonight, but I sure do wish I had a chili dog from the Dairy Queen on Main Street." He searched the night sky for a falling star to make the wish upon. Hell, any old star would do. Would kicking his heels together help get him home?

There was nothing more he wanted than to be parked at the Dairy Queen in Daddy's old red truck waiting on the server to bring out a bag of chili dogs and some fries—the short, crinkle ones that were crispy on the outside, yet soft in the middle. Was it a warning, a bad omen of things, yet to come? He saw visions of a prisoner being escorted to enjoy his last meal, a meal of chili dogs and crinkle-cut french fries. No, he told himself. He had made a promise to his momma, he was going to keep it.

Chapter Ten

The radio exploded to life a little after 0030 hours, interrupting the cadence of tree frogs and night crickets that echoed from the jungle of trees on the other side of the field where the fallen trees lay. Alton crawled out from under the APC as if a firecracker had been lit at his side. His boots kicked the dirt away from the hole he had been sleeping comfortably in for the better part of three hours and used his elbows as leverage to squeeze his body out from under the vehicle. Once his feet were clear of the under carriage, he clawed his way to his feet, never once losing his grip on his rifle, and grabbed for the radio mounted to the dash. It crackled as if it had been struck by lightning amidst the backdrop of gunfire and soldier's voices, some shouting orders, others crying out for assistance. He could not make out most of the words coming from the soldier on the other end of the radio, but he was able to delineate the name Schofield and NVA amid the men for assistance. "What are we doing?" Alton called back to his commander and looked anxiously over his shoulder for Walter and the rest of his platoon.

"Hold this line," the commander yelled back, barking orders to troop A as he ran from one APC and tank to the other. "Get that MK singing, soldier," he called back to Alton.

Alton was already in position. He fastened the strap of his bucket more securely under his chin and slung the chain of ammunition across his chest so that it would feed in a perfectly straight line into the gun. "Coordinates verified," Alton screamed to no one in particular before his gun erupted into action, fire pulsating from the chambers as expelled shells shot into the air like bees, but he gave them no mind. He was fixated on eliminating an enemy he could not see, one who hid out in the open under the guise of the night sky. There were no faces to haunt him his dreams and from the distance, no screams either. There was only the darkness and the smell of spent gunpowder as it dissipated into the air around him and traveled like a trojan horse into his lungs. He knew it was a part of him now and would be with him always.

****

The enemy did not withdraw until well after 04:30 after taking a beating that included more than two thousand artillery rounds being deployed and support from both gunships and AC-47 aircraft. At first light, a sweep of the area located over a hundred enemy casualties, several prisoners of war, and an assortment of NVA equipment.

Although Alton's APC had emerged intact, others closer to the line of engagement were not as fortunate, four APCs and two tanks were destroyed. He watched in silence as the commander waved the medics towards one of the APCs, but Alton knew from the expression on the Commander's face, it was just an exercise, a formality that had to be completed. The medic was not rushing to the soldier's side to offer assistance. He was there to pronounce him. All that was missing was the priest to deliver last rites.

It was a passing thought, there was no indication why the impression entered his mind. It just did. It sat upon his mind as a leaf might make its way from the highest tree branch to the ground. Had the State Trooper called an ambulance to the scene of Garnet's accident that night? Or had he radioed the funeral home, instead? He knew Daddy and Delmore went to the scene and watched as his brother's mangled car was pulled from between the trees that stood like soldiers along the bending road to Mannsville. Garnet's body, no doubt, was already in route to Parrot and Ramsey funeral home where Mr. Dabney would be waiting to process his remains. It was true, Alton's family was not overtly religious. There was no designated pew waiting for them at church on Sunday mornings, but they were a Christian family. They believed in the holy trinity, that Jesus was the father, son, and holy ghost. Had Garnet received last rites at the scene by Pastor Henry, the minister at Elkhorn Baptist Church? Had Mr. Dabney arranged for a prayer upon Garnet's arrival at the funeral home?

"Phillips?" his commander's voice loomed overhead, close enough so that Alton could feel his warm breath as he exhaled his question. "You alright?"

"Yes, Sir," Alton pulled his eyes away from the medic's retreating figure from the APC and waited for the commander to speak again.

"Did you know PFC Higgins?" The commander's voice was low, hushed, and sincere as if he were offering the benediction at the summation of a church service. "Was he a close friend?"

"I knew him, Sir," Alton swallowed the knot threatening to strangle the life from his throat, "but not well." What he really wanted was to look away while Higgins' platoon gently pulled his body from the APC, but he could not. It was as if his eyes were a magnet and the scene unfolding in front of him was the steel.

Defiant. It was the only word that came to his mind as he continued to monitor the scene at Higgins' APC. It was as if his brain wanted to recall every minute even as his heart instructed him to file it away and never think of it again. It was a directive he wished he could follow, but he knew, somewhere deep inside his body, buried beneath skin and bone, the memory would live on. With every beat of his heart, the ache of the loss would echo and resonate until the day he took his last breath.

It was a fact. The possibility of death was seldom far away. Back home, Pastor Henry was a distant reminder of the fragility of life. But here and now, in this place and time, the footsteps of death were near enough to hear the sweet melody of the angels around every turn. He was beginning to detest the sound of their songs, angelic or not.

It was true, he had not known Higgins well at all. A nod between the two at the canteen, a shoulder bump on way to the showers, that was all that connected them. Still, there it was again, that nagging feeling that there was meant to be more, maybe something that had not been written yet and now, never would be. Higgins' light was extinguished, his book unwritten. Was their intersect meant as a premonition that Alton might share a similar fate? The thought only lasted a second before his momma's smiling face bullied the consideration away.

Alton at Cu Chi Base Camp in Vietnam

Two weeks. It had been two weeks since Higgins' death and there had been little time to mourn him. Within twenty-four hours, his belongs were boxed up and dropped off with the commander's aid who was given the daunting task of cataloging every item in Higgins' possession, down to the number of cigarettes remaining in the opened pack. And within forty-eight hours, his bunk was reassigned to newcomer, Bailey Portman, who reigned from Beaumont, Texas. Portman's presence would serve as a bitter reminder that everyone was replaceable, it was simply a matter of changing out the bedsheets. And it was understood, there was no time to mourn.

Booby traps, almost every minute of the time succeeding Higgins' death had been consumed by dismantling and blowing booby traps placed in plain sight by the NVA along the main supply routes to Saigon. It was difficult to predict which mounds of dirt and curtains of palm leaves concealed chicom pressure mines underneath and which ones did not. Therefore, life and death depended upon managing each event as if the traps were armed with live devices.

"You would think they'd get tired of digging these stupid holes for nothing." Bailey groaned as he pulled at the long end of a tree stump and drug it away from the road, stopping short of the swampy grass and letting it drop with a thud.

"Takes us longer to assess the holes than it does for the VC to dig the hole," Alton offered, pausing only long enough to gulp greedily from his canteen. "So, maybe the ploy ain't as foolish as it seems." He wiped his forehead with the back of his hand and dropped back to his knees to review the next stockpile of dirt and grass debris. "They been gone for hours, probably back at their barracks drinking a beer and satisfied with how they've monkey-wrenched our day."

"Fire in the hole," one of the two nearby soldiers called out before blowing a newly uncovered pressure mine. Alton and Bailey dropped to the ground and covered their heads, waiting for the dirt and leaves that were blown into the sky to fall back to the ground.

"See," Alton pushed himself to his feet. "You become lax and take for granted there's no mine, you go home in pieces in a body bag." He turned to look at the newcomer. "Bailey, you listening to me?"

"Yeah, Ky," the young man brushed the dirt off his pants and watched as the other soldiers motioned him over. "I hear you. I gotta go help them clear the road."

Linwood Turner. Alton's thoughts wandered back to the other side of the world where his momma and daddy were, most likely sound asleep in their beds like everyone else within the county lines of Taylor County. Bailey Portman reminded Alton of Linwood Turner. Linwood was an only child, the son of the high school principal, who was indulged frequently with extravagant possessions, whether they were deserved or not. Linwood had taken a liking to Delmore's restored 53 Chevy, the car Alton drove routinely. When Delmore refused Mr. Turner's offer to purchase the vehicle, Linwood had been given an almost exact replica, with the exception of the hand painted names of his daughters on either side of the car.

That meant that when both cars were in the same vicinity of town, Alton was able to attract the attention of the local police officers in some mundane violation of law and then guide the officer to Linwood's vicinity and then dart behind one building or another so that the officer would unknowingly pull Linwood over for the offense.

Watching the surprise expression on Linwood's face as he was cited time after time, eventually lost its attraction for Alton and he moved on to another adventure. Looking back, should he have sought Linwood out and apologized for the youthful indiscretion? Or should Alton add the confession to the list of wrongs he would right upon his return home? He smiled and lit another cigarette, finding comfort in the knowledge that his apology could wait.

"Watch your step," Alton advised as his thoughts settled to the present time and place. He was uncomfortable with the tone in his warning to Bailey. Every day that passed he sounded less like himself and more like someone who was in charge. It was hard for him to recall much about Garnet, other than the stories Delmore and Sis told. One thing he did remember was the authoritative tone in Garnet's voice. It was the same decibel he heard in Delmore's sometimes, usually when Delmore was trying to either make a point or teach a lesson. Did Bailey hear the same attitude in Alton's words? He hoped not, he did not want to be in charge of anyone except himself. His singular goal was to get himself home safely. He did not want the responsibility of getting anyone else back safely.

****

Labor day came and went. He wondered if his family celebrated the holiday at Miller Park, as was their custom. There would have been little to prepare for the event. Baked beans and potato chips were inexpensive side dishes. And several packages of meat should be more than enough to celebrate the holiday. No doubt, the children would want hot dogs, hamburgers, and chicken for the adults. Steak was a rarity and too expensive, even if everyone pitched in a few dollars.

Discarded paper cups were perfect vehicles for the children to trap the tiny crawdads that roamed up and down the small creek running through Miller Park. The distraction afforded the adults some time to rest and reconnect as the children wandered up and down the creek bed chasing the crawdads.

Every dime counted, and a penny saved was a penny earned, as his daddy had said many times over the years. Paying Peter in real time, might mean borrowing from Paul later on. With Christmas around the corner, no one would have much to spare. Even Wilbur would be on a budget now too. He was a married man now and his stepchildren would need presents under the Christmas tree. Life had moved on for them, yet it had remained stagnant too. It was the same and different, all at once.

Alton did not want his deployment to Vietnam to change his family in any way. He hoped they had found the courage to celebrate the holiday in his absence and he hoped it was at the park as usual. Probably Sis had given some speech about how celebrating was the right thing to do and what Alton would expect of them. She was right, he did expect life to go on for them. Regardless of the war's outcome, their life on and around Elkhorn Hill should continue as was God's plan. It should move forward as it was written, with or without him.

****

"Steak," he mumbled under his breath and laughed to himself to conceal his amusement as the cook dropped a medium well steak atop Alton's plate. His thoughts fluttered back to the holiday picnic he had, in all likelihood, missed and hoped he could be in attendance some future year.

"I was hoping for hot dogs," Walter dropped into the empty place next to Alton. "My family does a picnic around the holiday." He stuffed a forkful of mashed potato salad into his mouth and waited for Alton to respond. "Did you get the road cleared?" He asked once it was obvious Alton was not adding to the conversation.

"Yeah," Alton nodded. "We moved the school benches off the road and blew the mine, but the crater would have impaired the traffic, so we filled it with laterite." He pointed to reams of paper, stacked in irregularly stacked piles. "There were hundreds of those fluttering about once the mine blew. We collected them per policy and brought them back to base camp for intelligence to study."

"Addressed to the US service men, again?" Walter asked.

Alton nodded, "Yes, and explains how we are fighting for causes not our own. And should lay down arms and return to our homes." He paused and sliced the steak into two even portions, wrapping the smallest piece in a cloth napkin and sliding it into his knapsack. "If only we could," he added as if the thought simply popped into his mind.

"For that mutt that followed us back to camp?" Walter asked, although by the way he asked the question, it was obvious he already knew the answer.

"It's three seconds away from starvation," Alton added. "No need to let it starve to death. I've had plenty." He pulled a cigarette from the opened pack and struck his Zippo lighter several times before a flame finally burned long enough to light his cigarette. "I like dogs, cats too, but I prefer dogs. We got a dog at home, a German Shepard. Daddy thinks she's smarter than some people we know." He smiled and leaned closer towards Walter. "Course, most times he's talking about my brother-in-law."

Alton pushed the crumbled pack back into his jacket pocket and blew the smoke away from Walter's face. "I applied to work with the dogs in the K9 unit. Haven't heard yet but I figure since I'm already here, it don't look good that I'll get one."

"You got a soft side, Ky," Walter stuffed. "Ain't saying there's anything wrong with it, unless it gets you killed." His eyes met Alton's before he went on. "Like those Vietnamese kids you bring pennies to?"

"It's just a handful of change. Ain't gonna break my bank," Alton looked away, his face flush from embarrassment. He tapped his pocket again where his lighter was. "I need to get one of them to fill it up for me. Marty said they'll do it for a quarter."

"No, it won't break you, but the tender side of you might be your downfall." Walter's tone was sounding an awful lot like Delmore's. Alton could not decide if the realization was comforting or disheartening. Before he could decide, Walter went on. "Can you do what you have to do if the situation calls for it?"

"I don't understand what you're asking, Walt?" Alton's face was blank as he dropped the rest of the plate atop the table not bothered by the remnants that fell from the plate to the tabletop.

"If that scrappy dog or one of those kids wanders into camp with a grenade strapped around their body, can you do what needs to be done to save yourself or your fellow soldiers?" Walter asked the question without taking a breath. It was obvious to Alton; Walter had not wanted to ask the question and to do so had caused him immense pain.

"I'm not the kind of man to shoot a kid even to save myself," Alton stood up, his face red and hands shaking. "If I did, there'd be nothing for me to go home to." He collected his knapsack. "I don't want to talk about this. God willing, none of us will ever have to make a choice like that." He pulled the knapsack across his shoulder, a signal he was ready to make his exit. "How did it go with the Commander?"

"Initially he thought enemy fire took out the APC; when it was discovered the damage was caused by Bailey's cigarette, he flipped. Had to modify his official report and all. I think he was embarrassed."

"All of us smoke in the APC," Alton explained. "Could have happened to any one of us."

"No one else has dropped a lit cigarette and incinerated the APC," Walter's words were succinct. He wasted no time in delivering his next directive. "To reinforce protocol compliance within troop A, we've waived our next two periods for furlough in exchange for vehicle maintenance and cleaning."

"What's that mean?" Alton looked behind to where Bailey and several other soldiers were finishing their meal. Bailey was not the youngest man in the troop, but he certainly did appear to be the most naïve. He was routinely being lured away by the others on some wild goose chase perceived by the others as a joke.

"We'll be cleaning the three-four's vehicles and checking tire pressure, fluid levels, etc." Walter's words were dry but without animosity. Alton knew Bailey was liked by everyone including Walter. But giving up two furloughs to wash the vehicles was not going to go over well with the rest of the platoon. Once again, Alton was humbled by Walter's ability to guide and lead the troop into a pre-determined way of reacting. He was an amazing leader and would no doubt make an amazing commander one day. Unfortunately, Alton had no intention of ever serving under his friend. Growth like that would require years and years of service, he was going home as soon as his time was up. There would never be any situation that could present itself where the outcome was anything other than a trip home to Elkhorn Hill.

****

"We gotta move," Bailey's voice over the radio was loud and anxious, but confident at the same time. The week since he had arrived at Cu Chi had aged him like a fine wine. "Need a dustoff," he explained. "the fifty-caliber machine gun blew up. We have a man down."

"Negative," the commander's voice, "need you to move out of the perimeter of Mo Duc. C troop has oxen and carts blocking the road but cannot engage until you change coordinates."

"Copy that," Alton responded into the radio before adding, "Holding for new coordinates." He waited as the APC changed direction. Dustoffs were designed to be an exception to the everyday routine of wartime operations. Only minor injuries were treated at Cu Chi Base Camp, any injury of great significance was managed at Da Nang military hospital or aboard one of the military hospital naval ships.

After the dustoff was complete, troop A moved to conduct a search and destroy mission into a series of bunkers. In the past, Alton's engagement had been above the ground and from inside the protective bubble of the APC. He had fired his weapon across an expansive distance into the jungles. There was a high probability his shells had collided with tree trunks, emersed themselves into the swampy water of the landscape, and whirled past the swaying grasses into the unknown abyss. More than likely, at least some of bullets that left his gun had found their mark and made contact with his enemy. At least, he thought there was a fair chance he had.

But this would be different. The thought of leaving the sanctuary of the APC and potentially coming face to face within the confines of the bunker with an NVA soldier, one he would be expected to kill, was weighing hard upon his mind. As familiar as death was to him, Alton had observed it from the safe distance of the first pew at the town's funeral home. Death had not come at his own hand, and he bore no responsibility for his brother's accident or subsequent death.

However, once he entered the bunker with his machine gun in his hand, there was only a single pathway once the enemy was encountered. He would have to kill or be killed. And he had made his momma a promise. It was one he planned on keeping.

****

"You ok?" Walter's words echoed in Alton's mind as if the syllables were running a race and his forehead was holding a checkered flag. His hands shook as his fingers fumbled with the cigarette pack and finally freed one from the crumbled package.

Alton nodded and pushed the cigarette between his lips, pausing to allow the nicotine-filled smoke to fill his lungs before exhaling it from his nose like lava. There were no words to express what he was feeling as he and his troop exited the bunker and climbed their way out of the tunnel to stand, once again, on solid ground and look up towards the sky as if it were an old friend.

The sun's rays were warm upon his face as he closed his eyes against the brightness of the light. Inside the bunker, it had been dark. The air was damp and smelly as if the moisture itself was trapped within the humid walls of the tunnel. It had taken great resolve not to reach out and lay hands upon its soft exterior but that would result in having only a single grip upon his weapon. And he knew the action would be in great contradiction to his training. Still, he longed to know if the mud was cool like the walls of the caves back home that lay hidden among the woods near where the Green River merged with Cumberland lake. His inquiry would remain a mystery as he tightened his grip on his gun and trudged deeper into the belly of the tunnel, praying the structure was just as it appeared, abandoned.

His prayer was lost amid the noise as flurries of machine gun fire echoed and crashed into one wall and then another as if someone had driven a train into the bunker and it collided nearby. Alton's weapon lurched forward in his arms as if had a lifeforce and a will of its own. There was little time for debate, his finger pulled repeatedly at the trigger until movement at his left and right stilled. It happened, simultaneously, in slow motion. The NVA soldiers fell to the ground and the firing ceased. The air was still, and it was quiet once again. There was little doubt, this time where his bullets had ended up. There were no trees, swamp grass, or bodies of water to absorb the shells. The answer was lying dead in the mud at his feet.

Alton watched as the bodies were drug through the tunnel and dropped atop the ground. He did not wait and watch while the bodies were searched for NVA paraphernalia. Instead, he turned, hoping to return to the APC and use the massive vehicle as a screen to cover his actions from prying eyes while he emptied his stomach. There was little doubt, he should have felt better once his stomach was bare, but he did not, and he eased himself to ground and rested his back against the side bumper to catch his breath. No doubt someone, probably Walter, would wander over to check on him.

"We need another dustoff," Walter barked once he got closer but still a safe distance from the odor of the vomitus.

"I'm fine," Alton wiped his mouth with the back of his hand. "I wasn't expecting he'd be so close that I could see his face." Alton inhaled a long breath of smoke from the cigarette. "His eyes," he paused and looked away from Walter. "I won't ever forget the way he looked at me."

"No Ky, you won't, but you'll learn to bury it inside yourself with all the other things you'll see here but never want to talk about." Walter pointed inside to the APC. "Call for the dustoff."

"I'm fine," Alton said again as he pulled himself to his feet and slung his gun over his shoulder.

"Not for you, for the new guy who arrived from Fort Jackson," Walter explained watching as several soldiers carried another soldier from the bunker. "He passed out when the shooting started and hit his head. He'll need to be evaluated by the doctor before coming back to the field."

"Surprised he didn't scare himself to death," one of the soldiers mumbled once he was closer to Walter and Alton. "Says he was sick before we went into the bunker, but I don't believe him." He turned to observe the young medic who was trying to stop the blood flowing from the other soldier's head wound.

"Nobody cares what you think, Sanford," the medic's words were only half kidding. "He engaged, that's all any of us can do."

"He didn't fire a shot," Sanford explained, "he fell like a sack of potatoes as soon as the first shot was fired." Sanford was a big burly man whose confidence gave him the appearance that he was much older than the others. In truth, he was not much older than the others, including Alton. "Not like my man, Ky, over here."

Once he was close enough, Sanford slapped Alton on the back as if they were on a football field at home on a Friday night. "I think you got him, Ky." If he noticed how quickly Alton's posture changed or how pale his face became, Sanford gave no indication.

"Bullets were flying everywhere," Alton swallowed down the bile gathering at the base of his stomach. "How could you possibly know that?" There was no doubt Alton had hit his target, but how could the kill shot be traced back to a particular soldier or bullet?

"You've got good reflexes," Sanford looked to Walter for confirmation. "Yours was the first shot. VC was already on their way down where the rest of us started firing." His cadence was paused only momentarily before he added. "Congratulations, you got your first kill. Lost your battle virginity."

"I'll call for the dustoff for the new guy," Alton slid between Walter and the hulking figure of Sanford and climbed into the APC, reaching for the radio before his backside was even comfortable in the seat. He held his breath for a minute as if the act might offer him the opportunity to go back in time, just a few minutes was all he needed. Back to the moment in the tunnel, right before his finger caressed the trigger. He would pause only long enough for someone else to take the first shot.

There had been a comfort in not knowing the outcome of his rifle discharges. Until now, they had been merely sounds, like firecrackers on the fourth of July. They were faceless actions whose presence were a necessity, one that brought him one step closer to going home to Elkhorn.

He exchanged a sideways look to Walter and Sanford, deep in conversation where he had left them. They were both good men, he knew this to be true. No doubt their time in Vietnam had changed them, made better able to accept the task at their hands. Had there been a time, not too long ago, when one or both had sneaked off the battlefield to empty their stomachs in private? Would he, himself, in the not-too-distant future, accept the action of war as a necessity and render it in any manner that afforded him the best probability of getting home in a single piece? He had boarded the plane in Louisville as a man with principles handed down from one generation to the other. Would he be the same man in eighteen months when the plane touched down in Louisville and brought him home? He prayed so.

Alton engaging with some local South Vietnamese children from a nearby Village, He frequently carried pennies in his pocket just to give to the children.

Chapter Eleven

Alton was no stranger to work in and around the farms on Elkhorn Hill. Although Daddy farmed only enough as to put food on the table, from an early age Alton earned his spending money by cutting and housing tobacco on his uncles' farms. In addition, Winfrey and Willard Lee's grandparents had a huge farm, there was always hay to be cut or tobacco to be stripped. Work was never scarce. Alton knew the value of a good day's work, traveling around the world did nothing to alter that perception.

It had been a harrowing few days since he and his platoon had cleared the bunker. During that time, they had provided support while the engineers swept sector seven A for mines, evacuated civilians from the wood line, and waited as other platoons searched spider holes in the sectors adjacent to where troop A was currently hunkered down for support. It was hard to determine which was more taxing on the nerves, the actual engagement of the war or waiting for it to break out again at the drop of a hat.

The sun had sunk behind the horizon several hours ago, but it was not yet dark. There was still enough light so that visibility for many miles was still adequate. Alton sat cross-legged on the ground with his dinner plate balanced on his lap and leaning at an angle to rest his back against the APC.

"Steak again, Ky?" Michael Lackney, SPC from a small town in Alabama, fell into the empty place next to Alton. "Don't you get tired of steak?" He indicated to his plate that was piled high with several pieces of fat, greasy fried chicken.

"We ate lots of chicken when we were growing up," Alton explained as he stuffed his mouth full of mashed potatoes. "Didn't always have an opportunity for steak," his words were staggered as he swallowed the potatoes and knifed a portion of steak onto his fork. "And we seldom had all we wanted. Daddy had a lot of mouths to feed."

He laughed, "I remember once when my brother, Delmore, was still a teenager. Momma and Daddy had bought a bunch of chickens to raise thinking they would slaughter half when the chickens was old enough and keep the other half for eggs."

"My brothers are great with cars but not so good with slaughtering," he laughed louder. "Anyway, Garnet and Daddy were going to do the actual killing while Delmore and Wilbur were supposed to be scalding the bodies and plucking the feathers before tossing them onto the mud porch for Momma and Sis to gut and salt."

"How many are we talking?" Lackney asked, grabbing the chicken between his fingers like it was a cob of corn and taking large bites.

"We didn't have a big freezer," Alton explained, "just the top part of the refrigerator. "They put up like fifteen or so at a time. There were five of us kids at home. And with four of us being boys, Momma and Daddy went through a bunch of food."

"Anyway, Momma and Sis took to cleaning out the insides and cutting them pieces into legs, breasts, thighs, and so on while Daddy and the boys cleaned up the mess." It was as if he read the look on Lackney's face. "Momma didn't want me to see the killing, plucking, or gutting. My task was to carry buckets of water from the creek and wash the blood off the porch." He set his mostly empty plate on the ground and eyed the smaller plate with a large piece of chocolate cake that took up most of the saucer. "Course, most of the blood seeped through the wooden planks so my job wasn't hard at all."

"How big is your Daddy's farm?" Walter joined in the conversation.

"Not big at all, few acres with a barn," he smiled. "And none of my brothers became farmers. They moved to the city and got jobs working in the plants. Sis works at the factory in town. I don't think none of them are cut out for farming."

"Why do you think that?" Lackney tossed the chicken bones towards the tree line.

"Because the only people in my family who ever ate any of that chicken was Momma, Daddy, and me," he laughed. "To this day, none are really fond of chicken."

"So, they bought all those chickens and only the three of you actually ate them?" Walter fought to hide his laughter.

"Pretty much," Alton sliced the cake into several large portions and made quick work of the task on the saucer. "So, Walter, are we holding here for the night?"

"Probably," Walter nodded. "Commander didn't imply we'd be moving out at least until morning light. You got a hot date waiting back at Cu Chi, Ky."

"No way, Ky's got that little honey back home," Sanford joked in a manner that made Alton think of Delmore. "What's her name, Kelly?"

"Kathy," Alton corrected, his mind flashing back to the last night they had spent together in Louisville. "And no, I thought if we are still here in the morning, I'm washing off in the culvert." He looked to his left to the body of water that ran under the roadway. Its stagnant, blue water was nothing like the rolling waves of the Green River, but it was clean and cool and it would feel good to take an actual bath versus washing off with a bar of soap during a rainstorm.

"Good thinking, Ky," Walter agreed. "We go two by two until everyone who wants to wash up has had a chance." His attention was drawn to the commander who stood about a hundred yards away with a radio clutched in his hand and motioned for Walter to join him.

"Ought oh," Alton said. "There goes my bath," his words were tinged with disappointment. Even though his daddy's house did not have indoor plumbing or an actual bathroom, they were able to bathe in the metal tub as often as was warranted, as long as water was pumped from the handpump or carted from the creek. One day, after he returned home, he was going to have an actual bathroom added to their house on the hill. And he added as an afterthought a real front porch for his momma.

"What is it?" Sanford asked once Walter was close enough to hear the question. "Are we moving out again?"

"Holding our position for now. Troop C spotted flashlights on the side of the road and fired on them but no fire was returned. However, the patrol moving east was ambushed with M16 and M60 fire that resulted in a secondary explosion probably by a mortar round." He paused to catch his breath, "Troop C patrol has observed several VC entering a hooch. They are engaging, we will support as needed but it doesn't sound like it will amount to much."

Alton was glad they were scheduled to be down for the night. It had been a long time since he had recollected the story about the chickens. Although he was not sure why all these long-forgotten memories were resurfacing into his thoughts, he liked the feeling. It was like his mind was home, even if his body was not.

****

Alton knew it was daylight even though there was no rooster to announce the coming of the new day. The break of a new dawn in Vietnam had a fragrance all its own. It was as if the rising sun carried with it on its back, the scent of gun powder and diesel fuel. No, neither an alarm clock nor the crow of a rooster's call was required. It was as if the curtain of night had been yanked away and the shutters thrown open in announcement.

"Okay men," the commander's words were forceful and direct as if he had been up all night and had yet to retire, even though Alton knew that was not the case. Like several of the other soldiers, Commander had slept upright in his APC, no doubt with one hand on the radio and the other on his sidearm. "We're heading out within the next two hours. Two at a time, if you want to wash up. Anyone not in the culvert be on the lookout for snipers." He scanned the area using his hand as a shield from the morning sun. "A6 track was hit during the night and the tanker traveling with it is on fire near the rubber plant." He exhaled and took a moment to study the young men who were gathering around him. "We've got some wounded and have called for a dustoff. Once the injured have been cleared from the area, we're going to tow the burning tanker out of the way so the supplies can get through."

He felt like a new man after his bath in the culvert. True, it was not as comforting as the shower at Delmore's house, but he'd enjoyed the cool water against his skin just the same. Alton did not hesitate to strip to his army issued long johns and bathe quickly so that everyone could have a turn. It was the luck of a draw really, whose platoon would come to a stop next to the culvert was like winning the lottery. It could be weeks even months before his APC might park close enough to take advantage of the clean, cool water. In lieu of the culvert, the only other option was to bathe in one of the many crater holes left by the war. The rainwater trapped within tended to evaporate quickly so even that option was limited most times.

****

The morning weather was nicer than other days, not that he took the time to notice very often. There was something different in the air that morning, it reminded him of waking up to the smell of Thanksgiving simmering in Momma's oven, except he was not in his momma's house and the fragrance of stale diesel fuel was the only prominent scent lingering in the air. Still, the morning seemed to be tapping against his shoulder as if to inquire that he come outside and play. And the realization left him anxious. It had been many years since he had enjoyed his time out of doors. It was both familiar and frightening at the same time. He was no longer a boy with a baseball glove in his hand. He was a man brandishing a weapon and he had taken a life, many lives. There was no longer any doubt where his bullet had landed. He wondered what had become of the boy he was, the man he was before he entered the bunker. He missed them both and he longed once again for the time when his boots were buried in Kentucky mud.

If he kept his head inside the APC, he could trick his mind into thinking he was taking the long country road from Taylor County to Lebanon. True, it was only about eleven miles from the county line to the Big John's mercantile across into Marion County. And with Taylor being a dry county, Alton, his brothers, and cousins made the trip frequently into Marion County to purchase beer. He could not count the number of times he had made the trip. Sometimes he would make the return trip with a six-pack or two tucked away in the truck. Other times, he had already indulged of the sweet nectar and was simply trying to make his way home. The road between the wet and dry county was fraught with bends and curves to such extent, it seemed as if God himself, had laid out an obstacle course meant to detour underage drinking.

Towards the end of the road, closer to Taylor County, the road straightened out and was lined with churches of all denominations. Over the years, it had earned the nickname, Sanctuary Road, partly due to the composition of religious institutions but mostly because the slightly intoxicated teenage drivers acknowledged their journey home, safe and sound. Alton would consider an alternate road from Louisville once his tour of duty was complete, one that would afford him the opportunity to approach the house on Elkhorn Hill from Sanctuary Road and acknowledge once again he had made it home safely.

"Why are we slowing down?" he asked his driver as the APC crawled to a stop. There was still a significant amount of road to sweep on the way to Phu Cuong.

"Commander just instructed us to pick up two of the six marching units from Long Binh and drop them at Cu Chi." He pointed ahead of the APC where the images of the soldiers moving to one side of the road were visible. "Copy that," he recanted into the radio. "And we're picking up six at Cu Chi for support at Phu Cuong to push the VC back towards the boats." He smiled, revealing a gap where one of his front teeth were missing. "Fish in a barrel."

"What about the tanker?" Alton asked, wishing not for the first time that he and Walter rode in the same APC. Walter always seemed to have the inside scoop on the plan. And Alton hated not knowing the plan, always had even as a kid. It was like having a wrapped present under the tree weeks prior to Christmas. As thrilling as it was to have a gift under the tree, the desire to discover its identity was overwhelming.

"It's been towed off the road, the troops are able to go around it," the driver advised, slowing down so that the troops could step onto the running boards and hitch a ride back to Cu Chi.

A flash of light off in the distance behind the tree line caught Alton's attention and he readied the M60 just in case. "HQ," he asked into the radio as he recited the coordinates. With his naked eye he could confirm there were no American troops or friendlies in the area. In fact, nothing seemed out of place except for the dozen or so ox carts that loitered along the edge of the road. It was as if they had been parked and the drivers were soon to return. "Permission to engage?" He waited patiently for confirmation.

"Negative," a deep, unfamiliar voice responded. "A troop elements confirmed just North of your coordinates. Return to Cu Chi."

"Copy that," Alton's words were succinct, tinged with anxiety as he scanned the area behind the fallen trees. Willard Lee had been wrong when he described Daddy's work with the grater on the trees that lined the road into Greensburg. He said they looked like a bomb had blown them up. It looked nothing like what's left after a bomb disburses tiny pieces and fragments within a blast area. Sometimes, there is nothing left to distinguish what was exploded, just shards of wood, metal, glass, flesh, and bone.

He wondered what road Daddy might be working on and pushed the thought as far away as he could. Although the work of the Roman plows made ambush by the NVC less probable, it was not impossible. Alton caressed the trigger of the M60 and stretched his neck as far as he could and still be contained within the safety of the APC. Nothing moved, not even the wind from the wings of a passing butterfly in route from one place to another. It was as if time itself had stopped. He could not help but check the hands of his daddy's old Timex watch to ensure they were still spinning around the dial.

"What is it?" Sanford, the driver asked, rubbing his hands up and down the steering wheel as if his palms were itching and only the hard leather of the wheel would ease his discomfort.

"Nothing," Alton pulled the strap of his helmet as tightly under his chin as he could and sat as if he were at attention. "Just feels off."

"You ain't been here long enough to have developed a sixth sense, Ky. It's just nerves."

"Remind me to tell you about my daddy and a mason jar of gold coins he found hidden inside of a rotten tree trunk when he was a young man."

"I love your stories, Ky. What's going to happen when you're plum out of stories?"

"I guess your nights will be long and quiet," Alton laughed. "Get us back to Cu Chi."

****

Sept 16th, 1968

Dear Momma and Daddy,
Finally got to the field. Spend most of the time patrolling the roads but we can't get off the road or we get hung up in the mush. Had to sleep on the road last night. Kids here sell cokes for 40 cents and 25 cents to fill up your lighter. Some things are cheap, others not. Sitting in a rubber plantation now, keeping the roads clear so the convoys can get through. Didn't get the dog trainer assignment. Please send me some of those green, wool army socks. Takes 7 days for the mail to get here. And send me a calendar.
Love, Alton

****

"You writing home again, Ky?" Michael Lackney pushed his body into the empty place next to Alton, careful not to drop his plate in Alton's lap. He folded his hands in silent prayer and scooped a thick spoonful of mashed potatoes into his mouth almost at the same time.

Lisa Colodny

Alton folded his writing pad closed and laid it atop a leather-like jacket folded neatly at his side. It was soft and ornate with Asian symbols along the back and the letters Vietnam sewn across the left side just below the collar. The town, Tay Ninh, nearby was known to house a number of expensive jackets, boots, and hats as well as some watches and chains. Alton did not care much for necklaces, although he was fond of the cross and chain his momma placed around his neck before she pulled away from Bob's Big Boy the last night she had seen him in Louisville. The jacket, however, had caught his eye from the very first moment he noticed some of the other soldiers wearing one. He had not thought much about taking mementos from the war home to Kentucky, but he very much liked the idea of a jacket to wear once the idea of the war was not so raw.

He had just enough time to make the trip into town and get back to Cu Chi before curfew. He had already been late once and had the dishpan hands to prove it. He hated kitchen duty; it was only slightly above cleaning the latrine. Luckily, that was not the current circumstance and he made it to the tiny shack that served as the camp bar in plenty of time. Apparently, many of his platoon had the same thought as well.

The cantina at Cu Chi was bustling with activity as soldiers ordered beer and enjoyed meals not routinely served in the field such as pizza and French fries. Time away from the field was few and far between and everyone enjoyed the downtime as best as they could. Music from the US streaming service pulsated from behind the counter where a pseudo barkeep and server marched back and forth distributing beer and food to the soldiers who were on furlough.

Lackney did not wait for Alton's response before continuing, allowing just enough space to talk around the lump of food in his mouth. "You get more mail than anyone I know." He swallowed, making loud gulping noises as the partially masticated food made its way down his throat. "I guess that's why you're always sending them out?"

"Actually," Alton tossed the pen against the table close to the untouched plate of food. The effects of the malaria pill he took once a week were at its worse the day after. Luckily, his diarrhea was resolving and hopefully his appetite would return. In the meantime, he took the last drink of beer from the nearly empty bottle. "I don't write as many as I get. My parents, sister, and brothers tend to share the letters with each other." He smiled seeing his sister's image in his mind's eye. The way she teased her hair across her forehead in the hope of concealing the widow's peak common to all the Phillips siblings. She did not wear a lot of makeup; she never had. It was one of the things he admired most about his sister. She was more than comfortable with who she was and where she was from.

"You're lucky," Lackney went on, his face contorting as if he had eaten something distasteful. "Some of us only get a few here and there. And that new guy in troop C, I don't think he ever gets any letters from home."

"You mean that Harold kid with the thick, black glasses?" Alton turned to scan the room as if he expected to see the recruit approaching their table.

"Yeah, he's been here three times as long as you and hasn't received a single letter," Lackney eyed the untouched chicken breast on Alton's plate. "You gonna eat that?"

Alton pushed the plate under his friend's nose. "Help yourself." Mosquitos seemed to swarm in packs when they were in the field. Thankfully, Chloroquine kept the disease an arm's length away. Lackney had just returned and, no doubt, consumed more than his share of the medication. How was he able to even think about food, let alone devour so much, knowing it would be making an appearance at the other end soon?

"Okay, Ky," Kyril Farmer fell into the seat across from Alton. "I want to hear about how you inherited your daddy's uncanny sense of premonition." Farmer was a tall, thin, young man with sun-kissed blond hair and piercing green eyes. He hailed from Franklin, Tennessee and his dialect was such Alton was more than comfortable in conversation with him. There were intermittent moments where he could trick his mind into thinking he was sitting in a booth at the corner drug store with Buck while they selected a song from the jukebox.

Basketball had been Kyril's game and, had he not been drafted, he would have embarked upon a full athletic scholarship at UCLA. But like so many other young men in his platoon, his life had been interrupted by the Vietnam war as new chapters opened and closed depending upon circumstances of the conflict.

"Ky don't have no sixth sense," Walter laughed and motioned his partially empty plate into the center of the table. "If he did, he'd have a better sense of the NVA and those damned booby traps."

Alton held up his hand and extended his fingers as open as he could. "Still got all my fingers, Walt." He pushed himself to his feet. "I'm getting another beer. Anyone else want one?"

"I got it," Walter jumped up as if a firecracker had been placed under the table. "Don't start the story without me," he warned as he hurried towards the barkeep. Seconds later, he returned grasping three bottles by the neck in each hand. He dropped them ceremoniously atop the table. "Wasn't sure how long the story's going to be."

"What story?" Alton reached for the bottle closest to him, wasting no time in delivering the bottle's sweet nectar past his lips.

"You said something about your Pa and some coins inside a tree," Lackney reminded him, perusing Walter's plate to see if there was anything on the plate worthy of eating. Finding nothing, his attention turned back to Alton.

"Just some old story my daddy told us kids once," Alton smiled, his thoughts filled with the image of his daddy and siblings gathered around, absorbed in every word that slid from his lips. For as long as he could recall, his daddy had entertained in the midst of rain and snowstorms with tales of running moonshine on the ridge and pushing the team across the deepest part of the Green River. But one story always stood apart from all the others.

"When my daddy was a young man," Alton began, "before any of us kids came along. He was on his way back from a full day's work in Mannsville." He took a long drink from the bottle and waited as the intoxicating liquid settled upon his recollection. "He was riding on horseback, no team or anything. Just him and old, Otis." Alton laughed in a way that reminded him of Delmore. "You should have heard Daddy talk about this horse. As far as Daddy could tell, Otis was smarter than some people he knew."

Alton paused for a moment to gauge the crowd—it would have been impossible not to notice how enthralled in the story his platoon was. He may have only been moments into the recollection, but they were already hooked, and he knew it. "Any way, the sun was setting but still prominent in the evening sky and as Daddy led Otis off the path to cut across the field, a flicker of light behind one of the big, old elm trees drew Daddy's attention."

Alton reached for another beer and continued with the accounts of the story. "At first, he thought it was simply his eyes playing tricks on him. But then he looked down at old Otis and knew the horse had seen it too." Alton looked from left to right to augment as if he himself were sitting atop Otis. "Daddy didn't see anyone else around, but he said he felt as if he was being watched. He made his way closer to the tree where he'd seen the light and dismounted."

Off in the distance, the sounds of war continued but no one paid it any heed. Instead, they waited patiently to hear the outcome of Alton's daddy's encounter with the unidentified light. "Daddy made his way to the tree and once he was close enough, he could tell the inside part of the tree was rotten. There was a place inside the trunk deep enough to fit a man's hand."

He paused, licking his dry lips, and reaching for the bottle once again. Minutes seemed like hours as he emptied the bottle and dropped it loudly against the table.

"What was inside the tree?" Walter asked as the others nodded in conspired agreement.

"An old mason jar with a rusted lid was stuffed inside the tree. The jar was filled with gold coins," Alton answered, pushing himself as far against the seat's back as he could and exhaling a long deliberate breath. He was beginning to understand his daddy's love of storytelling. It was like performing on center stage. And after being in the shadows of his older siblings for the better part of his life, he was liking the attention.

"Gold coins?" Lackney repeated. "Like real gold coins?" He snatched one of the bottles of beer from the center of the table and turned the bottle up to the sky as if the drink was an offering.

"Yeah," Alton nodded, "hundreds of dollars." His eyes grew wide with excitement as he went on. "More money than my daddy had ever seen."

"What did he do with it?" Walter asked, as engaged as the others at the table.

"He put it back where he found it, mounted his horse, and continued on his journey." Alton's words were like those that fade into the darkness of the big screen at the cinema on Main Street.

"He left it in the tree?" Kyril Farmer's words were incredulous. "All that money and he just left it even though no one would have known he took it?"

"Daddy said that even though he didn't see anyone, he felt as if someone was watching him. He said he knew that if he'd tried to keep it, they would have intercepted him." Alton said in conclusion as if he'd just argued for the defense at a trail's end.

"Did your daddy ever find out what it was or who it belonged to?" Walter pushed the last beer toward Alton and folded his arms across his chest.

"Not really, but a few years later," Alton went on, "some old guy told Daddy that outlaws used to pay each other and their conspirators off with coins in mason jars." He downed half of the beer in a single gulp. "The James Brothers had family nearby in Jamestown and they held up the stages in and around Horse Cave several times." He pushed the empty bottle back atop the table. "And I read once in school how the Confederate sympathizers in the North used to sequester monies for use against the Union army by hiding it in predetermine places. Kentucky was a very volatile state with farms next to one another who fought on opposite sides of the war."

"Wow," Lackney said. "What a story!" He ran his hands through the short hair against his scalp. "I appreciate you sharing it with us, Ky."

"My pleasure," Alton laughed as he pushed himself to his feet, using the table for support. The many beers he had consumed in such a short period of time had caught up to him and he hoped he would not be hung over in the morning. "Show's over for tonight, Boys. I'm hitting the head and calling it a night."

It had been many years since he had thought about that story. As a child it had been one of his favorites. And his daddy told it well, taking the time to ad lib facial expressions and emphasizing action with his hands and arms. For as much as he enjoyed being in the center and sharing the story, he would much have preferred listening to his daddy tell it in real time. Hopefully, one day in the not-too-distant future, he would hear it again.

Alton at Cu Chi Base camp in Vietnam

Chapter Twelve

The morning had started routinely enough with Alton's APC leading the convoy across the Phu Cuong bridge. Luckily the indulgence of the previous night left no after effect. In fact, he had experienced one of the best night's sleep he'd had since arriving at Cu Chi. Perhaps he should conclude each night with a memory from home on the forefront of his mind. Maybe, it might counterbalance the effects of the horrors that marred his waking hours. Might one wipe the other away? Only time would tell.

By fourteen hundred hours, the time had ticked away with limited enemy engagement and only minimal conversation. As a result, Alton's troop's orders were modified several times. The most recent finding themselves posted just outside the rubber plantation. The TC reminded them to stay focused as the jungle around the plantation served to shield dozens of NVA at any given time and to be alert for snipers.

The six or seven rounds that had been fired at the APC and half-tracks over the last hour seemed to be more of a diversion than an actual attack. By all accounts, a lone NVA soldier or two were simply target practicing somewhere within the jungle and the stray rounds a testament to their ineffectiveness.

Alton was grateful when we felt the gears of the APC pull its movement forward. "Where we headed, Farmer?" He knew it was too early to be headed back to base camp but was hopeful, nonetheless.

"Headed up the west side of the MSR," Farmer answered over the roar of the big machines. "Tank hit a mine. We're going to clear the rest of the road so the supplies can get through." He waved to his left as if they were cruising Main Street on a Saturday night. "TC says to be on the lookout. Lots of NVA in the woods behind the downed trees."

"Maybe the Rome plows should take out a few more acres to give us a little more breathing room there by the road?" Alton wiped the dust out of his eyes wishing once again for a pair of goggles. He hated to ask his parents to get them, but he had little choice. The commissary had none to purchase and no one had an extra pair to loan.

They had not gone far at all before the lead APC came upon a roadblock, consisting mostly of bamboo poles and banana leaves. One by one, the vehicles were emptied as the soldiers began the tedious job of checking for booby traps and clearing the road.

"That was a lot of time for nothing," Bailey remarked as he adjusted his rifle higher upon his shoulder and took heavy steps towards his vehicle. "Why do they make such a show of doing nothing?" He climbed into the APC and loosened the strap of his helmet. Even as the sun was beginning to set for the night, it was warm. So warm, the shirt under his full metal jacket was saturated like a wet diaper.

"Because as soon as you start thinking it's nothing, it will be something and you'll get yourself or one of us killed." Walter's words were harsh and angry as he climbed in behind Bailey. "Pull that strap tight under your chin, soldier."

"Copy that," Bailey mumbled as he adjusted the strap tight against his throat and sank as deep into the seat as the vehicle would allow.

"That boy is an accident waiting to happen," Lackney whispered as he and Alton climbed back into their APC. "If he comes through this alive, God must surely be watchin' over him."

"Hopefully, God's watchin' over all of us," Alton offered. "He's young and he's scared."

"We're all young, Ky, and scared," Farmer added. "And if we want to grow any older, we gotta whip that kid into shape." He pushed the heavy gear forward. "If we don't, he's bound to get one or all of us killed."

Farmer stole a glance at Alton. "You should take him under your wing, Ky. You'd be a good mentor."

"Don't want no responsibility for anybody but me," Alton answered before anyone else could offer additional interjections.

"You like kids, you're good with young uns. You got those pictures and poems from your nieces and nephew," Farmer argued, his words hopeful and confident.

"My sister sends me pictures of the kids to comfort me. And my niece, Gail, sent a poem to me that won her an award at school. That's it, short and simple," Alton explained.

"What about all those Vietnamese kids you're always engaging with?" Farmer argued.

"I give them pennies," Alton explained. "And pay them for fluid for my lighter and cans of coke. Same as the rest of you." He pulled the butt of the M60 as tight against his shoulder as he could, grateful for the dull ache against his bone from the weight of the gun. It was a distraction; one he was grateful for.

"No," Farmer's words were formidable as if the argument was over and he knew he had won. More importantly, Alton knew it too. "It's not the same."

****

"Not again," Bailey's disappointment was heard loud and clear over the radio as the platoon continued west. "More poles and leaves," his words resonated over the radio.

"Ky! Lackney!" Walter called from the other APC as all the vehicles rolled to a stop a safe distance from the roadblock. "Check it out. Everyone else on point for snipers."

A watering hole, Alton's thoughts drummed against his brain as if part of a cadence. The booby traps were all the same. Yet, they were all different at the same time. As Bailey had surmised, the roadblock was indeed comprised of bamboo poles and banana leaves. Unlike before, behind the row of bamboo poles was a shallow watering hole. Buried

Inside the watering hole was a mine. After careful assessment, it was determined there was no charge in the mine, it was a dud. Like before, Alton's platoon had not been in any real danger.

It was a different story, however, when two hours later one of the tanks hit a mine. Although, no one was severely injured, the tank was blown off the track and the team was not able to get it back on track. As a result, it would need a tow back to Cu Chi Base Camp. Therefore, their orders were to secure the area until motor pool could be dispatched and offer aid to the downed tank and its crew.

The waiting game had been in play for the better part of the morning with the APCs and lowboys gathered around the crippled tank. Alton, like the other soldiers, had taken his turn outside the APC as sentry, perusing the immediate area behind the downed tree line for movement of any kind. He moved his rifle from one shoulder to the other and tossed the spent cigarette to the ground with his free hand. It was hard to judge the distance to the jungle, especially with the trees that had fallen victim to the Rome plows, distorting the spaces in front of him.

Alton made a fist, imaging how the worn seems of his old baseball might feel against his fingertips. The leather against his palm would be soft and marred by the insult of Wilbur's old Louisville slugger bat. Would the fragrance of tobacco drying in the barn still be prominent if he held the ball to his nose? One, two, three times he threw an imaginary ball towards the tree line, watching as if he expected it to actually make contact with the ground.

"You like baseball?" Walter's words grew louder as he made his way from behind the other APC and stopped near Alton's side. He scanned the area as if he, too, were looking for the baseball.

"Played a little when I was younger," Alton answered without looking away from the tree line. He pulled the strap tight under his chin. "Was a pretty good hitter and I was a really fast baserunner." He turned to face Walter. "Course, that was just me playing with the kids on Elkhorn Hill. My parents couldn't afford for me to play in school. There was no money for uniforms and cleats or league fees at the park." He pulled another cigarette from a crumpled pack in his pocket and offered one of the few remaining to Walter. "What about you?"

"That's about all I could play when I was a kid." He made an obvious gesture to emphasize his height. Walter was then thin and shorter than most of the other soldiers. He would not have been effective at basketball or football. Baseball was most likely Walter's only option. "I played a bit before I entered high school but no way was I making the varsity team." He tapped his forehead. "I decided to focus on school and graduate so I could have a good life."

"And here we are," Alton added before Walter could finish. "Here in this hell hole, fighting in a war I'm not sure is ours to fight." He took a long drawl from the cigarette and exhaled the smoke slowly as if he didn't want it to escape. "We've got radios. We know what's happening back at home. What people are saying about us, what they are calling us."

"That's politics, Ky," Walter's hand fell against Alton's shoulder. "Ain't nothing good gonna come from any of that talk. We all got jobs to do. You have a job to do."

"And I'm doing it. Ain't I?" Alton's words were angry, and he was instantly sorry for his outburst. "How do you do it, Walt?" he moved uncomfortably from one foot to the other. "How do you stuff your feelings into a box and not let it not bother you?" He took a final drag from the cigarette and threw it away as if were burning his fingers. "I'm not built like that; I don't know how to cover it up." He needed a moment to collect his next thought before continuing. "My brother, Delmore, he's like that. He keeps everything inside. When he's happy or sad, it's all the same. You can't tell the difference."

"Are you more like your other brother?" Walter took a moment to scan the tree line before turning back to face Alton.

"About some things," Alton answered, his face wrinkling into a broad smile. "Wilbur keeps more to himself about most things in his life but he's calmer, more serious than me or Delmore. My cousin says I have a wild side like Delmore does."

"What about your sister," Walter was genuinely curious. Alton talked about his family all the time and his stories occupied most of the nights they were in the field. In some ways, Walter felt like he already knew them. "Who is she most like?"

"You know my sister is married, Walter, with kids and everything?" Alton joked. "Sis is like us all in one way or another." He looked away, his smile vanishing almost as quickly as it had appeared. "My momma's been sick for as long as I can recall. She's not always able to cook the meals or see to the laundry. Sis has had to step up and be sort of a substitute. Delmore, too, in some ways." His mind flashed to an image of Delmore in the back yard scrubbing the laundry against a wooden washboard in a small metal tub. He could not curtail his laughter and Walter waited for Alton to finish his story.

"Sis has a lot of responsibility with a husband and two children. She works full-time at the factory and cares for Momma in between all her other jobs. Yet, she still has a big sense of humor. She's quite the prankster, my sister. You'd like her."

"I'm sure I would," Walter admitted. "And I hope to meet her someday."

"I told you, Walt. She's married." Alton pushed at Walter's arm.

"Well," Walter shrugged his shoulders. "I hope to meet someone one day like her and live happily ever after." He directed Alton's attention to an approaching convoy, still a fair distance away.

"I can see you, Walt, dressed like one of those plastic figures on top of a wedding cake holding hands with some sweet thing." He turned to gauge the success of the motor brigade as they drew closer. "You'll look fine in a white tuxedo jacket."

"So will you, Ky." He moved closer to Alton and whispered. "Once we get out of here, we get our lives back. Just where we left off."

"I hope so," Alton turned away and waved to the approaching vehicles as they came to a stop. "I pray so."

****

Alton did not know any of the men in the APC that accompanied the vehicle delivering the soldiers from the motor pool. He recognized a few from Cu Chi, had seen them around the bar, drinking with the other men. However, as the soldier stepped down from the passenger side, there was no containing the smile that corrupted Alton's face.

One soldier was more than familiar to Alton, this was someone he knew, part of his extended family. "David!" he called out, moving quickly to address Sis' brother-in-law.

"Alton?" the solider answered, spinning around to confirm his recognition of Alton's voice. "Kenneth said you were part of the three-four but since I hadn't run upon you, I thought he might have the wrong platoon number." He took a moment to study Alton, his smile radiant on his face. "When did you get over?"

"Seems like forever, David," Alton shook the soldier's hand. "But has just been a few months. When did you get here?" Alton pointed towards the vehicle David had exited. "Sis said you were assigned to motor pool, but she wasn't sure where?"

"Been in Vietnam about six months but at Cu Chi only about five weeks," David motioned for the soldiers who had accompanied him to start working on the tank. David was smaller, like Walter, and looked younger. Even dressed in his battle fatigues, David looked less like a soldier and more like a high school student at Halloween. He was thin, his jet-black hair cropped tight around his ears and neck, and looked nothing like his brother even without the thick black glasses Kenneth, Sis' husband, wore.

"You look good," David hugged Alton, his smile fading to reveal a perfect set of white teeth. "Army has put some muscle on you." He pulled Alton an arm's length away as if he were measuring him for a suit. "Can't wait to tell Kenneth I finally ran into you."

Beside Alton, Walter cleared his throat and offered his hand. "Walter Piedmont. Nice to meet you." It was obvious, Walter was sizing up the newcomer, attempting to determine where in Alton's stories the young soldier fit.

"David's older brother, Kenneth, is married to my sister," Alton offered, pausing to give David the opportunity to elaborate if he desired.

"I recognize you from one of the pictures hanging at Ky's bunk." Walter took advantage of the silence. "I think there's one of you and your brother standing in front of a motorcycle?"

"Yeah," Alton added. "The last summer we were both at home, David rode his bike over to Sis' and we all took turns taking it for a ride over the hill." He raised his hand as if he were surrendering. "Sis sends me pictures with every letter." He smiled. "I think she hopes to make sure everyone in my life is represented in some way or another."

"I better get to work," David motioned to where his associates were busily working on the tank, "get this thing outta here."

Alton fell into step with him after surveying the tree line again. "Still getting letters from Janet?"

"Yeah," David nodded before dropping to his knees to offer assistance to the other mechanics already on the scene. "I'm not sure when I'll get some leave time, but I hope when I do, I can spend some time with your cousin."

"I hope you do too." Alton took his place beside the tank and positioned himself so that he could scan the tree line for movement. Losing any soldier was a tragedy, but losing a family member to the war would be something he could not imagine, especially on his watch.

****

"Okay," David words were muffled from under the tank. "Pull her out."

Alton stepped back as David emerged from under the tank just as it began its forward motion and the tank slid back onto the track. It took only minutes before the tank was fully aligned back on the track. David wiped the mud off his backside and watched as the tank made its way along the MSR, headed back to Cu Chi.

"Thanks, Man," Alton slapped at David's arm. "Wasn't sure how long they were going to keep us here babysitting that hunk of metal."

"No problem," David adjusted his helmet more evenly on his head and tugged at the strap under his chin as if needed to be tighter. "It was good to finally catch up to you again. I can't wait to tell Janet."

"Who will scurry to tell, Sis," Alton seemed worried. "I don't write how things really are here in my letters. I don't want them to worry."

"Neither do I," David cut him off. "Even though I'm in motor pool, it's not without risk. There's really no such thing as a safe job over here."

Alton thought again of Bentley Peters and his assignment to kitchen duty. David was correct. Even though the bulk of Bentley's day was spent safely behind the walls of the kitchen. At least twice a day, the crew made an appearance at the field to deliver breakfast and dinner. Either of those were an opportunity to be on the receiving end of an NVA sniper's bullet. David was right, no one's safety was guaranteed.

"A buddy of mine from training camp at Fort Knox was assigned to the motor pool. You know a soldier named Cooper Butterfield. He was up from around Hazard, I think."

"I don't know him," David assured him, "but I'll ask around. There's a bunch of us, you know. Something is always down somewhere." He stopped quickly as if he had stepped into something unpleasant. "If something opens up, I'll let you know? Fixing motor vehicles is in your genetics. You're a natural."

"That would be great, but I won't hold my breath," Alton repositioned his weapon, grabbing the neck tighter as if the load was too heavy to manage. "Those positions usually go to someone with some juice."

"Juice?" David repeated.

"Someone whose family has money or power. The waiting list is probably a mile long for those jobs." Alton stopped near David's ride and waited for David to open the vehicle's door.

"Lord knows my family doesn't have any juice," David's eyes were sad. "We come from the same place, you and me." He smiled. "And with God's grace, we'll both get back there."

"You take care of yourself, David," Alton offered his hand again.

"You, too Alton," David shook his hand and slid eagerly into the vehicle and motioned for the driver to move the vehicle out.

Alton turned his back, heading to the APC where no doubt new orders would be ready for them now that the tank was on its way back to Cu Chi.

"Hey wait up, Alton. Hold on." David's frantic voice echoed across the space between them until Alton spun around to lay eyes upon the departing vehicle. David spilled out of the vehicle and ran to Alton clutching something in his left hand. "I've had these in my pack for a while just in case I ran upon you."

"What is it?" Alton was hopeful, licking his lips involuntarily at the thought of what it might be. At this point in his stay at Cu Chi, a bite or two of his Momma's burned jam cake would be welcomed. He waited and watched as David dropped a bag of Brach's Maple Nut Goodies into Alton's hand.

"Where'd you get those?" Alton's excitement was evident as the words spilled over his tongue. "They are my favorite, but you can't get them here."

"Janet sent them to me for you, in the event we ran into one another." David turned back towards his vehicle. "Enjoy and I'll let your cousin know her package was delivered."

"Thank her for me," Alton stole another glance at the bag of candy in his hand before looking back at David's vehicle as the image became smaller on the road. "Take care of yourself, David," he said aloud even though no one was near enough to hear.

****

By the time Alton returned to the APC, Farmer had received their new assignment and the APC was sweeping North to head off anything coming out of Thai May. The terrain was flat with only an occasional patch or two of uneven areas to make the journey uncomfortable. It was spacious enough, there were only seven soldiers traveling inside. Since it could accommodate as many as nine, no one was uncomfortable stacked closely aside anyone else.

Still, it was unceremoniously quiet with only the updates streaming from the radio to break the monotony of the silent thoughts of the soldiers. Alton was no exception. It had been an amazing stroke of luck to run into David. He had often thought of how a rendezvous with a familiar face might occur, but until today, it only been a performance he repeated in his head. Sometimes, he imagined there was music to accompany the event. Other times, there was silence.

Seeing David today was as if he had been plucked from the hell hole of Vietnam and dropped momentarily back at home. It was both painful and pleasurable to the extent he was not sure his emotional state was strong enough to repeat the act at frequent intervals. Get your head straight, Alton heard Walter's words as clearly as if he were riding in the APC instead of occupying the adjacent one. By all accounts, he felt as anxious as he had upon first arriving to Cu Chi. It was as if God had hit the rewind button and restarted it back to Alton's arrival at Cu Chi.

"You gonna open that?" Farmer's words tore through the silence in the APC in a manner as if he had passed gas. "The candy," he added, after realizing Alton was not following the conversation. "You going to share those?"

"I have a tooth that's bothering me," Alton rubbed his left jaw to better illustrate his discomfort. "Unless you get a really fresh bag, they are hard on your teeth. If David's been carrying them around for a while, no doubt they are hard as a rock." He pulled that bag open and handed it to the soldiers in the back. "Save me a third of the bag for when my tooth is better." His thoughts traveled the miles once again to his home and imagined the sweet, crusty, maple flavor of the candies and how good they would taste with a bottle of soda from the cooler in his daddy's barn.

"Is this one of those Kentucky things, like fried chicken and bourbon?" Farmer asked as he tossed one of the candies in his mouth.

"No, not really," Alton answered, trying not to smile as Farmer crunched loudly upon the nut goodie and winced at the discomfort. "We didn't have much money growing up and trips into town were infrequent." His lips curved into a smile that spread across his cheeks and danced in the irises of his eyes. "Some Saturdays, however, Daddy would let me and some of the cousins ride into town with him. We'd pile into the back of his old red pickup and file out when he stopped at the light on Main Street. My cousin Janet and I would combine our change and usually have enough to buy one bag of those."

He smiled and reached behind him for the bag. "No one else liked them. Everyone else wanted something with chocolate but she and I always chose these." He folded what little was left in the bag up and stuffed it into the pocket of his jacket. "I hadn't thought about those trips into town in a long time. We were just kids."

"Heads up," someone, probably Lackney called from the back. "Movement up ahead."

It was as if a rubber band had been snapped how quickly the soldiers inside the APC snapped to attention, fingers triggered at the ready. The APC slowed to a crawl, finally stopping at the perimeter of the road that was unrecognizable as such because of the numerous mounds of dirt that were covering it. At the other end of the blockade, the South Vietnamese armies worked in place, sequentially blowing one mound and then another until the road was cleared.

Over the radio, Alton heard Walter's familiar voice inquiring of the commanders for the next series of assignments. Civilian traffic? Alton leaned in closer to the radio as if being in close proximity might make the translation clearer. Be alert, he was able to decipher. The orders were not specific, except to watch for eligible males.

Alton was on the alert as his APC drifted past the cleared area of the MSR. It was hard to differentiate the North and South Vietnamese soldiers from one another, especially if the NVA was banking on the confusion. It was the perfect circumstance for a surprise attack. Although the Vietnamese soldiers on site were blowing the booby-trapped mines along the road, it could have just as easily been a trap to lure the platoon into a false sense of security and make an attack as the convoy rode past.

True the soldiers were dressed in uniforms to represent the South, but Alton knew uniforms were easy to come by. In fact, clothing had been confiscated from nearly every bunker and hooch, he had secured so far. Because of their fear, the platoon was at the ready until the very last vehicle cleared the area where the South Vietnamese soldiers loitered about waving at the APCs and tanks as if they were old friends.

No doubt, everyone exhaled a sigh of relief, grateful the soldiers were exactly as they appeared, friendlies. As the platoon continued its sweep North, the terrain changed once again to an area where the Rome plows had only downed a single row or two of trees from the perimeter of the roadway. From the APC, Alton could hear the birds singing just off the road, watched as bees and butterflies jumped from bush to bush marking the territories as their own. Given the shade of the nearby trees, it did not seem as warm as when the trees were stomped at ground level. And then, there was the sweet breeze that blew across Alton's face. If not for the scent of gunpowder and diesel in the air and the sound of airborne vehicles in the sky, it might have been like fishing from the bank of the Green River on his daddy's farm.

The radio crackled to life again alerting them to activity a few miles ahead. One of the reconnaissance planes reported a number of individuals on foot and at the APC's current rate of speed, intersect would approximately be in three to five minutes. The plane was not able to determine if the individuals were friendly or not, or if they were armed or unarmed.

"Stay on the road," Walter's words were tense and urgent. "Field could be booby-trapped."

"There's so many of them," Farmer advised, "must be a hundred, maybe two."

"Copy that," another soldier, possibly Marty, in Walter's APC responded.

"Guns at the ready," Walter ordered. "Deploy on my count, 3, 2, 1." Alton wiped the dust away from his eyes, wishing once again for goggles, and rubbed his finger against the M60's trigger while the soldiers safely tucked inside the APC dismounted and targeted the newcomers.

The guns of the tanks whined and groaned as the tanks came to a stop and targeted the people who had ceased to move and stood with the hands in the air. One of the soldiers from South Vietnam spoke in their native language to inquire where they were from and where they were headed. An older man stepped forward and responded they were heading South for sanctuary from the NVA.

The soldier shook his head and waved them back in the direction from which they had come. The old man shook his head and pointed past the American convoy indicating they needed to pass and make their pilgrimage South.

No, the soldier warned him again. They had to turn around and return to their villages and homes for now. They had no other option, no choice but to return.

It took several minutes for the chatter to cease and the crowd to turn and initiate a journey back to where they had started. Alton would remember the look of despair on their faces for the rest of his life. These people were desperate, caught in the middle of a giant game of chess of which they would never be the victor.

The country was cut in half, delineated into the North and South, good and evil, right and wrong. There were farmers and civilians in both segments who wanted nothing more than to feed their families and provide a proper life. Everyone in the North was not brandishing weapons and setting booby traps. No doubt, there were occupants in the South who were sympathetic to the ways of the Viet Cong. It was not always possible to tell the good guys from the bad. And more than once since arriving to Cu Chi, Alton felt as if the task of deciding was little more than a toss of the dice. Afterall, he was here to protect people unable to make a stand for themselves. He was not comfortable with situations where harm came to those he was charged with protecting. And although it was hard to differentiate friend from foe, he prayed that God would continue to guide him towards the right choice, the one that would get him home to his family.

Chapter Thirteen

The sun had just begun its decline in the evening sky but there was still a fair amount of daylight left, as evidenced by the number of South Vietnamese farmers working to harvest the last basket of produce before nightfall. There were adults of all ages as well as children, with shovels and hoes in hand rushing to complete their tasks. There was more than enough daylight left to make it back to Cu Chi before dark. But that did not appear to be the plan. There was little doubt that Alton's platoon would spend yet another night in the field. Otherwise, they would already be headed back to camp.

At the last break, Alton's APC had relinquished the lead spot in the convoy and assumed the last position along the trail. Walter's APC was just ahead of the tank and the APC leading the convoy was being driven by a new guy who just arrived a few days ago. Edy Estel reigned from Northern California, wine country as he had said repeatedly. He was nice enough guy, friendly but in an ingenuine way. Over the course of the last few days, he claimed to be an ordained minister as well as an amateur race car driver. Problem was, his immediate task of action upon his arrival was to hang posters of naked blondes along the wall that bordered his bunk. And his driving was such, Walter had already alerted him that this was his last shift at the wheel, any wheel. As such, Alton was surprised Walter had put Edy's APC as the lead vehicle.

"You think we will go back to camp tomorrow?" Farmer asked, his face tinged with exhaustion. "We've been on assignment for like what, ten days straight?"

"I don't know buddy but I ain't asking the TC." Alton tried not to laugh. First platoon had an impeccable reputation for the getting their job done, quickly and efficiently. As a result, the TC seldom accompanied them on missions. And they waited for orders to come from Walter or the radio. There was never a circumstance where they knew in advance what the mission was or where they were bunking for the night.

"Why is Harold changing positions?" Farmer asked as the tank in front of them pulled out of line in an attempt to change places with the tank ahead. "I didn't hear anything come over the radio, did you?"

Alton shook his head and sat straighter in his seat to get a better view of the immediate area ahead of their APC. "Is there an update?" His words were succinct and anxious.

Before Walter could respond, there was an explosion as Harold's tank disappeared momentarily behind a cloud of smoke and debris and the area alongside the road imploded. "He hit a mine," Farmer screamed into the microphone against his chin.

Alton watched as the tank emerged from the flurry of smoke and dust to find it sitting lopsided by the side of the road missing two of its road wheels. "We can't fix that," he mumbled. "Going to need motor pool again. It will have to be towed."

"Any injuries?" Walter's words on the radio were impatient.

"Negative," Harold responded. "Everyone's ok."

Across the field, near to where the field had erupted, the sound of a woman's scream hung in the air like sirens on a police car. "Help," she screamed. "Help us, please." Everyone watched from their vehicles as the woman dropped to her knees to where the form of a small child had fallen.

"Stand down," Walter's voice on the radio was louder and brazen. His words coming in great gasps. "Feeney, dismount and assess the situation. Everyone else stay put."

Alton watched as Adam Feeney, platoon medic riding in the first APC, dismounted the vehicle and made his way cautiously to the field. With his head to the ground, he was careful to place his steps inside existing footprints until he made his way to the mother and child.

The child was unconscious, bleeding from the nose and ear. She was small and frail, with dark eyes and hair pulled back into a tiny ponytail. Her flowered frock was worn and dingy and torn away in such a way that may or may not had been caused by the explosion of the mine.

"We need a dustoff, ASAP." Feeney said into the radio as his hands worked frantically to assess the child and offer aid as best as he could. Within minutes, the blood trails from her ear and nose reappeared as quickly as he wiped it away. The gauze from his pack was soon exhausted and he called in the radio. "I need the first aid kit from one of the APC."

"I got it," Alton said into the handheld receiver attached to the dash before Walter could respond. Alton leaped out of the APC with his rifle in one hand and the first aid pack in the other and stepped delicately into Fenney's footprints. By the time he made his way to the medic and fallen child, a small crowd of Vietnamese, old and young, had gathered, watching as Feeney rendered aid.

"Here," he dropped the pack to Feeney's side and readied his weapon in the event the crowd became hostile. Although he was not sure what they were discussing, it was evident by their body language and words, they were angry.

"Accident," Feeney explained to them in their native tongue. "The tank hit a mine."

One of the farmers, who looked to be about Alton's age, stepped forward and waved his hand angrily at Feeney. The farmer was thin, frail almost, with stained trousers and shirt. His sandals were leather and worn, with strands missing between the toes. His toenails, like his fingernails, were unkempt and caked with mud.

"Step back," Alton advised, his hands caressing the rifle like a lover. He fought the urge to look back towards Walter's APC for guidance. The crowd appeared to be nothing more than angry farmers but looks were most times deceiving.

The farmer raised his eyes away from Feeney and the child to come face to face with Alton. It was the first opportunity Alton had to see his face. Like the rest of his body, it was thin, long and narrow with dark eyes. There was a faint, red, indignant, scar that ran from the tip of his lip to the bottom of his eye. There was a fleeting moment where he wondered the origin of the injury. If they were able to communicate, would the farmer explain how one of his brothers had accidently clip his jaw with a cutting knife while harvesting a crop or slaughtering livestock?

Alton fought the urge to pull up his army issued trousers and point to the scar across his calf where Wilbur had accidentally nailed him while cutting tobacco. See, he wanted to say, I have one too. But he did not break eye contact with the farmer or the crowd. Walter would alert them to the plan as was applicable.

"Set up a perimeter with Ky," Alton heard Walter's voice behind him and knew at least some of his platoon had vacated their vehicles and were joining him and Feeney. In his Peripheral vision, Alton saw Farmer and Bailey take position on either side.

"We're clearing an area for the dustoff," Walter advised once he was close enough for Alton and Feeney to hear. He pushed his way through the crowd and came to a stop across from where Alton was. "Chopper is a few minutes out. Can she travel?"

"I don't think we have a choice," Feeney advised without looking up from the child.

The farmer spoke again, moving anxiously through the crowd towards Walter.

"He's her brother," Feeney spoke, looking up at the farmer for the first time. "He wants to know what happened? Why the American army has shot a child?"

"Tell him it was an accident," Walter instructed as he edged his rifle between himself and the approaching farmer.

"I did," Feeney pushed himself to a standing position so that he was facing the farmer.

"Tell him again," Walter's response was abrupt. "And we didn't shoot her. A Vietnamese mine hurt her, one intended for us." He waited as

Feeney explained to the farmer the circumstances, but it was obvious the farmer was not satisfied with Feeney's response.

The farmer paced back and forth from Walter to where the child was, the words spilling from his mouth like rain and arms waving wildly. Alton did not understand what the farmer was saying but he understood the farmer was hurting, concerned for the welfare of his sister. The farmer was on the verge of tears and Alton wanted nothing more than to offer comfort to him.

"He says, his mother is sick and dying in a village just over the hill," Feeney explained. "He says if his sister dies, it will surely be the end of his mother as well."

"Tell him, we're sorry. And we will pray for both his sister and mother." Alton's words slid from his mouth so quickly, he seemed as surprised as anyone else.

Feeney paused, looking to Walter for confirmation.

"Tell him," Walter responded.

There was silence in the crowd as the impact of Feeney's words were absorbed and calmness settled over the crowd like nightfall.

"Chopper's here," Farmer spun around to the end of the road where a Huey was touching down. The crowd turned and watched as a soldier carrying a stretcher ran towards them.

Minutes later the child was strapped to the gurney and motioned to Walter that he needed help to transport the child to the chopper.

"Ky," Walter urged, "assist with the transport to the chopper." He turned back to Feeney, "ask him if he wants to go with her?"

Feeney translated and waited for the farmer to respond. "He says he can't leave his mother." They watched as the farmer pushed an older man towards Walter, speaking frantically in their native tongue. "He says, their grandfather will accompany her."

Walter nodded and motioned for the elderly man to follow him to the chopper. "Once the dustoff is complete, and the tank gets towed, we're moving out," Walter announced.

"Copy that," Alton waited for Farmer and Bailey to make their way back to the vehicles before following suit. A child, he thought to himself, probably no older than Allen or Robin. What was a child that age even doing in the middle of a war zone? And under what circumstances was it possible that a child could be injured, killed even. The world he was in had gone crazy. He wanted more than ever before to go home, back to burned jam cakes and a stinky outhouse.

He meant what he had said to the farmer earlier. He would pray for both the child and the mother, but he was going to pray for himself as well. A prayer that he would make it home to his momma and this country would eventually come together and heal from within.

****

It had been three days since the dustoff for the child. Since the event, Alton wondered many times the outcome of the child and the mother, Hell, he had even asked Walter for an update at least twice but the response had been the same each time. No information was forthcoming.

He supposed it made sense, they were fighting an unpopular war both here and at home. Any event, even those without intended harm, was scrutinized and critiqued ad nauseum here and abroad. Fault and blame were tossed around like a hot potato from one politician to another. The truth was inherently dependent upon who was reporting the story. And the facts varied from reporter to reporter, not necessarily meaning the media.

There was the truth and then there was what was true. Most times, he was not sure he could tell the difference. Alton had no choice but to trust his instincts and what was in his heart. And he prayed the Lord would continue to watch over him and felt confident in his fate as God planned.

"You're quiet this morning?" Walter's question seemed innocent enough, but Alton knew it was little more than a ploy, leading to a deeper conversation. True, troop A had been on furlough for the last seventy-two hours and Alton had seen Walter only twice, once at the commissary and again at the showers. It had been obvious to Alton; Walter did not want to talk shop during their time off.

The APC was lighter for the assignment at hand with Farmer at the wheel and Alton manning the M60. Walter, Lackney, and Bailey were locked and loaded in the back along with two other soldiers. Their path North would take them along the MSR towards Trang Bang.

"Still thinking about that kid." Alton answered taking a long drag from his cigarette before answering and exhaling afterwards. "Still don't know nothing?"

"I inquired twice for you and was told both times that no information was forthcoming." Walter sounded so formidable; Alton knew he was not happy with the continued line of questioning. "Why are so concerned about one kid, after all you've seen?"

"I have a niece about her age," Alton wiped his chin and adjusted his helmet more comfortably atop his head. "I haven't been able to think about anything except how I'd feel if that were Robin laying in that field or Allen."

"Casualties of war, Ky," Walter's words were solemn as if he were delivering the benediction at a church service. "They are all around us here." He paused and indicated ahead of the APC. "Look."

Just in front of the APC to the right of the road were three freshly dug graves, the dirt, dark and moist. About twenty yards away laying in the open were four or five decaying bodies staggered over several downed trees. From the APC, it was not possible to distinguish if the bodies were sympathetic to the North or South Vietnamese cause. Since the bodies were not American soldiers, no one had made an attempt to recover the remains.

"It bothers me to think the families of those men will never be sure of their loved one's fate. They will spend the rest of their lives wondering if the missing men are being held in some God-awful prison camp or living elsewhere without any prior knowledge of who they were before." Alton was sincere and his heart ached at the thought of his momma and daddy if the situation were different and they were unsure of his whereabouts.

"We can't save them all, Ky." Walter patted Alton's shoulder in sympathetic understanding.

"Walt," Farmer interrupted, "HQ says we got movement up ahead." He paused and listened to the incoming message. "Convoy of buses, intersect within five."

"Radio for support," Walt instructed, "just in case." He readied his weapon and waited for the APC to come to a full stop. "Stay on the M60, Ky, at the ready. Will take a few minutes for support to reach us."

Alton watched as Walter and the other soldiers formed a blockade across the road and waited as the first of four buses came to an abrupt stop. He approached the first bus and spoke briefly through the window to the driver before taking his place back in line.

"Will await reinforcement then begin search of each vehicle for eligible males." Walter's directive was specific and direct.

****

Four hours later, after the convoy consisting of four buses, one truck, and one car carrying approximately one hundred men, women, and children was turned around and directed back to Trang Bang, Troop A resumed its destination surveilling the MSR towards Trang Bang.

Graves were becoming commonplace and the seven freshly dug graves near the paddy dikes were not even worthy of investigation. The APCs and tanks barreled past without a second thought or additional discussion. It was becoming as common place as the seizing ground and fragrance of diesel in the air.

What was less common was the image of a Vietnamese child waving from the roadside off in the distance. Cautiously, the APC rolled to a stop and watched as the child leaned into the lead vehicle and pointed a short distance away from the road.

"Vehicle fifteen," HQ's order cracked over the radio. "Set up a Southern Barrier. Vehicle nine take the lead and set up a Northern perimeter. Vehicle thirteen lead the sweep to the west, we have intel for the whereabouts of a mine."

"Copy that," Walter replied, motioning for Alton and the others to disembark. Before their boots even hit the ground, another soldier was leading the Vietnamese child towards Walter and the others.

"This way," the child cited in broken English and waved, running towards the field as if a game was afoot and the platoon was his competition. He looked to be about twelve years old, his skin tanned dark, like his hair and eyes. He was barefooted, wearing ragged shorts and a short sleeved knit shirt that had been white once. However, it was so stained, it was mostly the color of the mud banks across the way.

"Hold on," Farmer clutched the child gently by the shoulder. "We have to move slowly."

"Only one mine," the child smiled, his teeth impeccably white against the contrast of his skin. "Over here." He struggled out of Farmer's grasp and skipped ahead about 200 yards, coming to a stop and dropping to his knees. "It's here." He pointed to ground where a small area of ground had been displaced, it's regrowth not consistent with the surrounding area. As a result, it was noticeably different.

"How do you know it's here?" Walter asked as he pulled the child a safe distance away.

"I watched them bury it. I hid behind the trees," He answered, pointing to trees behind him. "The soldiers from the North, they come before the rain."

"Let's blow it," Walter advised, pushing the child back towards the road. "Tell HQ we need two hundred pounds to pay for the intel." He turned to Alton, "Stay with him until he gets his reward."

"Copy that," Alton said waiting for the child to catch up to him. Then walked with him towards the first APC where they would await the arrival of the funds. It was not uncommon for the army to pay for intel as related to bunkers or mines. The word was out, and it was paramount that the army followed through.

"More mines buried over there," the child said, almost as an afterthought and pointed to the trees just ahead of where the convoy had come to a stop.

"You don't say," Alton smiled and reached into the APC, grabbing the receiver to update Walter almost at the same time. It was shaping into a very productive morning and not a single shot had been fired. Timing was perfect, Alton considered.

By the time they finished clearing the field and blowing the mines, it would be close to nightfall. This was a good area to set up camp for the night. The terrain was flat, with good visibility beyond the downed trees. And the culvert nearby would afford them a bit of a diversion. Troop A would need to wait with the child and ensure he was rewarded for the intel. Most times, the funds were flown in via a Huey. Walter had not mentioned anything about a night mission, so it was safe to assume the troop would bed down for the night once the mines were blown and the child compensated.

The Huey lifted off about the same time as the unit kitchen appeared on the horizon behind the troop. Barring any surprises, they would definitely bed down for the night. Before long, the convoy of jeeps with insulated mermite containers was parked and set up to distribute a pseudo hot dinner for the troops. It had not taken long for the kitchen troops to get everyone served and they usually waited for the men to request seconds or thirds, in some cases.

The downtime was a perfect opportunity to follow up and see if any one of the kitchen crew was familiar with Bentley Peters, his friend from basic training. Bentley was such a larger-than-life guy, no doubt he had made an impression, of some sort, if he had been in the area.

Alton tugged at his flak jacket and handed his empty plate back to the soldier leaning against the Jeep's open compartment. "Hey, buddy," Alton cleared his throat, "can I get another piece of that pie?"

"Sure thing," the young soldier unlatched another compartment and handed Alton a sealed container. "You want some whipped cream with that?" He readied his can of ready whip and waited for Alton's approval.

"No," Alton shook his head. "It's fine like it is." He was not going to eat it anyway; it was just a ruse to ask about Bentley. Truth was, he was stuffed, unable to swallow another bite. "Say, a buddy of mine from basic training is here somewhere." Alton moved the container to the other hand as if preparing to open it. "Was wondering if you know him?"

"What's his name?" the soldier snapped the compartment closed and waited for Alton to respond.

"Bentley Peters," Alton answered, smiling from ear to ear. He thought back to the help with marching that Cooper and Bentley afforded him. It would be good to see the old boy again. Maybe he could send a message back with the soldier and Bentley could plan to participate on kitchen unit detail for troop A sometime soon?

"Yeah," the soldier cleared his throat and turned his back to Alton, pretending to check that the compartment was latched. "I knew him," he turned back to Alton.

"Knew him?" Alton swallowed the know in his throat. What did he mean, knew him? Bentley's job was like delivering pizza. There was nothing safer than the food unit.

"It happened awhile back. He hadn't been here very long." The soldier looked away.

"What does that mean? What happened?" Alton's heart was about to jump out of his chest and he thought he was going to puke.

"About two weeks after he got over here, the jeep he was riding in took a mortar round," the soldier paused, his eyes closed. "Was a direct hit. I don't think he even knew what had happened."

"Were you there, in the field with him?" Alton's eyes were teary, his words strained as he pictured Bentley's smiling face and heard the laughter in his head.

"Riding in the jeep behind him," the soldier answered. "He was a good guy. I'm sorry for your loss."

Alton handed him back the container. There was no need to even pretend he was going to eat it. Bentley had been killed before Alton and Cooper had even left Fort Knox. All the time, Alton had spent being envious of Bentley's station in life and the "safe" job he had procured, his friend was already dead. No doubt, his body sent home in the same flag-draped pine box as everyone else. His money and affluence had meant nothing here in Vietnam. Bentley Peters' page in the book of life had been written and destined by the hand of God. It was as it was intended to be, but Alton cried for his friend, nonetheless.

Alton in the field, flexing for the camera.

Chapter Fourteen

The sun dropped below the horizon and motioned for the moon to make her ascent. It had not taken long for the word to get out, Ky was not himself, he was sad, and Ky was seldom anything except smiling. He had not shared the details of his friend's death, just that someone he knew from basic had been killed and he needed some time to process it all.

As the platoon closed the hatches in anticipation of nightfall, it was obvious to everyone, Alton needed some time on his own. There would be no story to fill in the hours between supper and lights out. Tonight, they were on their own.

Alton was grateful he had drawn first watch. He didn't feel like talking or even listening. And if they had been at base camp, he would have gotten drunk to help dull the pain of losing Bentley. Instead, he cuddled as close to his AK47 as best as he could without agitating the trigger and almost wished an altercation would present itself. It would be a welcomed distraction for his heart, something to extinguish the flame of guilt eating away at his soul. Why was he alive and well while Bentley, the chosen one, had fallen upon his arrival? It made no sense, then again, it seldom did. Garnet's had not either. Death was like that.

By the time the sun's light danced across the terrain, Alton had been awake for hours, even though he had completed his watch and retired for the night. What little sleep he grabbed was saturated with dreams of Cooper and Bentley and their time at Fort Campbell. It had been only five months since basic training. It felt like a lifetime ago, and his three months at Cu Chi had passed as slowly as three lifetimes. If he counted the many men he witnessed succumb to the battle, it was triple that many lifetimes. By the time his boots headed for home, he would be an aged man.

****

The air was humid, sticky like the tips of his fingers after consumption of a melted popsicle when he was younger. There was but a little breeze evident by the way the leaves brushed back and forth and even though there was silence, the fragrance of spent gun powder lingered like cologne. And not one he was familiar with, his daddy wore Old Spice, when he could afford the price of a bottle or two. Delmore was a fan of English Leather and Wilbur had several bottles of Faberge Brut lined atop his dresser. Alton enjoyed all three of the brands, especially if the bottle was pocketed from one of his brothers' or daddy's room. One of his friends from school wore Hai Karate beginning his freshman year until graduation. Truth be told, once he had a regular paycheck coming in, he would probably invest in a bottle or two of it. It sure did attract the girls back at school, like flies to a picnic gathering. He wondered what Kathy or Mary might have preferred and wished he had asked.

His stomach growled as he checked his watch in anticipation of breakfast once the kitchen units arrived on site. Overindulge, that was going to be the motto for the day starting with bacon, eggs, hashbrowns and pancakes. He would even throw in some fresh fruit and biscuits to cover all the food groups. He searched the road again and stole another glance at his watch. Where were they? For a moment, he considered breaking into his C rations for a snack. He knew there was several single servings still in his ruck sack. If he were lucky, one of them might contain a serving of peanut butter or cheese. If not, the crackers by themselves would make a tasty bite.

No, he told himself, he would wait for the kitchen units. Maybe he would encounter the soldier from dinner again, the one who had shared the news about Bentley. Although, there was no need to engage him again. Bentley was dead, his story was done.

"You planning on hibernating for the winter?" Bailey asked as he balanced his breakfast plate in one hand and slid into the empty place on the ground next to Alton before moving the ragged canteen to accommodate the long, lean length of his legs and backside. Before Alton could respond, Bailey smiled so deep his bottom row of teeth seemed to jump up to meet the top row. "That's a lot of food, Ky."

I'm celebrating the life of a fallen buddy," Alton stuffed the last quarter of two pancake stacks into his mouth and spun the plate around as if it were a roulette wheel so that he had better access to the pile of fluffy yellow eggs. "Bentley would eat chocolate cake for breakfast sometimes. Once, the morning after intensity training, he ate an entire banana split. Alton smiled, "Course, he puked it all up about halfway through the obstacle course."

"I'm sorry about your friend," Bailey's eyes were sad, the smile gone from his handsome face, as he waited for Alton to finish the eggs. "My granny would say, it was his time. And it just goes to show you, there's no safe job over here. We are all literally in God's hands."

"Your Granny sounds like a smart woman," Alton agreed.

Bailey eyed Alton's canteen. "Can you spare a drop or two of water?"

"You're supposed to bring two full ones," Alton handed the canteen to him and stuffed the last piece of bacon into his mouth.

"I did," Bailey nodded before setting his plate on the ground between then and uncapping the canteen. He brought it to his lips but only took a few sips before handing it back to Alton. "VC shot a hole plum through one. I know should be upset but I was so happy it went through the canteen and not my leg." He did not finish the sentence, there was no need to.

"Your other one's empty?" Alton looked back toward the soldiers putting the kitchen units away. He might be able to coax a plate of donuts or muffins from one of them, if he hurried.

"I had to fill it up from the culvert last night," Bailey turned to see what had Alton's attention and smiled as if he knew Alton was considering a breakfast to-go plate. "But even with the Kool-Aid, it still tastes so bad, I couldn't swallow it."

"Drink what you want," Alton handed it back to him, having decided against devouring any more delicacies. "You know animals piss in the culvert and we all bathe in it?"

"I know but it seemed a better option that going without." Bailey took several long gulps before handing it back to Alton.

"Keep my extra one till we get back to camp," Alton pushed himself to his feet and swatted at the dust on his backside. "But I want it back when we get to Cu Chi."

"Will do, Ky." Bailey anxiously jumped to stand beside Alton. "I appreciate it so much," he fumbled with his plate, juggling the canteen as if were hot to the touch. "I will definitely get this back to you."

"You better finish eating and get ready to push out before Walter comes looking for you again." Alton looked behind them to where the other soldiers were climbing into their vehicles. "Last time you had sentry duty every night that week. Best not, piss him off again."

"Thanks, Ky," Bailey dropped his plate to the ground and slung the canteen strap over his shoulder before his big feet stumbled toward his APC.

Alton collected the discarded paper cup and breakfast container and carted it under his arm towards his own APC for disposal. It was true the Viet Cong tracked the army's trail by the trash they abandoned along their route. C rations came twelve to a pack and once emptied were too cumbersome to be carried back to camp for disposal. In addition to being too much for the ruck sack, the cans, when emptied, had a tendency to clank together and divulge their positions to the enemy.

As a result, the soldiers tended to drop them out of necessity. Of course, sometimes the cans, once emptied, could be booby trapped with a grenade and the pin pulled upon movement of the can. It was common practice among the ranks to set the trash traps. It was not a practice Alton supported, there was no way to know who would happen upon the can. A child or hungry adult was just as likely to engage the trap as was the North Vietnamese. There was much pain and suffering in the country, death seemed to be around every door. Alton had no intention of adding to it any more than was necessary.

****

It should have been an easy night, even though the rain had started falling steadily over the two hours, the dry ground was a suitable collecting pool. It reminded Alton of the creek on Longbranch Road that Daddy used to take the children for swimming on the hottest of summer days. It was fairly shallow in most places except for the area around the big rocks. There, the water was deeper, the only place to pose a safety hazard to him and his siblings. It was here, on top of the big rock, that Daddy would sit and watch them as they dove from the big rocks and dunked one another into the dark waters. From this vantage, he was only a stone's throw away and the old red truck was parked on the dirt road just behind him, sitting idle at the ready in case a trip for emergency care was required.

It was natural, he supposed, to steal a glance over his shoulder, as if searching for sanctuary of Daddy on the big rocks. But there was nothing but the falling rain and wind in the trees. There were no mechanical sounds of APCs or tanks and no bursts of machine gun fire. The ground was still, absent of the riveting explosion of mortars colliding with the terrain. And the only fragrance in the air was the residual meaty scent of fried bacon, lingering in the air like a lover's caress. Would it be asking too much to loiter here in this space for just a little while? If he could not be at home on Elkhorn Hill, this place would do in a pinch.

****

Once the kitchen units pulled away and headed back towards Cu Chi, Alton figured the troop would either bed down for the night or trail the food trucks back to camp. He was more than surprised when the order came to move North and assist a troop recovery for a tank that drove into a rice paddy and was now stuck and sinking rapidly.

"How the hell did that happen?" Alton heard Walter's incredulous words scramble over the radio.

"Accelerator stuck while the driver was attempting to turn around and the tank drove straight into the water," an unidentified voice on the radio explained.

"I'll be damned," Alton whispered the words under his breath as if he had not meant to say it aloud and watched as the rain-saturated ground around the rice paddy accelerated the tanks descent. He could not help but consider the homemade raft he, Buck, and Wilbur had made when they were eight, maybe nine years old. All morning long, they had worked on building the vessel, using scrap pieces of wood from Callahan's furniture shop at the top of the hill. Just as the sun began to set for the evening, the three of them drug the raft towards the pond that sat on the land between Daddy's and Benningfield's. it had taken the boys longer to get their supplies loaded and the three of them on the raft than the time the raft spent atop the waterline. Just as soon as everyone was on board, it sank, like a rock. The boys emerged from the pond, covered in mud from chin to toe. It had been many years since he had thought about the event, but it brought a smile to his face just the same.

"Something amusing, Ky?" Jarvis' words cut through the layers of the years and just like that, Alton was back in the jungle, his hand itching against the M60 as he surveyed the tree line for snipers.

"Nah," Alton shook his head but did not look away from the area behind the downed trees. "Just thinking about a homemade raft my brother and I made once."

"Sounds fun," Estel pushed the big knobs of the gears into park and waited for further orders. "Not too much raft building going on in Northern California." He smiled. "My cousin and I used to steal paper cups of wine from the winery and sneak off behind the barn to drink it." He adjusted his strap under his chubby chin so that it was less snug and added. "Bet that was fun being on the water, you guys were like Huck Finn and Tom Sawyer."

"Not exactly," Alton smiled, "it sank about two minutes after we launched."

"I see," Estel motioned towards the tank to where the engineers were deep in thought. "All the rain has made the ground too wet. No way is that thing coming out without a tow any time soon."

"Look," Alton pointed to a convoy of soldiers as they lined up next to the tank. "They going to unload it." He nodded his head. "Better not leave those radios and share all our intel with the NVA."

"We're going to be here for a while, Ky. Watch the tree line for snipers." Estel warned.

Alton pulled his tired body to attention and focused his thoughts once again on the tree line behind the downed trees. "Copy that."

Bailey had been right; the Rome plows should have taken out another few rows of trees and provided the troops a better field of vision. Besides, the distance from where they were currently positioned would not have been much of a challenge for a sniper. Hell, his grandpa could have hit a tin can from this distance. And his grandpa was not a marksman, he was a farmer with a keen eye for hunting. Alton imagined many of the NVA could say the same.

****
November 5, 1968

Dear Sis,

Thank you for the green army socks, I am glad to get them. Am okay, nothing happening right now but feel that will change in a second. Smoke and lead are about to fall as we are up North now. Found a mortar, blew it cause Charlie booby traps things like that. People here are like dogs. Three MVA soldiers were killed and left in the street. It's sickening but you get used to seeing things like that. Ran into David Clark, was good to see him. He's lucky to be in motor pool but there really is no safe place over here. Found out my friend from Fort Campbell, Bentley Peters was killed only a few days after arriving. He worked in the kitchen unit and was killed while delivering meals to the field when a mortar hit his unit. He was a good guy, I will miss him. I'm going to ask Momma and Daddy for some goggles, you may have to help them round some up. Tell them hello and Gail and Allen to be good. Love, Alton.

****

The ground near the rice paddy was drier by the time Troop A returned with the engineers and a tow to pull the tank out of the water. Even though it had only been a few days, it was evident the tank had not been left alone during that time, anything not latched down had been confiscated by the VC. Taking the communication and scouting equipment from the downed vehicle had been a wise tactical decision.

Although Alton could not be certain, more than likely the delay had been a result of the increased Viet Cong activity in the areas in and around Cu Chi. The upcoming election in the United States had left the Viet Cong anxious and more aggressive than ever before, staging massive roadblocks and deploying an enormous number of booby traps. All of the troops, not just Troop A, were working double shifts clearing the roads and detonating bombs that pocked the MSR.

Everyone was on pins and needles, hanging on to an imaginary ledge and hoping once the election results were announced, the familiar tone of the war would return. Alton was no exception; he had matured since he had stepped off the cargo plane from Saigon—changed in a manner that was not evident at first glance. But his momma would see it, there just under his skin like a blister. And she would know her baby was gone, reborn in the spider holes and underground bunkers of Vietnam.

"Am I being punished for something?" Alton asked as Bailey slid into the seat behind the M60 and snapped the buckle tight around his chest. It was no secret, Alton always rode in truck thirteen with Lackney, Kris, Marty, and the others. During his time in Vietnam, he had come to think of the rig as his, the same way a fireman or paramedic might be assigned to a truck.

"No," Walter walked hurriedly towards his APC, "of course not." He pulled Alton to the side and motioned for the other soldiers to proceed to their vehicles. "We got a lot of intel over these last few days about a major offensive towards the end of the month." He pushed his bucket higher on his head and dropped one hand against his hip. It reminded Alton of one of his teachers at school, she taught math and after several attempts of showing him how to set up the equation, she would strike that same pose. He wondered what had happened to her. Had she retired or was she still teaching?

"Our unit is sound, Ky," Walter's words echoed through Alton's recollection and broke his train of thought. "Except for Bailey, he's our weak link." Before Alton could respond, Walter went on, "I need his skills evaluated by someone who can be objective. He's going to ride with Lackney and Kris for a few shifts so we can determine if the three-four is the right place for him."

"You don't think I can assess him?" Alton was not questioning Walter's directive, he truly wanted to know the answer. He trusted and respected Walter and knew he would be truthful.

"No, I don't think you can," Walter shifted his weight from one foot to another. "You like him, he's a sweet kid, one you're trying to mentor."

"Because you guys asked me to," Alton cut in.

"I know and I appreciate that you stepped up and took on the responsibility. That's why I don't think you can be objective, not about him and not about this." He smacked Alton's back, "it's only for a few shifts. And you'll ride with me in fourteen in the meantime."

Alton smiled and followed Walter to the waiting APC, "Great, the band's back together."

"Hurry," Walter pulled himself up and into the APC, "Base camp is going on lockdown." He waved to the vehicle that pulled the tank from the rice paddy and secured it for the tow back to Cu Chi. True, it had been stripped of anything of any value, but the tank could be repaired and most importantly, it could not be used against the American soldiers. "Let's get this tank to the mechanics and secure the bunkers."

"Copy that," Alton pulled himself in the seat behind the M60 gunner and made himself comfortable. Other than sleeping, he could not recall being in the back before. It was a new experience; one he was not embracing with open arms. One thing he had learned since arriving to Vietnam was consistency. He was a man who craved the familiar and he was good at being consistent. Nevertheless, he swallowed his tongue and prayed Bailey's assessment would come and go quickly and Alton could get back in his seat on truck thirteen.

"Bridge up ahead," Farmer called out, turning his head so that Walter and the others in the back could hear him better. "Does HQ want us to go in a certain order?"

Up ahead, Alton could barely make out the outline of an old bridge and although he could not see its end, he knew the bridge was only a mile or less across. It stretched across the river along the Northern side of the MSR. The roadway was not traveled by the three-four as often as those further South. As a result, there were many unknowns.

He enjoyed traveling across the old bridges at home, some more than others. The one in Greensburg was old and rickety with metal planks and rails that could only permit one vehicle at a time to cross. The approach at one end was steep and the progress slow as the vehicle crawled to a stop at the top, only to discover another vehicle was crossing already. The approaching vehicle had no choice but to place the vehicle in reverse and back down the steep incline to a safer junction down below.

The old iron bridge near Tebbs bend was a remarkable sight to see as well and it was only a few miles away from his hometown. He had ridden across it numerous times as a boy and young man.

Others like the old wooden one near Saloma whined and groaned as if the weight of Delmore's old car was just too much to bear. Although the wooden ones were pleasing to the eye, those were the ones he had the least faith in. They were, afterall, made of wood that came from trees. And Vietnam was littered with downed trees that collapsed under the forceful arm of the Rome plow. He had every reason to trust them even less after his wartime experience.

"No particular order," Walter's voice hummed through the APC. "Just work your way behind Lackney and follow him across."

"Copy that," Farmer nodded and tapped the break so that truck thirteen could slide in front of them. "Don't know about you boys, but I'm looking forward to some cold beers once we get to camp for the night."

"We'll be on lock down," Walter explained. "No one's indulging at the cantina tonight."

"Shit," Farmer slid the APC into a higher gear and accelerated to keep on Lackney's tail. It was a game they played, a love tap here and there, sort of like a twelve-ton game of tag. "We've been working doubles for over a week."

"I understand," Walter's words were soothing, "but tensions are still high even after the Tet offensive. We've got to make the best of it."

"My God," Farmer's words were far away. "Abort, truck thirteen," he screamed into his receiver.

"What is it?" Alton and Walter asked in unison, stretching as far into the front as they could.

"I saw movement on the bridge on one of the lower rafters," Farmer warned. "Lackney, there's someone on the bridge. It could be an ambush. Abort!"

There were no words, it was as if the occupants of truck fourteen were watching the events unfold on the big screen as if truck thirteen was part of a Hollywood movie. It seemed to happen in slow motion. Then again, it was as if a fast forward button was activated, and everything happened at the same time. There was a feeling of helplessness as a small, frail, arm appeared from one of the bridge's beams and dropped a grenade into the open cockpit of the APC. Mere seconds passed before the APC exploded, spinning around several times before slipping onto its side. Smoke and metal fragments filled the air and fell like rain into a debris field that was surprisingly small.

Alton watched in horror as some of the men of truck thirteen crawled out, their bodies compromised by both flames and smoke. "Four by four," Walter screamed into his walkie talkie device and was among one of the first out of the APC, his rifle at the ready as the remaining three set up a perimeter and the other four soldiers piled out of truck fourteen to assist in the recovery from truck thirteen.

The sound of gunfire erupted all around the convoy, as the soldiers fired at anything and everything that moved from the tree line to the bridge and including the NVA juvenile who had dropped the grenade into the APC. His small body hardly made a sound as it fell from the bridge rafter to the ground level. The small artillery fire that came as a result was no match for the M60s and the tanks. Within minutes it was silenced, and the area grew quiet again.

It was a child, Alton confirmed, a baby, only slightly older than Allen or Robin. This child should not be here, his inner voice screamed. He should be at home coloring and eating crumbled cookies and drinking milk. Where was the justice in this child's death? Was there no honor in this place?

"Ky," Walter called from the downed APC. "Call for a dustoff." His image disappeared into the interior of the APC.

"The child is dead, Walt. He don't need a dustoff." Alton knelt to where Lackney had crawled, his clothes were burned away so that his right arm and leg were visible, the skin charred away like burned paper. Adam Feeney, the medic, was starting an IV line in Lackney's good arm and motioned for Alton to hold the IV bag so it could infuse quicker.

Alton watched as Feeney injected Lackney with something and dropped the spent syringe into his bag. "I gave him some morphine. Just hold the bag and try and keep him calm."

"I'll do what I can," Alton admitted as his eyes traveled back to where the child's body grew cold. "Everyone else ok?" His eyes darted back to the spot Walter had disappeared only moments ago and yet to reappear.

"Looks like only two escaped without major injuries, just bumps and bruises. We'll escort them back to base camp to be seen in the infirmary." He paused and listened to whoever was speaking to him from inside truck thirteen, probably Walter.

"We got three more critical and one DOA," Feeney repeated. "Call for four dustoffs, Ky, and another one for the NVA child."

"DOA?" Alton repeated, unable to actually utter the word. "Who?" He paused, was it Kris or Marty? God, he closed his eyes, his heart facing. Who else was in truck thirteen? Bailey's name spilled from his lips in silent remorse. Bailey had taken his seat in the APC.

"Feeney?" Alton yelled to the medic's retreating figure, "Who's the DOA?" he had to know, he could not wait a moment longer.

"Harold," Feeney answered, his words barely above a whisper. "Everyone who was in the front is critical including Lackney, Bailey, Kris, and Marty."

Alton's knees gave way and he dropped to the ground, wishing he could either lie down or find a bush to vomit into. He was either going to pass out or throw up, maybe both. Harold, the guy with the thick black glasses who did not send or receive any mail. One minute he was alive, smoking a cigarette with the rest of the platoon and the next minute he was gone, washed away like the snow after a rain.

The image of Garnet's snow angel on the ground bullied its way into his mind. Would Harold's be smaller or bigger than that of his brother? And how would that compare in relation to the size of his grave? Would there be a grand gathering at the funeral home for Harold like there had been for his brother? Or would his immediate family pay their respects at an intimate burial at the graveside? Was there a situation where one incidence was better than another? Did it matter to Harold anymore? Had it made a difference to Garnet?

It had taken most of the remainder of the night to transport the wounded from the scene at the bridge. Surprisingly, there was little damage to the bridge, a few planks blown away here and there, but easy enough to patch and replace. The bridge, once inspected by the engineer, would be usable by daybreak.

There was little chance any of the supplies headed in either direction would be delayed. A waste, Alton surmised, blowing the bridge had not brought the North Vietnamese any military advantage. All they had done is murder a young soldier and seriously wound four others. Not to mention the child, the one who had been coaxed into lying in the shadows and dropping the grenade into the APC. His was probably the most tragic of them all. He has a child who trusted the adults around him to protect him. Instead, he was used as weapon of war. Had he known what the outcome would be? His blood was as much on the hands of the NVA as it was on troop A's.

Alton looked down upon his own hands, still shaking from the ordeal. He knew it was there, the child's blood, there on his hands like a glove.

He could not see it but knew it was there just the same. Many bullets had been fired by the troop before the child fell from the bridge. His death could have come from any one of thirty or so soldiers. Or it could have come from Alton's weapon. There would never be an opportunity to know for sure. Then again, did he really want to know?

Chapter Fifteen

"Not much to send home, Huh?" Estel pulled the box of Harold's belongings closer to afford himself a better look. "How'd you get stuck with this detail?"

"Harold didn't hang out with us a lot," Alton dropped an identical pair of thick, black glasses into the box, a backup pair no doubt. "No one stepped up when the Lieutenant asked for a volunteer." He rolled several pair of faded boxer shorts into a roll and stuffed them into the box with the glasses. "I didn't want some stranger from support services in here, gathering his things and asking us if we're okay."

"We aren't," Estel offered, "but we will be, in a bit." He shrugged his shoulder and chewed the nail of his index finger on his right hand in a way that reminded Alton of Delmore. "We'll say a prayer tomorrow when the Lieutenant comes back to pick up Harold's stuff and offer his condolences and wait to greet the guy who claims the bunk next. It's a cycle, like spokes on a wheel."

"Seems like there should be something more, something else we do to honor him and the others." Alton closed his eyes as he finished the thought and saw Lackney's raw, oozing flesh sliding away from the bones as he was moved from the APC to the gurney. His cries and pleas echoed louder than the roar of the helicopter blades as Feeney and the other medics transported him into the treatment bay.

Like Lackney, Kris and Marty were burned, their skin charred in patches that covered their entire appendages, Most of Marty's hair was gone and his scalp burned in places down to the skull. When he first was pulled from the APC, Alton was sure he was dead, his body limp as a rag doll as if his bones themselves had disintegrated. But once Marty was placed upon the stretcher, he cried out for his mother and tried to sit up as if reaching out to touch her. Everyone in troop A who was close to Marty knew his mother was dead. She had passed while he was still in high school. Was it possible his mother was welcoming him from the grave, comforting him for his trip across the River Styx to the other side?

Alton's heart ached again for Marty's mother, for Harold, and for his brother, Garnet. Who was there for Garnet when he made the trip?

"All we can do is pray for their souls," Estel spoke barely above a whisper, "and pray we don't share a similar fate." He watched as Alton folded the last remnant of clothing from the footlocker under Harold's bunk. "Speaking of fate, how are you doing?" He bit his bottom lip, his eyes darting back and forth as if he thought Alton might fall prey to a swarm of bees or some other predator from behind.

"Same as everyone else," Alton folded the ends of the box together and reached for the packing tape to bind the box. "I didn't know Harold well at all." He dropped the fat roll of tape against Harold's bunk. "Hell, did any of us, know him?"

"I mean about Bailey?" Estel glanced across the room to Walter who was just crossing the threshold into the barrack and warned him off with his eyes.

Walter hesitated at the doorway, pulling his jacket as tightly around his waist as he could and leaning against the frame as Estel went on. "I mean if Bailey hadn't been switched to ride

in thirteen," he paused, as his tongue fought against his lips. "I mean, it would have been you, right?" He shook his head and dropped his chin to his chest. "We all feel badly for you. That's quite a load to carry."

"I been thinkin' about that," Alton explained, noticing for the first time that Walter was nearby. "If you believe that the hand of God controls us all, you have to have faith in his plan." Alton could tell by the expression on Estel's face, he was confused, did not understand the point

Alton was trying to make. "Bailey's going home. I reckon his job here was done and mine ain't."

The ground rocked under their boots as a mortar breeched the nearby sector into the base camp and threw Alton and Estel to the floorboards as if they were rag dolls. Dime size particles of plaster fell from the ceiling like snow leaving the room blanketed in fog-like haze that made visibility from one end of the room to the other almost impossible. So much so, Alton wiped the soot away from his eyes and twisted his body around Estel's as he pushed himself, dazed and stunned, to his feet.

"Cu Chi's under attack," Estel forced the words from his bloody mouth. "We've got to get to the bunkers." He grabbed Alton's arm and pulled him through the rubble.

"Wait!" Alton yanked free. "Walter?" he called out, staggering toward the last place Walter had been and pulling frantically at the pieces of the ceiling that occupied Walter's previous place. "Walter," he called again, pulling as much of the debris as he could away until he was able to make out the tip of Walter's boot.

"Estel!" Alton screamed, pulling as hard as he could on a portion of the middle part of the rood with the beam still attached. "Help me!" Behind them, another explosion blew out the window on the other side of the wall, spraying glass as like a lawn mower cutting through tall grass.

"I'll lift it up," Estel yelled trying to be heard over the ocean of screaming and sirens blaring from the camp. "And you pull him out." Estel clutched onto the beam and pushed at the beam until it gave way enough for Alton to slide Walter by his ankles from the rubble.

Once Walter was clear of the rubble, Estel dropped the beam and took a step back to collect his breath. "I'll sweep around behind the building and make sure no one else is trapped. Can you get him to the bunker?"

"Yeah," Alton nodded and wrapped Walter's arm around his shoulder and walked him towards the open area where the back wall had been.

"What happened?" Walter's words were slurred as if he had been drinking. "When did we go back into the field?"

"Where are back at camp," Alton explained. "Cu Chi is taking mortar rounds. We were packing up Harold's things, remember?"

"Oh yeah," Walter laughed and spit a mouthful of blood at the ground almost hitting his own boot. "You okay, Ky? You're bleeding," he indicated to Alton's head where blood dripped from a small, jagged cut over his eyebrow.

"I'm good, Walt." Alton pulled him through the opening in the wall and down the alleyway toward the bunkers. Feeney, the medic, waved them into the bunker just as another mortar crashed into the wall of the mess hall.

"When is air support going to make their strike?" Feeney asked of no one as he pulled Walter into the bunker and waited as Alton slid down unabated. "Either of you lose consciousness?"

"No," Alton shook his head and pointed to Walter. "I don't know about Walt. He was buried underneath the ceiling. I'm not sure."

"I didn't," Walter piped in, spitting another mouthful of blood from his mouth. "Bit my lip and the weight of the ceiling knocked the breath out of me. I couldn't get a word out."

"I need to suture your lip, Walter." Feeney reached into his pack for a pain killer.

"Just sew it up," Walter grimaced and moved closer to Feeney. "If you shoot me up with that stuff, I won't be able to work." He looked around where a dozen or so soldiers, some wounded, others not, had taken refuge in the bunker. "And I think we'll be heading out soon to give a little payback."

It only took a few stitches to close the wound on Walter's lip and even less time to complete the act. "Your turn, Ky."

"Ain't nothing to worry on," Alton answered. "Look after one of the others," he indicated to the soldiers gathered behind them.

"If you want to be on shift to even things up, Ky," Walter argued, "let him stitch you up 'cause I don't want you bleeding all over my rig."

Reluctantly, Alton stationed himself within an arm's reach of Feeney. "Copy that."

"Ky," Walter added, his cadence even and tempered. "Thank you for pulling me out."

"Estel did most of the heavy lifting, I just pulled you out." Alton reminded him.

"But you were the one who came back for me." Walter fought back his tears. "Thank you, Ky."

"You'd have done the same," Alton winced as Feeney finished the last of the sutures and reached for the morphine. "I don't want that either, Feen. I'm going to the field as soon as the sirens clear."

Feeney dropped the unopened vial of morphine back in his pack and moved towards the back of the bunker to reassess a soldier who was moaning and thrashing about.

"Ky," Walter clutched Alton's shoulder. "I'm grateful your job here wasn't done, yet. I owe you, brother."

****

November 7, 1968

Dear Sis,

Am fine, had to move from the field back to Cu Chi cause things were getting hot here. VC blew the bridge and mortared Cu Chi base camp. VC dropped a grenade into one of the APC's and got one of our guys, his name was Harold. Hurt four others. VC was just a kid, only a bit older than Allen. This place is always causing trouble – keep messing with us until we wipe them off the map. Had KP from 3:30 am till 7:30 the other night, tell Momma I'm an expert now. Wallace isn't doing well in the election guess Nixon will win it. Wrote Hartley Skaggs and Tommie Hunt letters. When I'm not in the APC, I'm packing that radio everywhere – breaking my back. Bought me a nice jacket, will send it home. Would like to have it dry cleaned and put up for when I get home. Tell Gail and Allen to be good.

Love Alton

****

It had taken several days to put Cu Chi back together and like Humpty Dumpty, there were ragged scars on the ground where barracks and other support buildings had once stood. All the debris had been pushed behind the camp and most of it set ablaze so that the entire camp was camouflaged by thick, grey smoke and ash. It was like being in a waking dream and walking through the pits of hell.

Walter's injuries were minimal as were Alton's but still, they were required to forego action in the field until a troop physician could be flown in from Da Nang and clear them for active duty. Until then, both were currently assigned to preparing the insulated containers of food for the kitchen units that supported the troops in the field with breakfast and dinner.

Ironic, Alton thought, if Bentley had not been killed, there would a have been a good chance they would have run into one another. Perhaps, even worked alongside each other again like when they were back at Fort Campbell. It felt longer than nine months, it seemed like a lifetime ago. It was impossible to consider Bentley and not also think of Cooper Butterfield. They were peas in a pod, the three of them. Alton wondered if David had managed to locate him and prayed both were safe and well.

"Thinking about your friend again?" Walter asked, sliding the last of the breakfast mermites into the kitchen unit and slamming the door as if he had herded out cats.

"Yeah," Alton nodded. "I ran into a guy in the back washing dishes who knew him." Alton smiled a genuine smile as if Walter had told the most humorous story. "Said Bentley told them about a friend back at Fort Campbell who couldn't march well. And how the TC would kick at the soldier's ankles to keep him in step with the rest of the platoon."

"That you?" Walter pulled two bottles of Cola from the refrigerator just inside the kitchen and handed one to Alton.

"Yeah," Alton pushed the cold bottle to his lips and emptied it in several large gulps. It was not as cold or as good as the one he enjoyed in his daddy's barn with Winfrey, Willard Lee, and Buck but it would do. "If he and Cooper hadn't helped me, I guess I'd be crippled by now."

His attention fell upon a soldier dressed to the nines in dress blues, making his way past the debris to the commander's barracks. "Someone important must be coming through." Alton looked around the immediate area for anyone else out of place. "I hope it's Ann Margaret. Feeney said she and Bob Hope make regular appearances here."

"Settle down, Romeo. The celebrities don't usually come by until the holidays." Walter motioned toward the fire that seemed to be growing by the minute. "We're supposed to be tending that fire. Last thing we need is to be responsible for burning the rest of Cu Chi to the ground."

"Thanksgiving is only a few weeks away," Alton followed Walter closer to the fire. "Maybe he's like the one that comes through and makes sure everything is ready for the show?"

"Nah," Walter pushed the burning material towards the center of the mass with a huge metal rake. "I think he's here for Harold." Walter stopped to collect his breath, "or at least for his belongings to send home to his family."

"Oh," Alton stopped and turned to watch the soldier as he came to a stop outside the commander's barrack. It felt like being in church and waiting for the minister to finish the benediction before the congregation vacated the sanctuary. And Alton felt like he should place his hand over his heart as a show of respect as the soldier passed by with an office sized container under his arm.

No doubt, the box Alton had put together was inside, along with army issued letters and papers. What else Alton wondered? He wished he had known how the process worked, he would have slipped a note inside for Harold's family, sending them his condolences.

"I wonder who Harold gave his letter to?" Walter's words were barely above a whisper and Alton questioned if Walter had meant to ask the question aloud. He motioned for Alton to address a small fire that had started outside the perimeter of the main fire. No doubt, it had been fueled by the little of breeze that danced between them.

There was no need to reach for the bucket of water nearby, Alton was able to stomp it out with little effort. "What letter?" He took several steps back, his thoughts entranced by the way the fire hissed and sang, its waves of flame licking the top of a wilted tree whose few leaves were black and charred, yet still hanging onto the branch.

"The letter he wrote to his family, in case something happened to him." Walter answered, pausing only long enough to watch the soldier in blue slide into his army-issued vehicle and head towards the guard gate. Once the jeep pulled away, Walter continued raking the burning embers into the center of the fire. "A lot of the guys write letters, just in case they don't make it home."

"You have a letter?" Alton asked, sounding almost juvenile.

"Yeah," he stopped again and wiped the dripping sweat from his brow, leaving a slimy trail of soot across his forehead. "I didn't until we watched them pull Higgins from the wreck. He was a good guy, a great soldier." There was a brief pause as if Walter did not want to finish his thought, but he did. "I thought if Higgins can get hit."

He did not have to finish his sentence. Alton knew exactly what he was going to say. Anyone of them was at risk of dying, every minute of every day. No one was immune.

"How does the letter get to them?" The question came out before Alton could stop it. Simply having the conversation would upset his momma. He had promised her, he'd come home to her. There was no need for him to pen a letter to her.

"You ask someone to hold it who has a safer job than you, like someone in the kitchen or motor pool or in an administrative role." He paused. "It's addressed and everything with whatever you want them to know. If something happens to you, they mail it for you."

"I'm not writing a death letter," Alton dropped his rake abruptly to the ground. "Cause I'm going home in one piece." He walked towards the latrine. "I'm going to take a piss, be right back."

****

By the time Alton returned, the fire was once again more manageable and Walter had leaned both of the rakes up against the wall of the only building without some kind of damage. He had dropped to his backside, bucket strap hanging lose under his chin, with his eyes closed as if he were sleeping. "You feeling better?" Walter sipped lazily from a worn canteen laying against his thigh. "I didn't mean to upset you, I was just thinking out loud."

Alton stopped close enough to touch Walter but didn't. He slid down the wall to his backside and motioned for Walter to toss him the canteen, "I didn't know about the letters." He closed his eyes and took a long swig as if the liquid that caressed his lips and throat was something other than water. "Makes sense, I guess. Just in case."

"No," Walter shook his head. "Not everyone writes a letter. You keep on doing what you've been doing, Ky. You have your own beliefs, your own way of doing things." He nudged Alton's shoulder with his own. "It's part of who you are, and you shouldn't change anything about who you are. Not over here."

He pulled the canteen from Alton's hands and took another drink. He pretended not to have tears in his eyes and Alton pretended not to notice he did. Walter went on. "You keep being you, stories and all."

"I'm hungry," Alton half laughed, half cried. "We loaded up all that food and kept nothing out for ourselves." The discussion of the letter had ended. It was no more, gone like the ash that burned off the main blaze and was lifted into the air like smoke merging with the clouds.

"Let's go around to the other side and grab a seat, see what's being served for breakfast?" Walter suggested pushing himself to his feet as if it were taking all his effort to move.

"I was thinking about hotdogs," Alton cringed before joining him into a standing position but turning to look once more upon the fire. Or pinto beans with cornbread and a ham bone, he wanted to add, but did not.

"The ones with chili that you and your friends would get at the restaurant?" Walter slid his hands into his jacket pocket and collected his rifle from its reclining position against the shack.

"No," Alton smiled and folded his arms across his chest as if he had all the time in the world. "Before that when we were younger, kids growing up on the hill. Willard Lee and Winfrey's momma worked at the sewing factory in town, but she worked in the cafeteria, instead of on the production floor. She used to bring home these hot dogs; she got them by the case." He moved his hands about ten inches one from the other before continuing on. "They were huge. And somedays when she was at work and we were playing at their house, we get into those hotdogs and roasted them outside near the barn." He took a few steps backwards but did not look away from the fire. "Sometimes we had buns and mustard, little bit of ketchup. Other times we ate the hot dogs by themselves. Most times, we'd eat the whole case, all twelve dogs. Was some good eatin'."

"You're makin' me hungrier, Ky," Walter joked. "Now I'm craving hot dogs."

"Their grandparents lived next door," Alton went on, as if Walter had been dismissed. "And Aunt Sarah had an old handpump that pumped fresh water from an old spring behind the house. It was cold as ice especially on a hot summer day."

It was as if he could not get the words out fast enough. They tumbled from his mouth like a landslide, "After we'd eaten the hot dogs, we'd run over to Aunt Sarah's and drink water from our hands out of the handpump and pull fresh grapes off the vine that grew wild along the outer wall of the barn. It was shady there and you could yank them off the vine by the handful."

He made a big fist with his hand not brandishing a rifle. "You'd come away with a bunch of fat, juicy grapes. They were sweet as a piece of chocolate." He looked away, his face tinged with surprise. "I haven't thought about those grapes in a long time. I'd actually forgotten until just now." He wondered what else he might have forgotten over the years and under what circumstances he might recall other lapsed memories. It was both a blessing and a curse to walk the line between the past and present. He clung to the stories like a child holds a favorite blanket, its tiny grip reluctant to let the worn fabric go even briefly. He knew, like the child, a time would come when he would outgrow the stories and they would lay folded and creased, tucked away for safe keeping, never to be considered again.

****

Lisa Colodny

November 11, 1968

Dear Momma and Daddy,
Am Back in Cu Chi, will get to a dentist soon. Cheese spread was good, but potted meat and deviled ham – couldn't be eaten. Don't want to waste what is sent. 328 days left, seems like forever. I have to take a Malaria pill every Monday and it gives me diarrhea. When we're in Tay Ninh, we take a different malaria pill daily but it doesn't affect me the same way cause it's a different type of malaria. We get molded bread and have to pinch it off. Kids bring "food" with maggots that someone else has already thrown away. Write again soon.
Love, Alton

****

Over the next few days, it was as if the strike on Cu Chi never happened as if it were little more than an imagined event. Any minimal damage was repaired and disguised with a fresh coat of paint while the severely damaged buildings were pushed away into a mound of burned and broken wood, plaster, and electrical fixtures with octopi arms of wires that hung deflated from the stack.

Buried within the collection of items yet to be burned included mattresses from the destroyed barracks as well as photos, calendars, and notes that had once adorned the walls. It was perplexing why the soldiers had not collected their mementos prior to the building being demolished. Was it possible they had been injured during the ambush and were unable to return to the camp? Had others paid the ultimate price and the earthly souvenirs of life were no longer a necessity?

Although the artillery had ceased to fall, the fragrance of burned wood and ash hung stagnant in the air. It was a purulent mixture of diesel fuel, spent gunpowder, and fresh paint. The combination of odors left him nauseous, it was as if he had overdosed on the malaria medications. His stomach churned and groaned in angry protest and Alton excused himself to make an impromptu trip to the latrine before heading back out to the field.

His former APC was still in the shop, the damage being more significant than initially thought. For now, he would have to be content with the alternative vehicle. Although vehicle fourteen was identical in every way to thirteen, it was different. Everything about it was unique, especially the way the bulky material of the seat felt against his backside and back. It should have been comfortable, but it was not. It was too thick in some places that pressed against his spine as if he had sat upon a porcupine.

It reminded him of an old tractor with a metal seat that Daddy let him drive when he was about nine years old. The leather and foam cushion had been ripped away years earlier, leaving the rusted, metal skeleton to rest one's backside upon. The cold, metallic throne was by far more pleasing than the chair of the APC. Perhaps, the aggravation was only in his mind, he resented being back in the APC, thirteen or fourteen, it did not matter. Not really, one could be as easily targeted as another. Bentley was proof, there was no such thing as a safe place.

He wondered not for the first time about his buddies, the ones who had fallen prey to the bomber on their last assignment to the field. He had not been able to see them once they were transported to the waiting choppers. All six dustoffs had taken less than fifteen minutes. And even though everyone, except for Harold's belongings were still safe and secured in the foot lockers under their bunks, he doubted any of them would return to Cu Chi.

Lackney's burns were so severe, there was little doubt his destination would at some point be home to Alabama. There were several fine rehabilitation centers in Dallas, Alton was certain Bailey would spend many long months learning to walk again and regain the use of his left arm. The thought left him with a tinge of jealousy, if he and Bailey had not traded places, Alton would be homeward bound once he was stabilized. Did it make him a bad person that he was envious of Bailey? Injuries, and all, were better than walking a tightrope between life and death over here. It was a fact. Bailey's letter would not need to be sent home to Texas. He could contact whoever was holding it for him over here and let them know to destroy it. Alton wondered If whoever was holding Harold's letter was aware he was one of the casualties at the Phu My bridge. Was the letter still safe and secure with the keeper or was it already on its way to Harold's parents.

The airplane ride to Tennessee would surely be crowded with both Kris and Marty heading home to recover privately with family and friends at their bedside. Before Vietnam, Memphis and Nashville seemed worlds apart but the distance felt shorter in this space and time. Alton pondered the probability if, after their recovery, they might make an attempt to reconnect with one another? Or would they opt to bury recollections of the time spent in this hell hole and with each other so deeply the memories might never see the light of day?

"Situated up there?" Walter asked from the rear as Farmer started the engine and waited for Alton to buckle up against the M60. There were several new transfers into Troop A. Only one soldier was a new recruit, Alex Platt, from Boston, Massachusetts. He was tall and lanky, with blonde hair that looked more red sans the sunshine and intense green eyes that looked more feline than human. He had been at Cu Chi only a few days and had spent every free minute in his barracks with a book under his nose. His dialect was unique in that car and far, sounded more like "cah" and "fah". And he had mentioned more than once as the last twelve hours of furlough had ticked away that the pizzer at the cantina tasted like shit on white bread, Alton fought the urge to inquire if he knew this hypothetically or if he had in fact devoured Wonder bread topped feces prior to his assignment within Cu Chi.

Next to Platt, loaded with a radio-ladened backpack that prohibited him from sitting fully against the back of the seat was Frank Wade. If not for the fifty-pound radio strapped to his back, Wade looked more like an expectant father anxiously awaiting his child's entrance into the world than a soldier. He was tall and thick, with only a shadow outline of dark curly hair on his head and a thin patch of hair that looked more like he had missed a few days of shaving than an actual mustache.

One dark hand clutched at the rifle, standing between his legs while the other drummed anxiously against his knee as if his fingers were drumsticks and his foot tapped out a complimentary rhythm.

"You play the drums?" Walter asked, in an attempt to break the uncomfortable silence that was deafening with the APC.

Wade nodded, "I was really excited about becoming a redcoat but that's all on hold now."

"Redcoat?" another soldier, Sam Williams, in the back questioned. "You in a movie or something?"

"University of Atlanta marching band," Wade answered, sliding his drumming hand under his knee. "I got second chair drum corps three days after I received my draft notice."

"You from Georgia?" Williams asked, offering his hand.

"Yeah, small town in Cooke County, couldn't wait to get out of there." Wade exhaled as if the act of breathing was a hardship. "I suppose anywhere is better than there."

"Doubt that," Walter whispered under his breath, leaning forward to determine how close to the Phu My bridge they were. Their orders were to sweep to Mui Lon and set up a perimeter. "What about you?" he turned to Williams. "Where do you call home?"

"Detroit," Williams smiled a toothy grin, his grin seeming almost too large for his face as if he was the wolf dressed in granny's red hood. "Pleasure to meet you fellows," he smiled again and nodded, his chin so prominent, it was as if he was purposefully mimicking Gomer Pyle.

"Detroit?" Platt chimed in, looking up from a tiny book he had been studying. "Best cahs in the world, right there, brother." He stole a quick glance at his book again. "You drive a Chevy or Ford?"

"Ford," Williams responded, looking anxiously around as if he had said something wrong and was awaiting the fallout. "What about you guys?" he asked to the remaining soldiers in the APC.

"Chevy," Jake Curtis from Phoenix, Arizona leaned across the open space and shook hands with Williams first and then Wade. The distance to Platt was too far to make contact without standing up. He nodded to Platt instead and waited for the last soldier to introduce himself.

"Drew Allen, I drive a beat up 1964 baby blue Dodge pickup truck and have spent most all my life working on my family's dairy farm in

Nevada." Allen, the last soldier, spoke with such elegance, he should have been spinning vinyl at the local radio station near Las Vegas.

"Walt?" Farmer called from the front, "Phu My bridge coming up on the right," as the APC crawled nearly to a stop. It looked almost the same as the last time they been near it. Yet, it was different, new, unfamiliar. Were the souls of Harold and the VC kid lurking about, waiting to make their presence known?

It felt as if they were passing through an abandoned town, one occupied by ghosts. The way the wooden beams of the old bridge groaned and whined against the gentle breeze that blew past was as if an omnipresent force had floated from the clouds and settled upon the bridge, itself. Should a prayer be said? Was the place sacred?

The grenade's explosion had been mostly contained within the APC but there were telltale signs of the attack. The wooden floorboards of the bridge had charred wood where the child's body had fallen and the rafter where he had laid in waiting was pocked prominently with holes where the machine gun's aim had been true.

"Ky," Walter warned, "At the ready, finger on the trigger." He barked instructions to the team in the other APC behind them. "Estel, pull ahead two hundred yards and be on the lookout for booby traps. No one on foot, everyone rides."

"Copy that," Alton hugged the M60 as tightly as he could and tightened the strap under his chin until he could barely breathe. He could feel the static electricity in the air, smell the burn as clearly as if the ground was ablaze, and hear the pounding of his heart against his chest.

"Roger," Estel's affirmation was mechanical as it resounded over the radio. "Be advised," he spoke again, "we have fifteen to twenty mounds of dirt blocking the road up ahead."

"Let's stop here and clear it," Walter barked into the receiver. "Black and Sanford from vehicle fifteen make a perimeter in the front of the APC's. Allen and Platt, set up a perimeter in the rear. Ky and Estel man the M60's. Everyone else is on point to clear the mounds. Disembark and stay sharp."

Walt paused and then added quickly. "We lost a lot of our troop this week, let's see to it we don't suffer any more losses."

Alton did not need to look behind him to confirm, he knew Walter was praying his words would be truth and God would watch over them all.

Chapter Sixteen

Alton watched from his vantage point within the APC as the other members of the troop dropped to their knees and began the tedious task of filtering the dirt and attesting the hole was clear of any explosive devices. Nothing moved within the blankets of green jungle behind them. He did not notice a bird landing upon a fluffy branch or a butterfly dance by to rest upon a nearby bush or tiny, yellow flowers.

Time came to a stop while the road was cleared. Was it that way for his momma and daddy while he was away? Did their worn bodies push forward through the waking hours while their minds lorded over the night as if on autopilot?

Alton had been prescriptive in his letters home, careful not to share images of the war that would worry his momma. Her health was fragile, like a fine porcelain vase. He did not want to be the bull in her china shop. It was different with Sis. There was something cathartic about the letters he sent home to her. His pen to paper was therapeutic, medicinal.

"Dozens of child-like footprints," Alton overheard Wade's voice on the radio.

"Say again," Alton spoke into the receiver, his niece and her broken cookies popped into his mind as if an instamatic camera flash had been initiated. He rubbed his eyes in response and squinted towards the road now cleared and passable.

"Area was saturated with dozens of small footprints as if the booby traps were set by children." Wade explained, his words growing louder as his image appeared along Alton. "I say the VC used the kids to dig the holes as a decoy."

Alton considered the VC child who dropped the grenade into the APC and killed Harold. He recoiled, remembering the sound the child's body made as it slammed onto the bridge and echoed above the roar of gunfire from the M60's. Had he, like the builders of the road decoys, been forced to lay in wait for an opportunity to attack the American forces? Or had he volunteered, hoping to gain celestial rewards in the life after this one?

****

The explosion rocked the APC, but not to the extent that thirteen had been pummeled earlier. Alton, Walter, Curtis, and Williams were stunned and bruised. No doubt, they would be sore and swollen in the morning where they had been slammed against the interior of the APC. And the troop would need to wait on the engineers to get the track back on the APC. Other than that, the biggest challenge in the immediate future was dinner. They were expected back at Cu Chi before nightfall. Therefore, a kitchen unit had not been dispatched. They were hungry, but not enough to indulge in the C rations they carted in their backpack.

"I'm going to open one and hope it's spaghetti," Alton explained, holding his left shoulder so still it looked as if it were made of stone. He was certain once the camp medic provided something for the discomfort, he would be fine. His injury was not significant enough to warrant to trip to Da Nang. Alton was certain his therapy would not extend outside of Cu Chi. He fell on his backside and pulled his ruck sack to rest between his legs so that he could better dig through its contents.

"With the luck we're having, I'm thinking you're more likely to lay hands on a joker," Walter exhaled and joined the circle of soldiers as if they were going to roast marshmallows. No one liked the containers with chopped ham and eggs. Even if you could forego the smell, the taste was downright blinding. Despite its appearance, the taste was unforgettable. Hence, the combination had been tagged the "Joker." He tossed two unmarked C ration containers towards Alton. "Can you light those up for me, Ky?"

"Sure," Alton pulled out a few pieces of dime sized C4 and ignited it under the rations, careful to hold the cans by its metal ring. "No jokers here," he announced to Walter and handed the heated spaghetti cans to Walter. Alton held his breath and pushed the devil ham and eggs into his mouth as quickly as possible before his colleagues could identity what constituted his meal. It was a talent he had honed many times over the years. Food was not always plentiful on their table, and he could devour it without pausing long enough to taste it. There had been many situations in his youth where he had simply nourished his body. It was a similar situation with the Jokers.

****

November 21, 1968

Dear Sis,

I'm okay but skinned up. Fools blew up my track with a 35-pound mine, we ran over it. Track was lost, radio still working. Several guys from the Phu My bridge got purple hearts – haven't seen them since we were hit. Don't tell mom or dad, they will only worry. I sent my jacket home, would like it cleaned and hung up for me when I get home. Tell Gail and Allen to be good, Alton

****

About four miles west of the Saigon River lay the Bo Ho Woods. It consisted of rubber plantations, sparse to dense woods, and open rice paddies with dikes as high as one to two meters. It was a well-known secret that the VC used parts of the woods as a base camp with extensive bunkers and tunnels, some with levels that ran two or three deep.

Since the day he had stepped foot in Cu Chi Base Camp, Alton had heard the stories about the Bo Ho Woods and how in July of 1966 several platoons were dropped at a landing zone within the woods and came under intense sniper fire for many hours. There were significant

American losses and when support from Cu Chi arrived the next morning to recover the bodies, they found them neatly lined up and stripped of all weapons and equipment. It was a mental picture, once imagined was hard to shake.

Alton was no exception. He had heard the stories from the South Vietnamese as well as the seasoned soldiers of Cu Chi and cringed with every tall tale. He had felt death many times in his youth beginning with his brother and seen it firsthand since arriving in Vietnam. Still, the thought of patrolling Bo Ho Woods amidst its bunkers and spider tunnels gnawed on his last nerve. He thought, once again, of his promise to his momma and considered, perhaps, he should have saved a letter for home, especially after his APC had hit the mine. Death was knocking at the door, and he wondered how many more times he could ignore the noise?

It was dark in the tunnel, even once it opened up into the room, it was hard to see the interior of the room. Once the torch was lit, Alton was able to make out fresh ashes at his feet. Sweat pooled from his forehead, down his neck, and saturated his shirt. Even though it was cool inside the bunker, he could feel the droplets parading down his neck and back.

"Clear," he whispered to Wade, waiting for the others to fan out and cover the rest of the room.

"Got a grenade, pin is still in it," Wade explained. "Back wall is temporary," he added, moving further into the room.

"It's a mud wall," Walter explained. "Ky, break thru it and let's see what's on the other side." He motioned to Platt and Curtis. "Cover him."

Alton approached the wall, holding the butt of his rifle like it was an ax. He waited as Platt and Curtis took their position before breaking thru. If he could have closed his eyes, he would have but he did not. Instead, he barreled thru, using his rifle to clear a pathway for his boot. The wall gave way with little effort, he probably could have kicked it down without the aid of his rifle. And when the pieces of mud and sticks fell from where the wall had been into the empty room, he opened his eyes and was relieved to discover it was empty. He had kept his promise to his momma, once again.

"This one's not that old," Alton explained as Allen and William collected the contents of the bunker: two grenades, four bottles of lotion, one VC hat, and one bottle of unidentified pills. Once Alton had documented the contents, he turned to Walter. "Detonate the grenades and burn the rest?"

Walter nodded and motioned for the troop to evacuate the bunker. "We're done here, boys. Let's set up a perimeter for the night. Wade, make sure that radio is set and cranked. If we need support, they'll need to get here quickly." He scanned the darkness of the night, aware the jungle edge was close by, too close. Charlie would be on top of them in a flash. "Ky, you and Farmer set some booby traps just enough to give us a heads up. We'll yank them in the morning before we head back to Cu Chi."

It was well into nightfall when Alton and Platt returned from scouting the area beyond the perimeter and setting a booby trap to announce any visitors that might come calling. The platoon quickly saw to the business of setting up a defensive night position, similar to how wagons as they traveled the treacherous plains of the old west used to form a circle to keep the Indians on the outside.

Several of the soldiers set their stations up for the night, some guarding the perimeter outside the circle, others standing on foot with their AK47 tucked like a lover against their chest. They took turns sleeping, patrolling, and eating. It was like a well-oiled machine as each cog engaged a spring at just the right moment, except they were not machines, they were men. They needed rest, water, and food.

"What are the chances this ain't a joker?" Curtis held up several C rations in his hand and waved them as if they were playing cards. "Cause I'm not hungry enough to eat that shit."

"If it is, just keep opening them till you find one with spaghetti or peaches," Farmer explained, "the cheese and crackers ain't bad."

"I'd feel bad about wasting them," Charlie Black offered, digging through his ruck pack as if he had just returned from trick or treating and was assessing what candies we had hauled in. Black had been quiet since Harold's death. It was true, Black and Harold had not been close friends, but it seemed to Alton as if Black felt guilty commenting about Harold's lack of mail, implying he had little family or friends. They were all just barely existing in the pseudo-lives they had carved out here in this place. Once back in their innate environment, would one recognize the other? Or might a head turn away in pretentious anonymity upon an encounter once the war was little more than a memory?

"Just pick up the empties," Walter barked as he passed by and caught the last of the conversation. "Don't want the VC using them as booby traps, especially with so many new soldiers coming into the field. They might see the containers as familiar, safe."

"And wrap them so they don't rattle together in your pack," Farmer added. "Last month, that new kid from New Jersey sounded like a marching band when we were out on patrol." Farmer leaned his rifle against the APC and dug into his ruck sack, smiling as his hand wrapped around the remnants of Alton's maple nut goodies. There was less than a quarter of the package left and the bag and been folded upon itself to preserve the little that was left.

"Ky," he offered the package to Alton. "You want the rest of these? Your cousin may not get anymore to you anytime soon."

Alton, who had remained inside the APC with the strap of the M60 secured around his body, had drawn first watch. His eyes never broke away from the dark images of the tree line. Even by the light of the moon, there was little visibility. He shook his head and rubbed at his chin. "I wish I could but with this tooth, it would be like adding gasoline to a brushfire."

"You want me to drop them in your ruck pack?" Farmer asked, moving towards the back to acquire Alton's pack.

"Nah," Alton pushed the crinkled bag back to Farmer. "You guys finish them, they won't be good much longer, be too hard to eat, bad tooth or not." He smiled mischievously, thinking of Janet. "Maybe my cousin will send you a package if you ask her?"

"Is she the one with the dark hair in that photo your sister sent?" Farmer unrolled the bag and finger grabbed two pieces before handing the package off to Wade.

"Yes," Alton nodded in agreement, more than aware that Farmer knew which girl in the photo was his cousin, Janet. He had caught him admiring the photo as it hung on the wall near his bunk more than once.

"She's pretty," Farmer said, trying to sound as noncommittal as was possible. His attempt fell short, especially since he had started the conversation in the first place. "See if she'll write to me?"

"Sure," the words slurred from Alton's mouth, it took minutes for his brain to catch up to his tongue. What about David Clark? It was no secret she had feelings for David and he for her. And they were practically family already. David was Kenneth's brother and Kenneth was married to Sis. What then did that make Alton and David, other than friends?

It was too much to sort out behind the M60. Later, when a distraction might not sacrifice a life, he would sort it out. Or Janet could, either way, it would not be up to him. Like so many other chapters of life, it would evolve as it was written.

****

The second day in the Bo Ho Woods reaped the revelation of more spider tunnels and intricate bunkers that seemed to be more ghostly than inhabitable, It did not appear as if anyone had occupied the bunkers in a very long time. The same could not be said of the tunnels, though. There was enough evidence to support their use up until, at least, a few days ago, including cigarette butts and spent ash where fires had been burning.

Alton felt as if he had been on a scavenger hunt, only no one had provided the eclectic list of items up front. In fact, it was more like a seek and find than a hunt. As he and the others entered and cleared tunnel after tunnel, it was clear there was little rhyme or reason for the contents they found and confiscated. Old bandages, rice canisters, bamboo basket, two saws, rain jackets, shower shoes, fresh meat, Chicom grenades, and several bins of rice were carried out and displayed like prizes on the ground near the tunnel's entrance.

Nearby, leaning against a tree was a pole, flattened on one end as if it were being used as a paddle for a sampan. Tucked behind another tree, nearly hidden from sight was an old well partially covered with a wooden chair seat. Since there was a portion of a soap bar and a worn brittle brush placed neatly atop the well's cover, it was a safe bet to assume someone had been in the area recently.

The others watched from a safe distance as Alton pulled the pin from one grenade and threw in as far into the jungle as he could. He waited for the blast zone to settle before repeating the act of the second grenade. It was like throwing baseballs. Yet, it was nothing like that at all. Back home, the World Series had just finished in October. He thought he remembered someone saying the Detroit Tigers had won. And that it had been a close game. He could not recall who their opponent was or anything else about the game. His life before was a world away and he wished he could wrap his arms around it and pull it against his chest, even if for a little while. In the meantime, he would ask Williams about the game. He would know if Detroit had, indeed won.

It was a coordinated effort to blow the tunnels and bunkers and it required perfect placement of the C4 to ensure the structure imploded upon itself. The Americans and South Vietnamese had no need for the bunkers or the tunnels. The intent was to ensure the NVA could not use them either. That had been the strategy to date. Every bunker or tunnel they had encountered had been destroyed with the expectation, eventually the NVA would run out of places to hide and fight out in the open, man to man.

"Load up," Walter called out, once the smoke and debris from the blown tunnels and bunkers cleared and settled like snow upon the ground. "We've been called back to Cu Chi for furlough till after Thanksgiving." He turned back to face Alton, "I think I read on some flyer that we're having a guest."

"Ann Margaret?" Alton's face lit up like a fourth of July bottle rocket.

"I don't think so, Ky." Walter fought back the urge to laugh. "But she'll be back at some time. We've named a gate after her. I believe Colonel McGowan is joining us for dinner at Cu Chi."

****

Lisa Colodny

November 24, 1968

Dear Momma and Daddy,
Dry season is here. Leaving base camp to sweep the woods, will be very busy – wanted to write while had the chance. Leaving in 2 hours – if you get a letter with only 3 lines, don't be surprised. Lucky if I get the time to write that much. Thank you for the goggles – they are nice. And for giving Marguerite the money to clean the jacket. How is work with the state? You'd think big trucks and graters could go anywhere but if its damp, they will bury themselves in the mud. Course, a lot of it depends on the man behind the wheel. I watch them hook things up here and they don't do it like you would have. Heard Mom's X-rays were good – take care of yourselves. Won't be able to send anyone anything for Christmas cause my money is tight and I haven't been into Tay Ning in a while. Hope everyone enjoys Thanksgiving in a few days. Save me some jam cake. I wish I was there with you all.
Love, Alton

****

Was there an agreement made by the leaders of the North and South Vietnamese that no fighting would occur on Thanksgiving? If they had made just an agreement, could they not make another and concede to just call the whole war thing off and let everyone go home? Home to a slightly overcooked turkey, lumpy mashed potatoes (mashed with real milk not powdered milk or water) and fresh corn off the stalk of Mr. Benningfield's farm. Alton would even welcome Momma's jam cake and fruit cake.

True, he had never been a fan of pumpkin pie, although Sis and Wilbur could eat their weight in it. Still, nothing would taste better than a piece of Aunt Sarah's pumpkin pie and cold glass of milk right now. Afterwards, he and Delmore would sneak off to the barn with Uncle Ira's bottle of spiked eggnog hidden under a jacket. Daddy and Wilbur would soon join them, and Sis's appearance would come soon after she put her kids to bed. Then, they would put just enough wood into the old stove to barely outlast the bottle and take turns at it until they were warmed from the inside out and the eggnog was gone.

It would not be long before everyone would sneak back in through the kitchen door (Momma would pretend to be asleep and not know) and retire to the bedrooms upstairs. But not Alton, it was a tradition since getting his driver's license. He would pick up Willard Lee and Winfrey and head into town to cruise up and down main street. Sometimes, they would hook up with local girls from school. Other times, they would make new friends from the neighboring counties of Green or Adair County. They would pile into Delmore's old car, flipping spent cigarettes out of the window and sharing as many bottles of coke spiked with rum as the boys could afford. Once the cigarettes and liquor were exhausted, their dates would be returned to their own vehicles and the boys would make their way home to Elkhorn Hill.

How many mailboxes had been damaged along that road as he and his cousins made their way home, his vision blurred by alcohol and lack of sleep? More than once, he was only a half mile ahead of the Deputy and Mr. Watson had the tire tracks across his front yard to prove it.

Mr. Watson's farm had the great misfortune of being situated in the curve of a hair pin turn. It was not uncommon for him, or one of his brothers, to cut the curve short and leave a trail of mud about six inches deep in the yard as the car's tires chewed through it. This was the Thanksgiving celebration he longed to get back to, not the one currently ongoing on the Cu Chi base camp.

The mess hall was pretty much standing room only, his troop gathered at an L shaped table near the back of the room. Officers and enlisted men ate together, the officers making a point to wander around the room and interact with the men under their command.

Chefs dressed in long white stained aprons retreated back behind tall metal carts with racks of buttery sliced turkey and sugary ham dripping in thick sauces and roamed up and down the spaces between the tables forking healthy portions onto the soldiers' plates.

Groups of young people, some in ROTC uniforms, others dressed in white kitchen pants and shirts drifted behind the chefs pulling smaller carts, some with mashed potatoes or cornbread stuffing. Others meandered across the room dropping bread and cranberry sauce in smaller plates on the tables for the soldiers to distribute to one another.

There were dozens of pitchers of iced tea, lemonade, as well as cans of Coca Cola sitting in tubs of melting ice, but most of the drinks were left untouched. Instead, the individual tables were littered with beer bottles, some empty, waiting to be collected by one of the servers. Others partially full, waiting to be replaced with another bottle. In the center of the room, Colonel McGowan scooped out ice cream for the troops in appreciation for their sacrifice.

It was loud, mostly from the chatter of the soldiers but partially from the cheers coming from several televisions stationed along the back wall. The Philadelphia Eagles were pulverizing the Detroit Lions and from the look on Sam Williams' face, all hope was lost.

****

November 28, 1968

Dear Sis,

It's Thanksgiving Day, dry season is in full swing, holding outside of Cu Chi and the Saigon River. VC are everywhere. Found an RPG case and stuff set up about 2 nights ago. We are getting closer on them. Found 2 spider holes, one was old, the other had spent cig butts & ashes no more than a week old. I dropped a grenade in it and blew it up. Pulling the pin makes me nervous, several guys got messed up when they pull the pin and it explodes too soon. Will be on my 9 month in a few days, things get hot here quickly. Tell Allen to keep himself straight and thank Gail for the poem.

Chapter Seventeen

After Thanksgiving, because the terrain was too soft for the tanks, A Troop minus the tanks moved North of Fire Support Base Patton and Trung Lap into the Ho Bo Woods once again. They had not gotten too far into the woods when small arms fired was encountered. They returned fire until the NVA retreated and ceased fire.

It was getting easier, Alton considered, engaging, returning fire, killing, and retreating. Whereas, he had puked his guts out after his first kill, the most recent encounter had left him feeling little, if anything. He could have just as well been thrown a tie around his neck and went into an office to complete his day's work. His lack of empathy was concerning. Yet, he knew, it was a way of coping. But was it the right way?

The Troop continued to move forward, deeper into the woods until Lt Kody's APC hit a mine. The driver, Lieutenant, and another soldier were medevacked by helicopter from the Ho Bo Woods. Once the dustoffs were complete, the tanks once again moved forward to set up a night defensive position and link up with the Colonel's track and three of the tanks already positioned within the woods.

Just as the three tanks were about to leave the dirt road to link up, they sank in the soft ground all the way to their sponson boxes. The remaining tanks were redirected to Fire Station Base Patton while A Troop set up a night defensive position around the three stuck tanks.

"We sure seem to do lots of babysitting," Curtis joked, moving closer against the APC to afford better cover. The jungle was dark and threatening. It seemed to stretch far beyond the expanse of the field and everyone's attention was focused on the normal night sounds.

"We can't have our equipment fall into the VC's hands," Alton explained. "We'd blow it ourselves before giving it to them."

"Let's hope it doesn't come to that," Walter explained, scanning the area again for anything out of place.

****

Troop B tracked back South to escort the kitchen units to the night defensive position to provide hot meals and replenish supplies. Shortly after sunset, just as Col. McGowan's helicopter was about to touch down within the night defensive position, it took on fire from an NVA rocket launcher that pierced the fuel tank and blew through, then out the other side. The helicopter smashed into the ground like a child's toy as fire exploded from the vehicle leaving the night sky looking like a fourth of July celebration.

"Incoming!" Walter screamed, yelling orders into the radio as the sky exploded above them and the ground belched mud and debris into the air as artillery hit the ground around them.

"It's coming from the Northeast side," Alton pointed his M60 in the direction to return fire, hoping to draw second blood. The troops fired in the direction of the woods from which the rocket propelled grenade launcher had been expelled. But there was no further exchange of fire, the rocket had most likely come from over a half mile away, well outside the range of the AK47s.

Instead, Walter directed attention towards the successful rescue of Colonel McGowan, the two pilots, and gunners. Their injuries were minor, and they were able to be treated by Feeney at the site until transport out could be coordinated in the morning.

Morning came quickly as Alton, Wade, Williams, and Platt went to work busily burying the remains of the Huey, including the rotor blades, and left front door. The engineers could not get to the site until the afternoon to retrieve the stuck tanks from the mud. Platt expressed concern with drawing "babysitting" duty again, but the warning glance from Walter diminished any feedback that might have been forthcoming.

During the wait, a Russian-type pressure mine wrapped in green plastic was located underwater on the side of the road. Lt Gowan gave the order to blow it in place that resulted in a crater about four feet in diameter. The explosion caused the perimeter of the rice paddies at either side of the road to break and as a result, the road flooded.

"The road is impassable," Alton explained, and an alternative supply route would be required. One that required more time and patience prior to reaching Cu Chi.

He was anxious to get back to Cu Chi where he would participate in a ceremony to receive a combat infantry badge. It was his first "award" since arriving to Cu Chi. He wished he had not sent his camera home. Momma would have enjoyed seeing a picture of him getting the badge. It was true, she had little interest in the war, unless it pertained to her "baby" and his coming home. But somehow, he thought, the award might make her happy, might make her smile.

****

November 30, 1968

Dear Momma and Daddy,

Dry season is here and we are getting ready to sweep the roads. Intelligence reports reveal the NVA moving from the North and heading for Saigon. We are watching it and if it hasn't happened by the time you receive the letter, Saigon will be in the middle of a big breakout by Christmas and they will be coming at us. They put me in for a combat infantry badge. Had a ceremony yesterday and they distributed some bronze stars and about 25 purple hearts. My JC received one (he has like 3 now). He was also put in for a bronze star. Can't recall Buddy Clark but there are probably lots of people from school I don't remember.

Love, Alton

****

Even though most of Troop A received the combat infantry badge, the ceremony did not take long at all. And they were once again back on the road, patrolling the MSR and looking out for anything and everything unusual. There were the usual encounters with tunnels and bunkers, gullies and trenches that had become almost mundane, like working in a factory on an assembly line on the production floor.

Life was funny like that, Alton guessed. Sis had worked at the Union Underwear factory since she was a teenager. Now at twenty-six, married with two children, she had made a lateral move, three sewing machines over where she enjoyed little more than a two percent or less annual cost of living raise each year.

Delmore and Phyllis had both worked at the factory when they were a family of three. But after Robin was born, the cost of babysitting for two children was more than Phyllis made in a week. And the young family could not survive on Delmore's salary alone. Therefore, they relocated to Louisville where Delmore could work at Ford Motor Company and earn more independently than he and Phyllis' combined Union Underwear salaries.

Wilbur soon followed his big brother's example and made the hundred mile move to Louisville and Ford Motor Company. Like Hansel and Gretel and breadcrumbs, Alton followed not long after. Only Sis remained. It seemed she never got too far away from Momma or Daddy. She was there, next door, keeping an eye on them and the house. She never spoke of leaving or wanting anything more than what she had. She was content with her life on Elkhorn Hill.

Alton knew every waking thought was consumed of going home, back to his roots from which he came. But once the celebration wore off, would he be content making his life near Sis or would he return to Louisville and build his life there closer to Kathy and his brothers?

He had never given thought to college. Lord knew he barely graduated high school, but vocational school was a possibility. Like his brothers, he excelled at working with cars and motors. Perhaps, officially learning a trade would put him in a better financial state than his present one. And being recognized for his civil service was a step in the right direction.

Alton heard the words Col McGowan, whose hands were bandaged from the Huey crash, read as his assistant pinned the badge upon Alton's chest. "Assigned to infantry while the unit is engaged in active ground combat to close with and destroy the enemy with direct fire." The metal badge was long and rectangular with a blue background and silver rifle with the muzzle pointing to the left. A silver shoe horse like garland poked out from the top and hung visibly from below.

Try as he might, he could not recall ever winning anything, ever. There had been no stellar essays or cross-country acknowledgements in his past. It was a unique and gratifying experience; one he could not wait to share with his momma. It might also be of some assistance if an opening were to present itself at the fire support base. Even if those stations were temporary, they were more permanent than riding or walking up and down the MSR.

There were, also, the atypical encounters that, more than likely, he would not worry his momma with the details of. The old campfire on the edge of the defoliated tree line was not on its own unusual. What was unexpected was the can of Vietnamese food and the punji pit with at least twenty visible stakes protruding from its sides. It was a gruesome death for sure, the pit was dug about six feet deep and fitted with razor sharp stakes along the sizes and at the base of the hole.

The hole would then be covered loosely with branches and flimsy tree limbs so that the structure would give way once even a small amount of weight was placed atop it. The unsuspecting soldier would then fall to a slow and painful death as they were impaled upon the stakes.

Although several of his troop snapped pictures of the defunct death trap, Alton had no desire to have a memento of any kind of the pit. Even empty and rotting away, it radiated evil as if the souls of those it had already taken laid claim to this place. He did, however, volunteer to blow it. And did so with great pleasure.

****

Lisa Colodny

December 10, 1968

Dear Sis,
Trying to put in a fire base support but will probably get pulled off to do something else soon. Place is filled with mines and booby traps. Haven't gotten our new track up yet but probably will in a few days. Got Christmas box from Jimmy Cable, wasn't much but it helped. Don't send Kool Aid, everyone throws it out, you cannot drink it. Tell Allen and Gail hi.

****

It is hard to imagine that Christmas was only two weeks away. No doubt, the big church on Main Street already had that old nativity scene out. You would think they would invest in a new one or at least throw some paint over the places where it has peeled away and raw plaster was visible.

Momma and Daddy had never had the money to invest in lights or decorations for the outside, but Daddy was always able to drag in a tree, usually either from Uncle Ira or Mr. Benningfield's farm.

Over the years, someone, Delmore or Garnet had brought in a few strands of lights. It was seldom enough to cover the whole tree, like the one in the window at the drug store. But if the few lights were strung up the middle, the tree and its lights made an attractive, festive statement for the holidays.

What Momma loved the most were the ornaments. A few were store bought with places in the ball where the paint had rubbed away. Others were made by Garnet and Delmore when they were younger. Wilbur and Sis had contributed, as well, once they were old enough. But the majority were made by Alton and the grandchildren. Momma kept them all, wrapped in tissue paper and secured safely in a thick box that sat on the top shelf of the closet in the bedroom. The ornaments were one of her favorite parts of Christmas. The other was having everyone under the same roof to share a meal.

It pained him to consider that she would not get her wish this year and it would be the first time ever that a chair sat vacant at her table. The best he could do was a phone call and even that was iffy.

There were not many Christmas trees at Cu Chi. Other than the scrawny looking one that stood in the mess hall, Alton could not think of any others. Maybe it was a better plan not to have reminders of that life pulling one's thoughts away from the task at hand. This life and the life he had left back at home were irreconcilable—one a polar opposite of the other.

Walter had advised him within minutes of his arrival to Cu Chi not to be distracted. He had advised against thinking about home or its people. Yet, Alton ignored the warning. Instead, he had woven his stories of home into his and his platoon's wartime lives. His own hope for a life beyond Vietnam had become theirs, as well. And once he got the opportunity, he would devour Momma's burned jam cake, independently. Nothing would taste as good as that cake and his mouth salivated at the thought.

****

There were seldom explanations for all the circumstances of life, why things happened the way they did as opposed to occurring in a way that was expected. For example, who could have predicted that a soldier would lose one arm and part of his leg after lighting a new explosive and attempting to try and throw it in to the river at the Trang Bang Bridge.

However, that is exactly what happened, and Alton could not help but consider the irony of it all as the troop waited for a dustoff at the bridge. The soldier was not from Troop A but the hush that fell over the platoon as the helicopter lifted off with him was just as if he had been. He knew that moving forward, every time he pulled the pin from a grenade, he would think once again of the soldier.

The current situation, however, was to provide security for a downed lowboy and dozer just outside the main gate, the Ann Margaret gate. There was no point in hoping anymore. If she did not make an appearance before Christmas, the chance of her coming after that was low.

Lisa Colodny

****

December 11, 1968

Dear Sis,
Had some extra time to finish writing. Been sweeping today – saw a tank and PC get on a mine. Was a mess, 2 guys were messed up, one left on a stretcher, the other in a poncho. They are saying the gooks are taking over in Jan and they will start pulling troops out. Doubt I will be that lucky. Will be glad when this nightmare is over.

****

The explosion several meters away made him jump and he looked to determine if anyone else had noticed. Before Alton could ask, he heard someone on the radio explain how someone in troop A had tripped a mine, a booby trap.

From his vantage point, he could not tell who the injured man was, but he could see the others moving to render aid. The smoke settled and he could barely make out the image of a downed soldier near the ground at the edge of the naked tree line. Damned agent orange, he cursed to no one. When it was dropped upon the jungle, it stripped away every blade of grass and hanging leaf, leaving a vast wasteland of death and destruction in its wake.

"We need a dustoff," the voice on the radio advised. Alton did not recognize the name of the soldier. Even though he was in Troop A, he was not familiar with everyone in the troop, but he said a prayer just the same.

****

December 13, 1968

Dear Sis
Haven't gotten messed up yet. Got the letter about Mom, if anything happens – get with the Red Cross cause they can get me home quick, especially if my visit might help her. Saw some guys get killed and will probably see a lot more over

the next few days. It's a mess over here in the field but I never hit anything lucky. Letters will be short over the next few months. Remember call the Red Cross if you need to get me home quickly. Tell Allen and Gail to be good.

****

There was a general concern about the numerous lights spotted in the Ho Bo and Boi Loi Woods. As a result, troops were advised to engage and report any lights or movement that occurred within the vicinity. It was believed that the sighting were parts of a larger force hiding in the area. On a whim, someone from troop A, reported to be the Lieutenant, left the VC a message pinned to a hooch near a deserted hamlet.

The Strategic Hamlet Program was a collaborative plan to isolate the rural population from the VC influence by providing economic growth to the communities and strengthening ties with the South Vietnamese. Surprisingly, the VC wrote back with a warning to go home.

Alton wanted to raise his arms and proclaim. "Okay, when's the next bus home!" For as badly as the VC wanted the Americans out of Vietnam, the soldiers wanted it more.

Alton conducting guard duty at Cu Chi Base Camp

Chapter Eighteen

Another sweep of the MSR was underway as the second platoon moved out of Fire Support Base Stuart near Trang Bang. During the move, the turret on one of the tanks lurched violently and accidentally discharged the main gun with one round in the chamber.

From the newly repaired APC thirteen, Alton watched in horror as a young, eight-year-old girl walking on the edge of the road was tragically killed as a result of a concussive head wound. The canister round also impacted and damaged a nearby Buddhist Temple.

Within seconds, Adam Feeney was on his feet and headed to the roadside to offer his medical assistance. However, there was nothing that could be done for the child, she died instantly at the site. Alton saw the image of the child from the bridge in his mind's eye once again, as well as the tiny five-year-old faces of his niece and nephew at home. He could not imagine the pain his own family would endure if something were to happen to them and his heart bled for the family of the little girl. Regardless of how this war played out, there would be no winners or losers.

****

It was an engagement like no other and Alton's entire body was rocked by the machine gun as it chewed thru bullet after bullet, spitting the empty shells out like seeds. He was terrified but there was no time to fully consider what that meant. Aim and shoot, aim and shoot, his brain screamed at the rest of his body. Do not think or feel, just kill. Shoot at anything that moved and continue to fire until nothing moved. It was him or them and he had made a promise to his momma, a promise he prayed with every battle he walked into, he could keep.

The sheer number of enemy troops was massive, and as a result, Companies C, B, and D aligned with Alton's troop into the area of contact. Air strikes, Light Fire Teams, and artillery were called in to offer support. And one by one the VC forces fell until the battlefield was a red sea of blood. And it was quiet, almost peaceful as the fragrance of gunpowder clung on the breeze and the smoke bubbled up like a whirlwind.

Once the smoke cleared, the fire support base near Tay Ninh was littered with hundreds of bodies, friendlies, as well as VC. Miscellaneous weapons and equipment were sequestered and cleared. Troops remained in Tay Ninh to quell any reactionary attacks that might be forthcoming.

****

December 24, 1968

Dear Sis,

Hanging around Tay Ninh as part of the reactionary force for the base camp and the convoys for Dang Tung whose mission is to take the Rubbers (Largest rubber plantation in the world). My unit went through a 3 mile ambush and kicked their asses! I was scared, we'd been in there 3 times already but they didn't hit us. Watch the TV, we are going to Saigon and led will be flying. My truck is number 13 and I will be on the left 60 machine gun. There will be pictures taken, last year when the ¾ leveled Saberville, TV cameras were there to film it. Should be a war bond there by the last of December, have Daddy cash it. Tell Allen and Gail, hi.

****

The troops remained on blocking positions around Tay Ninh fire base station. Instead of having the Christmas meal served at Cu Chi as had occurred for Thanksgiving, it was served at Tay Ninh base camp, instead. To accommodate the entertainers from the Bob Hope Show, an A10 replacement track from Cu Chi was moved to Tay Ninh and set up next to the stage.

Not Ann Margaret, Alton's heart sank, but any kind of break from the fighting was welcomed. And Bob Hope had always made him laugh.

The fireworks display in Tay Ninh on Christmas Eve was phenomenal with exploding colors as bright as any Alton had ever seen that seem to absorb into the expanse of the entire night sky. It was like a live drive-in movie with the horizon acting as backdrop for the largest projection screen. And it was loud, too loud. In fact, once his time in Vietnam was over, he doubted he would ever look at the Fourth of July celebrations in the same light as before his time in the army.

The real sounds of war were nothing like the projected holiday celebrations. The explosions were usually followed by insufferable pain and misery. Once his time was done here, he had no desire to bear witness to the sky being lit up like fire. He had seen enough of that to last a lifetime.

****

December 25, 1968

Dear Sis,

Merry Christmas, here's some pictures. Tell Janet the boy in this picture would like for her to write him. He's my driver and he has her picture in his driver's hatch. Got the Christmas package and one from Hartley Skaggs. Heading to Saigon to knock out windows with my M60 machine gun. South Viet gov don't want us down there 'cause they got buildings just like in the rest of the world. Three–four cav shoots up the place when they have sniper rounds, but we have a job to do. Little man will scare you so badly you don't know your name. Many a man has prayed with a can of oil in one hand and his fingers on the trigger of the other. He will hit us with everything he has and if he doesn't the war will be over. He won't get far and will get his ass kicked when he tries it. Tell Allen and Gail hello. Seems as if I have been over here for three years and then again, it feels as if I just got here yesterday.

****

Troop A was on a scavenger hunt again, stopping along the way to Saigon to collect VC paraphernalia and destroy as many bunkers, tunnels, and foxholes as was evident from the MSR. Some of the foxholes were connected by tunnels as long as fifteen feet long. Others went nowhere, they were deep holes that did not seem to have been used in a while. One of the longest tunnels had holes for candles and contained canteens, belts, toothbrushes, toothpaste with NVA writing on the tube, and AK47 rounds. The tunnels and bunkers were imploded with grenades, the round detonated, and everything else burned into ashes.

Things got hotter after lunch when one of the APCs of Troop A hit a mine that tore a hole through the driver's compartment and wiped out the road wheel and instrument panel. The APC was a complete loss and would need a tow to the Stuart fire station base. The driver of vehicle sixteen was a new guy who Alton had not had a chance to get to know very well. In fact, all Alton knew about Tory Kingston was that he was from Lincoln Nebraska. And now, Tory was probably headed home.

While they waited for the tow, Allen, who was scouting for snipers, radioed to Walter that he had encountered a booby-trapped C ration and requested permission to detonate it. Alton listened closely as Allen explained the C ration had a grenade stuck inside and that the pin had already been pulled.

"Roger," Walter's words over the radio were clear. "Permission to detonate granted. Ensure area is cleared."

Alton scanned the area to his right watching for the small plume of smoke he knew would be forthcoming. And was not surprised minutes later when the sound of the grenade's explosion echoed from the West followed by a small tornado of smoke, dirt, and debris.

"All clear," Allen's words crackled throughout the APC and Alton was grateful there had been no surprises. He did not like them anymore.

As Written

****

The platoon then moved North in the Mushroom to conduct reconnaissance-in-force along the banks of the Saigon River. There they encountered a bunker complex with the NVA who were dug in with their backs to river. Troop A began a sweep operations in the lower Boi Loi, west of the mushroom.

The troops encountered small arms and RPG fire that, despite three attempts, they could not hold the line. One of the tanks received an RPG in the turret and was forced to withdraw to evacuate the wounded. Wayne Velaquez and Andrew Bellos of troop B were medevacked from the area. While Drew Allen of troop A was treated in the field by Medic Feeney.

Division Commander Williamson landed within the operational field and ordered a third assault on an NVA fortified position of the previous day. With a last final push forward, the NVA position was breeched. In three different bunkers, Troop A confiscated 1800lbs of rice, 12,600lbs of rice, and 17,200lbs of rice, all in bad condition that resulted in it being burned in place. Alton also located a foxhole, large enough to be used for a sleeping area. He sat charges and watched as the bunkers blew.

Alton had never seen so much rice in his entire life. And the smell as it burned was atrocious, something akin to cow manure and sulfur. He had never been a big fan of rice, he preferred potatoes. As the fires burned it away, what was left was a foul smelling, soapy mush. He was certain rice would continue to be an enigma. He would stick with French fries or mashed potatoes, from this point forward.

****

January 12, 1969

Dear Sis,
Am fine. Found 3.5 tons of rice in an empty bunker. Three soldiers were injured. One was my buddy Drew from Nevada but he's not hurt bad. The other two from another troop were more serious and they are headed home. Wish I was

215

headed home. I know some guys (maybe David) are extending their enlistment and can serve less time over here. Would have to be half nuts to extend it. David's assigned to motor pool, he's not on the line, like me. I'm not staying over here a minute longer than I have to. Tired of getting the wrong end of the stick in life. Am anxious to come home. I may not be able to answer all of your letters for a while cause it's getting thick over here but I will write as often as I can. Say Hi to Gail and Allen, Love Alton.

****

January 12, 1969

Dear Momma and Daddy,
Am fine, will be moving out in a few minutes so will be a short letter. Found 3.5 tons of rice in an empty bunker the little man had hidden in the ground. War bond should be there in a few weeks, at least the middle of Jan. Don't buy a (camera) for me, already spent enough on it. Have some money hidden away. I only keep enough for soda and cigarettes, everything else is packed away. Don't blame Billy Jo for not wanting to come over here. Take care of yourselves and Daddy – don't get a ticket in that old truck.
Love to you both, Alton

****

As the sun rose over the lower Boi Loi, west of the mushroom operational field, Troop A conducted a bomb damage assessment and discovered several old bomb craters filled with water. Alton was pleased, it was an opportunity for the troop to take turns bathing.

Alton wasted no time in stripping down to his boxer shorts when his turn came around. The warm rainwater felt cool against the sunburned skin of his back and arms. Months of being in the tropical climate had tanned his pale, pinkly skin into a golden bronze. And he had built muscle where leaner body mass had previously been. Would his family even recognize him when he stepped off the plane in Louisville when his time in this hell hole was over?

The water was invigorating as the sticky film of saturated sweat, grime and dirt was washed off and he felt like a man reborn. If was like being baptized again and he found himself looking up from the water in search of Pastor Henry, the minister of his church at the top of Elkhorn Hill.

And it was January no less, and he was swimming, nearly naked in a crater hole. Back home there was snow on the ground, but here the weather was warm, hot even. And he was swimming.

What would the beach in Sydney, Australia be like he wondered? Australia, home to kangaroos and koala bears, a place he had only read about. Never did he think the opportunity to vacation there, might present itself. But it had, and if he could come up with the money, he could request some rest and relaxation on a private military beach in Sydney with other members of the Allied armed forces. It was definitely something to consider.

****

January 14, 1969

Dear Momma and Daddy,

Am well, everything over here is the same. I would like to see some snow on the ground, but the heat is ok once you get used to it. I doubt I will run into Billy Jo, probably won't be assigned to my unit but will be on the lookout for him. I'm trying to save some money to take R&R to Sidney, Australia. Some guys take 4 – 5 hundred but I would only take 2 hundred dollars because that is the least you can have per the government. Might go now and again later. Maybe not, wouldn't be the end of the world. Asking my JC to put me in for SPC 4 (JC is leaving in 2 days for Sidney). Also trying to save for when I get out of here. Can't drive Delmore's old car forever, Say hi to everyone.

Love Alton

****

First light found the entire squadron engaged in a major battle eight and a half kilometers east of Bao Don as troops A and C, who were bedded down for the night in a combined laager, received RPG and small arms fire just as the sun was breaking through the clouds.

Although startled, both troops returned fire as the soldiers scrambled to get to their vehicles and engage weaponry. A troop conducted a reconnaissance-in-force in the area of enemy firing to identify any vulnerabilities while troop C remained in position and awaited long range reconnaissance patrol reports before maneuvering to push ahead of troop A.

"Where are they?" Alton screamed, sweeping his M60 from left to right, spraying the area with liquid fire that poured from his gun like rain. He heard Walter barking into the radio for tracks fifteen and seventeen to pull around and support fourteen and twelve, who were taking a beating. It was like the VC were everywhere and nowhere at the same time. The damned bunkers he reasoned with himself; they must have set up the laager atop NVA bunkers. It was the only way the enemy could move in and out so effectively.

As troop B moved closer to the heartbeat of the battle, an NVA force in web gear and helmets appeared as if by magic and attacked just as troop B initiated its forward movement. Not expecting the surge, the soldiers fell to the ground, some wounded, others dead. Like fish in a barrel, the soldiers had nowhere to retreat to.

Alton's troop was faring no better, as it encountered fortified bunkers whose perimeters seemed to be impassable, and more casualties accumulated for the squadron. Alton fired and fired at the VC line, but it was like watching one of those old science fiction movies where the machines had taken over and as quickly as one is destroyed or dismantled, two more appear to assume its place.

Alton felt his heart skip a beat when he heard McGowan direct Troop C to move abreast of A Troop on its right flank for support. Alton knew the long-range reconnaissance patrol dispatched last night had been recalled to link up with the Colonel. As valuable as the information would be, it would take a while to gather it all and formulate a plan. Amidst the chaos and confusion, the continued ambulation caused A and C troops to cross fire on each other.

"Friendlies," Alton heard the announcement in echo as the notification sounded. It was as if he were attending a high school football game, the way the crowd went crazy. It was as if both troops A and C realized what the NVA had contrived and scurried to make the correction.

Colonel McGowan ordered a cease fire and directed A Troop to complete a 180 degree turn back towards their night defensive position. Two of the platoons respond and initiated the turn but the third platoon had an issue with one of the tanks and could not gain the traction required to move from the area. Colonel McGowan's troop, as well as the medic track, remained with the tank for support and called for air support to push the VC back.

It was the first time since arriving to Cu Chi that Alton felt as if all was lost. To know the American forces had lost the engagement was a heavy burden, one he hoped he would not carry again. There was no way to know the significance of the contact or just how much had been lost. He was pretty sure troop A had lost at least one tank and one guy from one of the other tracks. He did not know the guy, not really, but he felt for his family's loss just the same. He could not help but wonder if the soldier had someone holding a letter for him.

One thing was for sure, at sunrise, the intel would be available and the VC would pay for the intrusion.

Lisa Colodny

Alton at Cu Chi Base Camp, Vietnam

****

January 21, 1969

Dear Sis,
Just got out of the boonies and a 6.5 hour firefight. Waiting for the order to stand down. Getting a new type of tank but doubt going back into the thick of it for a while. Did Daddy get the war bond? I'll have some money saved when I get back and will repay you for the camera. Got to sign off as my unit is heading out. Am back, we just moved down the road a small ways to a rice paddy to set up for the night. Firefight with the 268 was intense, thought they were done but the NVA came back to engage again but we messed up the plan. We lost one guy and a tank. It was scary, everything was burning and shrapnel blew everywhere. Those Gooks thought they got three hits but I grabbed my M60 kept my head low and they only scored one. Unit in on security now for artillery but the assignment won't last long. Tell Allen and Gail hi.

****

By the end of January, the NVA unit had infiltrated a hamlet stretching into South Vietnam by crossing the Cambodian border and forming a strong hold for training and setting up base camps. As a result, the troop worked Southwest of Go Dau Ha to secure a series of small bridges and culverts (two to three tracks per outpost or culvert) that bordered the Cambodian border. The battle that ensued was brutal, but the American troops broke the NVA stronghold and reclaimed Parrot's Beak. Payback, Alton thought, and Walter agreed, it was payback for the retreat in the Bo Ho Woods.

It was almost impossible to consider he had been at home this time last year. Garnet's car tucked inside Daddy's barn was a constant thought that hung onto the ledge of his mind with every waking thought. And with every firefight or battle, Alton was reminded of life's frailty.

Troop A would be in the field for the next ninety days, engaging and facing the enemy at every twist and turn. The promise Alton had made to Momma and Sis echoed on the wind, chanted in sync with the music in his dreams while he slept, and imprinted itself upon his heart like a tattoo.

****

January 27, 1969

Dear Momma and Daddy,

Am fine, nothing much to write. Going on stand down for 3 days to test a new tank. Will get the new tank in Feb. In April when the wet season begins. Will be back on the road in May or June. Been there 4 months, seems like 4 years sometimes and other times, like I just arrived. Will be glad to get out and stop being treated like a kid, not having bunch of people on my back all the time. Take care or yourselves and I'll do the same. Love you both, Alton.

****

Lisa Colodny

January 31, 1968

Dear Sis,
Things have been real quiet. Getting ready to stand down for 3 nights and no guard duty. Will probably go to Cu Chi for some cigarettes – won't have another chance for 90 days. Unsure what to expect, if I had $200 would go on R&R. I walked over an anti-tank mine. So much stuff to learn, you can't catch it all. Just live and learn. Tell Mom I have a calendar, she won't need to send one. How old is Allen now, I can't recall? Tell Gail to do well in school, she's a girl so she should do better than Allen. How's Kenneth?

****

The altercation began around 10 am as one of the sister platoons engaged the NVA near the rubber plantation. Troop A, who was assigned to convoy duty on MSR near the Ben Cui Plantation was released from convoy duty to reinforce the right flank of Troop C. As the battle continued over the next seven hours, Troop B was released from providing security to fire support base Hampton and moved up on the flank of Troop A while the South Vietnamese Marines reinforced Troop C.

Edy Estel attempted to clear his M2 50 caliber machine gun and return the enemy's fire. He did not realize what had happened as his APC took a 100mm recoilless rifle through its side about the same time as it fell victim to several more RPG hits. As a result, three crewmembers were blown from the backdoor and wounded.

"My God," Alton was speechless as the APC spun and leaped from the ground before sliding to a halt on its side. The three crewmembers who were thrown from the blast were nowhere to be seen. And Estel? Alton fought back the tears. The probability Estel had survived was low. Judging by the stillness of the APC once its momentum ceased, no one else was going to crawl out.

Alton laid down cover fire as platoon medic, Adam Feeney, jumped from track thirteen and darted across the debris field as if he were crossing an interstate highway during rush hour. He moved in and out of the smoke cloud until finally dropping to his knees upon discovering one of the injured crewmen.

"Watch out, Feeney," Alton screamed over the roar of the machine gun discharge and watched the situation go from bad to worse in a matter of seconds. Track seventeen was on fire. Its rear end was opened and flames leaped from the open space, leaving a breadcrumb trail of thick, black smoke that reached up into the sky like a flag. Driver Justin Davenport, who was wounded, and firing back at the enemy attempted to back the burning APC from the kill zone.

Through the smoke and debris, Davenport could not see Feeney or the injured crewman he was attending to on the ground. If APCs came with a horn, it might have helped but it was doubtful. The roar of the machine guns and the discharge of the turrets as the tanks advanced on the enemy seem to absorb all other sounds. Davenport did not even see Feeney on the ground, even as the track rolled over his leg.

Private Seigal was positioned on the back deck of track sixteen with his M60 machine gun in his hands, making his best attempt to take out as many VC as he could. Like Estel, he did not see the RPG as it collided with his gun, and it exploded almost where it was attached to his hand. He died instantly, his body mangled and bleeding near the culvert where his squadron had bathed in the night before.

A second RPG hit track sixteen, the blast knocking Private Altman off the back deck. He flew several hundred yards into the air, his body lifeless and unmoving before disappearing behind a thick dark cloud of debris. It was impossible, Alton screamed to himself, to keep track of everyone, where they had ended up.

And then there was the other new kid, Richards who hailed from South Carolina. A southern gentleman, the others called him, because of his impeccable Southern manners. He talked with a drawl but his was sophisticated, like in the movies at the cinema back home. Richards was the newest member of troop A; it was his first time out in the field. Such a loss, Alton thought about crying but before he could, he realized, it would be pointless. He had no more tears to shed, he was empty.

Seigal and Richards, it pained Alton to say their names. Their arrival to Cu Chi had been more recent but both had fit nicely into the pattern and rituals of this troop. And Estel, his time in Cu Chi was nearly done. Within the next few weeks, he was headed home.

Nearly seven hours, Alton walked briskly through the kill zone, not bothered by the fire that continued to burn or the smoky haze that clung close to the ground as if it were covering the scene. Subconsciously, he considered maybe it would be better if like a bandage, the sore was revealed a little at a time versus yanking it away all at once.

Walter requested assistance with Estel and the other soldiers from troop A who were killed. It was odd in that even in death, Edy Estel had a smile on his face as if he were back home in Northern California, sipping a fine wine with his college buddies and offering advice on which cheese paired best with that particular Merlot.

Alton closed his eyes and hoped the image of his friend's battered and broken body would not haunt him any longer than was necessary. And then, there was the letter, again. It presented itself like a splinter that has scabbed over but is still tender to the touch. Alton knew Estel had written a letter for home in the event of his death and had told him as much.

It was here near the Ben Cui Plantation, Alton decided to write a letter of his own.

Chapter Nineteen

The withdraw from the vast area of the woods into a night defensive position had taken well into the early hours of the morning. The first priority had been to see to their wounded and they were a medic short since Feeney had been injured. The casualties could wait, there was nothing that could be done for them anyway. Their souls were free, in a place without pain, suffering, or gunfire. Luckily, medics from C and B were able to assist and the numerous dustoffs were completed before daybreak.

Removing those who had been killed in action became the next priority as the body bags were laid out on the ground in a line so straight, it seemed as if the soldiers were still standing at attention. Alton had been assigned the taxing task of removing one of the dog tags from the deceased soldier's set around his neck and attaching it through the strap on the outside of the body bag so that identification did not require repeated zipping and unzipping of the bag. It was also Alton's chance to say a final farewell to Estel, as well as Seigal and Richards. And he did so with great remorse.

Alton pushed his tired body to his feet and walked along the line of fallen soldiers to ensure he had not skipped anyone. It was the last thing he would ever do for these brave soldiers who gave the ultimate sacrifice. He needed to make sure he got it right.

Walter stepped up behind him so quietly, Alton almost did not hear him approach. Walter was pale, ashen even with soot and blood stains defacing his jacket. His hand shook as he pulled a nearly spent cigarette from his lips and tossed it away. He came to a stop near Alton and placed his hands on his hips as if his legs could not support the weight of this torso on their own.

"What is it, Walt?" Alton asked, hoping it was something more than the obvious. The squadron had suffered a significant blow and many lives had been lost, even more mangled and crippled in a way that would leave them permanently scarred and broken, like the cook from the kitchen unit this morning who had picked up what he thought was an empty cartridge, only to have the booby trap blow up in his hand. The cook had survived but had lost several fingers on the affected hand. How effective he wondered could a chef without all his fingers be outside of the bubble of Vietnam?

"Colonel Tyrone was one of the casualties," the words flew from Walter's mouth as if he feared he could not get them past his lips.

"From troop B?" Alton asked, craning his head to where many members of troop C were gathered with the heads bowed in prayer.

Walter nodded and reached in his jacket for another cigarette. It seemed like it took forever for him to find his zippo lighter and ignite the end. He inhaled long and hard, closing his eyes as the smoke rushed from his lungs and past his lips.

"So, who's in charge now?" Alton asked, his eyes scanning the area for one of the other officers. No doubt, the VC would be back and soon. The squadron needed to regroup and request support. Otherwise, it would be a massacre this time.

"Lieutenant Crowe," Walter's eyes were tired and red, no doubt irritated from the smoke and his lack of sleep. "He's assumed command until Colonel Gowan can get here. Until then, new intel from the long-range reconnaissance patrol has come in and HQ is assessing." He paused, "Patrol found Altman on the way back."

"You mean his body?" Alton reached behind him for a new plastic body bag.

"No," Walter forced a tired smile across his face. "The patrol encountered him on the way back. He was confused and dazed, wandering behind enemy lines." He shrugged his shoulders as if he wanted to laugh but could not. "Medics are checking him out, he's fine."

"Thank God, he's safe." Alton nodded, wishing he had paid better attention in church and had something more appropriate to say in praise and comfort. Instead, he turned his attention to the recovery. "Is support in route, airships, Huey's, the kitchen sink?" Alton pointed towards the still smoldering APC that Estel had died inside of. "Won't take much to finish us off."

"We've got a carrier nearby with our coordinates and an airstrike at the ready." He tossed his cigarette away and stepped away. "Will be a very different engagement, this time."

Alton turned back towards the deceased soldiers, "I pray so."

****

Despite waiting on pins and needles for what seemed like a lifetime, the VC did not return to the Ben Cui Woods near the rubber plantation. And once the area was cleared, Troop A returned to its business of managing operations along MSR.

"It was cooler than some of the other days since the troop had returned to the field after the holiday celebrations. Alton knew the bunks and belongings of Estel, Seigal, and Richards had been cleared from the barracks in preparation for the new soldiers who had been assigned as their replacements. Jacob Willaby was a seasoned medic from another squadron who had willingly transferred into troop A in exchange for three months knocked off his time in Vietnam. It was a deal, one Alton himself would have accepted if he had any kind of medical training.

Ethan Bark, was a mountain of a man who hailed from New York City and spent almost any free time he had, strumming an old guitar with a string missing. Found it in a trash can at the airport, he had said, smiling so that the white of his teeth was stark and bold against the dark complexion of his skin. His hands were huge, and fit the wheel of the APC perfectly, just as Estel's had.

Lisa Colodny

Kyle Butler had been born and bred in Salt Lake City, Utah but had just completed his first year at the Art Institute in Chicago when he was drafted. His movie star good lucks had certainly made him a hit with the girls in high school and later in college. However, once the army barber shaved off the long, blonde locks of his hair, he looked just like everyone else in troop A. What was unique about him, was his artistic talent as he could in a manner of minutes sketch out a likeness of the local landscape or nearby village. And in the week since arriving to the three-four cavalry, he had sketched nearly everyone who routinely rode in Alton's APC and loved adding depictions of the places from Alton's stories to the collection of photos that decorated Alton's bunk In addition, Butler was among the first of the soldiers to be trained on the new M551 Sheridan tanks.

Barn as envisioned by Private Kyle Butler
Drawing courtesy of Liam O'Brien, great nephew to Alton

As Troop A made its way from the Ben Cui Woods after the firefight with the NVA, they did so without their M48 tanks, as the tanks had been driven to Cu Chi and retired in anticipation of the M551 Sheridan integration. M48 crewmen were given the options of transferring to another track or troop headquarters. Once again, Alton wished he had some specialized training, a cushy assignment at troop HQ to wait out the last few months of his time in Vietnam would have been like a gift!

****

February 14, 1969

Dear Sis,

Received box and sent some stuff in the mail home that you should have received by now. TET will start in a few days and lord only knows what will happen. Be glad when this mess is over. Cook picked up a 79 round, it was a dud but went off. Dusted off 6 guys including a Colonel. Really hurt because they were command leaders with experience and that is what counts over there. A lot of the old guys have left and the remaining few will be leaving soon. Maybe will have to assume JC position – hope not, I don't want that responsibility. Colonel just came down and looked them over. Is David taking leave in March? I sent camera home to keep it safe. When a tank is blown, they can barely get the men out. Everything else burns up inside. Saw a man burn up in one, they put him in a sandbag. How are Gail and Allen doing? I will wear four presidential citations home.

****

It was like a symphony erupted in the Boi Loi Woods as the Tokay Gecko chanted a breathless, "FAA-CUE, FAA Cue," in duet with Blue Eared Barbet bird's deep baritone, "REEE-UP, REEE-UP". A chorus of crickets and tree frogs in perfect cadence making the woods feel and sound more alive than usual. "REEE-UP, FAA-CUE", they chanted in perfect synchrony and Alton snarled at the implication. No thank you, he thought to himself.

The night was warm, and even though there was a slight breeze, it was still humid. Alton could feel rows of sweat dripping down his back and pooling behind his knees. Without the gear he wore, it would still have been warm, too warm. But removing it was not an option, he was the first defense against the VC. It was his responsibility to keep the troop safe as they slept, and he took great pride in that responsibility.

There were streams of moonlight that broke through the clouds and cast eerie shadows between the rows of huge trees that had fallen victim to the Rome plows. It reminded him of bodies rotting on the battlefield. Why did they not repurpose the trees for lumber? Those trees would fetch a fine price back home. Mr. Watson had made a fortune off the timber rights for his spread. And his trees where small compared to these. Not to mention, the sheer number of trees that had been cut down would retire a man many times over.

Behind the fallen trees, a black curtain of jungle hung like a wall whose sole purpose was to keep outsiders on the other side, protect the perimeter from trespass. However, the jungle's veil of darkness had another motive as well, it served as the perfect veil to distort the comings and goings of the NVA. It was as if the ground around Cu Chi had been laid atop a series of complex bunkers and tunnels. They were everywhere, the entrances hidden in plain sight, under rocks and flowering bushes.

Many had been identified and destroyed. Still, others remained. It was impossible to know when and where the enemy might pop out of a bunker and appear above ground. Six feet or six inches, there was no way to predict where the VC might infiltrate the perimeter, his perimeter.

****

It was not a flash of light that caught his eye. Instead, it was more like the lit end of a cigarette. Was the faint odor of smoke simply his mind playing a trick? Had he imaged the smell of cigarettes? Alton did not move a muscle, he could not. He froze in place, his eyes peeled into the darkness, watching for a sign, anything to indicate he was not alone.

Then it happened, the dull snap of a twig under a boot was barely discernible from the cadence of the jungle nightlife. He knew by the way the hairs on the back of his neck stood at attention, he had not imagined it. There was someone else in the woods. Someone who did not want their presence known.

He followed the sound and the cigarette's perfume through the darkness and rested his finger against the trigger, just in case. Alton wanted to call for back-up, alert the troop that he was tracking someone through the jungle. But that was not possible, the intruder was close, not more than seventy-five yards away. They would surely hear his pleas for reinforcement.

Best, he weighed his options, to wait until the target was close enough to guarantee a kill shot. No need to give them a chance to fire a shot off. Even a shot fired as a reflex could weave through the darkness and find its mark.

Two, he watched as the one burning cigarette became two. There were two of them. Alton waited until they were close enough where he could make out their images in the silhouette of the moonlight. They were young, his age, and one was wearing a lighter colored shirt, meaning the other man was probably wearing a dark colored one.

They were close enough so that he could smell the residual scent of fish, their dinner, no doubt. He had eaten fried chicken with several helpings of mashed potatoes. Was that aroma leading them closer to him as they tracked within fifty yards of where he stood in hiding?

The air around him lit up with smoke and fire from his machine gun as Alton aimed at the last place he had seen them and swept the area, spraying it with bullets that fell like rain. There were no other sounds, no return of fire or the sound of bodies falling to the ground.

"Status?" Walter's voice on the radio was frantic. "Reinforcement is in route to your last reported coordinates."

"Copy that," Alton continued to fire, mowing branches from the nearby trees as if they were butter and the bullets, hot knives. When he finally stopped firing, Curtis, Platt, and Bark came crashing to a stop beside him.

"Draw back, two hundred yards and reset perimeter," Walter's words echoed through the jungle, seeping into the spaces between the fallen trees and settling upon the rice paddies like a water lily. "Ky, assume JC until daybreak."

"Copy that," Alton whispered into the receiver wishing he could pretend as if he had not heard Walter's directive. JC, he replayed the words in his head. Junior commander, the soldiers who came in as reinforcements were now under his command until morning when the assignment was over. His mind's eye saw Bailey's mangled body as he had been pulled from track thirteen. He did not want to be responsible for other people. Most times, he did not even like being responsible for himself.

****

As dawn broke over the horizon, a quick search of the area did not reveal any enemy bodies. In fact, other than the tree branches that had been chewed away by Alton's machine gun, nothing seemed out of place. There was a moment of panic when he considered, perhaps he had imagined the encounter with the NVA. It was a side effect brought upon by the trauma and stress of being on the battlefield for nearly thirty straight days.

"There's some blood on the tree over there," Platt explained, trapsing through the tall grass as he made his way closer. "You pinched at least one." He shook his head. "I don't see any drag marks on the ground so he must have walked away."

"Did you see footprints?" Alton asked, squinting his eyes against the morning sun and flipping a spent cigarette away.

Platt shook his head that he did not.

"Tunnels," Alton whispered, reaching for his radio to update Walter. The VC had not just disappeared into thin air. They had to have made their escape down into a nearby tunnel. The area would need to be searched until the tunnels could be located, cleared, and blown, especially if the troop was not called to another destination. Last thing the troop needed was another surprise attack during the night.

One Chicom grenade, one butterfly bomb, four bunkers with fighting positions, trench line, four rice pots, two ponchos, and four punji pits discretely placed nearby, these were the fruits of troop A's labor for the morning. And Alton took great pleasure in being the one to blow the bunkers and wipe away any trace of the VC. He felt nothing, no remorse and no empathy.

****

February 25, 1969

Dear Sis,

TET is here and things are getting hot, but they haven't hit our laager yet. On watch night before last, about 250 meters away, gook was spotted moving. Waited and watched. However, a second gook was spotted, requested follow up as the gooks had spotted me. Waited until the gooks were 75 meters away and opened fire before running back to the laager. I did not see any bodies, just some blood. Can't believe David extended his time for 6 months and respectfully, David hasn't seen what I have seen or he'd been long gone. I made SPEC 4, will have to take over JC position. Lots of new guys now, lots of dustoffs and send back to the world. Tell Gail and Allen to be good.

****

It was one of the largest scale operations to date as Troop A quickly and silently went to full alert after the M551 Sheridans scanned the area and confirmed a large number of NVA advancing towards the squadron's night defensive position. The main gun fired towards the NVA's recoilless rifle crew and engaged the NVA gun position. Seconds later the entire Troop opened fire while the Sheridans fired canister rounds into NVA positions.

The NVA broke ranks and retreated after only fifteen minutes of sustained fire by troop A. To Alton's relief, there was very little fire returned. Wade called out as the last of the VC disappeared into the thicket. "They are running! Do we pursue?"

"Negative," Alton scanned the immediate area. There was a sea of bloody, enemy bodies scattered across the battle scene. It was too much for words, he had none. Upon his arrival, he had been almost sympathetic to the war-torn peoples of Vietnam. Two sides, he remembered hearing himself say. There are two sides to every story and every conflict. His naivety had turned into hatred and anger after Bailey's death. By the time, Estel died, Alton was paralyzed with fear. Now, he was simply numb.

****

Although the mood in the field was celebratory, Alton was not of the same mindset. True, his troop's sweep of the area resulted in over forty enemy casualties including a company and battalion commander, but still it did not feel right. The smell of blood was thick in the air, he fought back the urge to gag. What would the others think if he emptied his stomach, especially after so much time in the field had passed? His troop was celebrating a major victory, why was he not?

In addition to the high kill number, the battle was the first major combat test of the M551 Sheridans and they had performed exemplary. In contrast to the high number of VC casualties, there were only two soldiers with minor wounds. Both Wade and Allen were treated at the scene by the medic, Willaby. All in all, the campaign had gone flawlessly. Why, then, did he feel so badly?

****

March 9, 1969

Dear Sis,
Very late (after pm) will be a short letter. Got the new clip, will have to wait till morning to see it clearly. Sheridan is working well and not too hot. We had major contacts on Jan 8 and again on March 8 with body count of 50. A dustoff is wounded in action (WIA) that needs to be transported out of Cu Chi. Several

of my troop have had to have dustoffs, most have not returned. Some were KIA. I hope there would be no more. Will get a doll for Mom at base camp before I leave here.

Love, Alton.

****

There had not been as many engagements lately and Alton was grateful for the reprieve. He was tired of the bombs, of the blood, and of the killing. He had spent so much time over the last year, praying to find his way back home. It had never occurred to him how different he would be once he was back home in the lush, green hills of Kentucky.

How quickly would the life he left be returned to him? Would it ever really be his again? Might the sounds and anxiety of his time here fighting this war leave him as a mirror image of a man he no longer recognized? Someone he did not know. Could he really go back?

****

"Alton?" a familiar voice called from across the way.

Alton threw his hand up to block the afternoon sun and watched as an outline emerged from behind the Colonel's track. At first, he could not make out the caller's identity but once the soldier was close enough, he smiled and waved. "Ralphy?" Alton's greeting was almost juvenile as the driver for the Colonel drew close enough for an embrace but did not. "What are you doing here? Not much to see, it's pretty quiet now."

"Colonel wanted to rendezvous and catch the last part of the mortar training before we head back," Ralph Mings explained. Because of a shortage of qualified personnel, mortar crews had been filled with other military service men. Each "volunteer" was required to fifteen hours of training. Mings turned his attention across the way to where the gunners were completing live fire exercises.

He waved at Alton's APC, "Your antennae's down?"

"RPG hit the track, jungled us around a bit and snapped the antennae in half," Alton explained. He rolled his shoulder front and back as if her were doing yoga. "Sore as hell, but gratefully, I'll live. Was a good haul, too."

"I heard," Mings finished Alton's thought. "Seven hundred pounds of rice in what appears to be a tunnel being used as a distribution point."

"Yeah," Alton added before Mings could take a breath. "And another forty-one hundred pounds with a rice trail headed east. Long-range reconnaissance patrol is following the trail as we speak."

"Hope it's not a trap," Mings said looking hurriedly back and forth to where his Colonel was exchanging pleasantries with the Lieutenant and other soldiers. "I gotta go," he jumped almost to attention and took large steps away. "You take care and I'll see you when we get home?"

"Not if I see you first," Alton smiled thinking of fireflies trapped in mason jars and sipping iced tea from a wooden chair that sat under Momma's shade tree in front of the house.

Mings did not look back, Alton knew he would not. It was better that way, looking back was a liability. One Alton tested, almost daily.

****

March 14, 1969

Dear Sis,

Ran into Arlin Ming's boy, was glad to see him and he me. He drives my colonel's track, he's in fair shape but he probably won't see any action. Getting ready for a 3 day stand down. All the work is done so will probably just goof off. Went on sweep yesterday, confiscated 700 pounds of rice and 2 gooks in bunkers. Unit came in last night, grateful wet season is coming early. Track was hit, fire flew everywhere, broke our antenna. My joints hurt from the shaking and sitting for so long soaking wet. I know I need to send letters home and will send some during my during stand down. Will definitely write to Momma.

Love, Alton

Chapter Twenty

Alton was at a loss for words, they were back at the Boi Loi Woods. Last time, the fire fight had lasted six and a half hours, and they had lost Estel. Alton did not know the others very well, but he knew Estel and missed him every day.

The commotion from behind the trees startled him and he hoped no one close by saw him jump, saw that he had been startled. Someone was yelling, judging by the Bostonian dialect, it was Platt. Alton broke through the overgrowth to see a young woman flailing on the ground while two other soldiers tried to restrain her.

She was young with long dark, stringy hair, matted with leaves and twigs that hung over her face making her look more like a wild animal than a civilized person. There was little doubt she was a civilian, most evident by the NVA uniform she wore.

"Back up," Walter pushed through the crowd and came to an abrupt stop at the unfolding scene on the ground. "Get her up and secured," Walter barked, stepping closer to the woman. "Get Dau," Walter asked of Alton, referring to the South Vietnamese Lieutenant who was on the scene. "Protocol is, she's turned over to him for interrogation."

"I'll get him," Alton slung his rifle over his shoulder and disappeared back through the bush. His thoughts bounced like a jumping bean from thought to thought. It was like his mind was ice on fire, and with each step, his concern became more frenzied. "A woman," he said his thoughts aloud. "How would an interrogation be conducted on her?" After all, he had witnessed the questioning of NVA soldiers in the past. It was not pretty. Surely, a woman would be treated differently. He prayed so.

****

March 19, 1969

Dear Sis,

Radio went out on the track, unit is staying in for the repair. Planning on catching up on sleep. Stand Down postponed, was supposed to be the 26th of march. Big ceremony planned for the cavalry to celebrate soldiers who received the bronze star or purple heart. I should get an award for making it 6 months (just kidding) and hope I can make it 6 more without any incident. Thinking still about R&R, I need to get away, if I don't get away soon, I fear I'll go crazy. The time away would be great but I would dread having to return. Is David home or did he reenlist? He must be crazy, too to reenlist. We are back to where we were on Jan 17 and fought for 6.5 hours but not going as deep into the Boi Loi woods as before. Little guy is everywhere now and try to overrun us. They were spotted and slaughtered, gook bodies were everywhere. And in the am when you open the rice patty, he comes at you again, he's not afraid of us at all. Don't mind my rambling, it's a mess I know.

Alton

****

Alton reread his letter to Sis, thinking maybe we should discard it and write another one, a gentler, calmer one like the ones he wrote to Momma. But he could not, Sis was his sounding board, the only person he could share what he was feeling with. She had always known what his needs were, even when he was not himself aware.

Growing up, when Momma was sick, it was Sis (and sometimes Delmore) who scrubbed the stains out of his old worn trousers using Momma's old wooden washboard. No doubt, she would have preferred to be somewhere else, with a friend or on a date? More times than not, she was close by, seeing to everyone's needs.

As Written

"Where you guys going?" Alton asked as Wade and Allen jogged by with rifles pressed tight against their chests. He stuffed Sis' letter into an envelope and trailed behind them to see what the ruckus was.

"The Lieutenant asked for volunteers to help the South Vietnamese search for the other four or five males who was working with the female we picked up earlier."

"A Sapper team?" Alton was intrigued, he had heard about these teams who infiltrated the United States and South Vietnamese posts and planted explosive devices.

"Yeah," Wade said, "POWs told Dau, she was part of a group who were assigned to booby trap key positions." Wade stopped abruptly, "Walter asked for three, you want to come along?"

For a split second, Alton nearly nodded his head that he did but hesitated. Instead, he shook his head that he did not want to. He heard his momma's sweet voice in his head. "Don't you volunteer for nothing," she had pleaded. "You keep your hand down and come home to me."

"No," Alton rubbed his jaw and feigned an ache. "My tooth is still bothering me."

"You better get that looked that," Wade added before disappearing from Alton's space. "Be back soon."

"Happy hunting," Alton fell back atop his sleeping bag and reviewed Sis' letter. For now, it would have to suffice. He was no longer in the mood to rewrite it. Instead, he was going to close his eyes and pray sleep came easier tonight than it had in nights past.

The nights went by quicker, if he was able to dream. Some nights, he did, others, he thought, he did not. Then, there was this vast space of uncertainty where he was not sure. He just knew, one minute he was asleep and then, the next minute he was not. It was black and white.

It was the only thing in his life, presently, that was.

****

Lisa Colodny

March 24, 1969

Dear Sis,
Doing okay. Made contact twice more. Eight more days till down time. David must be home by now. Wish I was, tired of fighting and getting shot at. Little man will do it to you simple, you get blown away and they turn you into a MIA, saw it happen many of times. Place is a big game of tag, you either get it or you don't. 90 days since they were at base camp, probably going to cheat me out of time off. Radio is on and there's good music which makes me happy, but it also makes me homesick. Wet season is coming, lord knows I will be glad to see only mud and no dry places. Acting as a track commander, unsure if it will be permanent or not, has many good and bad points. Will try and get Momma a doll before I leave and a jacket for you. The jacket is made from a poncho liner and purchased on the black market from the Gooks. I promise to get you a plain one and send it home before I leave.

****

Ever since the Division resupply convoy was ambushed near the village of Uio Cao, the contact with the NVA along the MSR was heavy. So much so, the long-range reconnaissance patrol was extracted and the troop conducted a reconnaissance in force to pinpoint where to focus the aero rifle's attention.

Alton watched in silent wonder as the helicopter appeared as if from the clouds and aimed its efforts at protecting the convoy who was now under heavy fire. In response, the troop moved east and engaged NVA in the trenches near the wood line where bamboo trees lined up as standing at attention.

His APC maneuvered in perfect synchrony between the convoy and NVA strongholds, providing cover as the convoy passed safely. Alton heard the explosion before he saw the APC in front of his take the hit. He knew it was a solid hit, he could tell by the sound the RPG made as it contacted with the metal of the APC.

He only vaguely remembered hearing Walter from behind as he called for air strike to assault the NVA trench and bunker complex in the wood line. The sky lit up as if a light was switched on somewhere high in the sky as Napalm was dropped on the wood line.

"My God," Alton mouthed the words. He had seen napalm dropped before but never at such a close distance. Its unique odor, a mixture of gasoline and laundry detergent, was pungent as if oxygen in the air had been replaced. He felt the heat as the gelatinous liquid burned and heard the screams and pleas for help from what had been the bamboo tree line. Like the fires, the screams did not last long and once again there was silence as a stillness settled upon the scene.

Ten minutes later, the fires had burned out leaving behind gray clouds of smoke heavily inundated with black ash. "We need a dustoff," he heard Sanford's voice loud and clear as if he were standing at his side. "Black is down," Sanford continued, his voice thick with tears.

Charlie Black, Alton said his name and approached as close to the APC as he could. The medic, Willaby, had already crawled inside to attend to the wounded. Black's time in Vietnam was coming to a close. He, Walter, and Farmer, were among the only ones who had been in the platoon when Alton arrived at Cu Chi. Most everyone else came later. Alton slid down into a sitting position, rifle between his legs, and prayed Black and the others would not be yet more casualties of this war.

Once the smoke settled and the air cleared, forty-two NVA bodies were collected from the bamboo line and five POWs were readied for transport. Three of the soldiers in the APC required a dustoff, two were treated at the scene by Willaby, and one soldier lost his life.

Troop A stood in silence as Black's body was pulled from the APC. There was no rush, no need to prioritize him over the others who were wounded. His earthly presence was gone; his body wrapped in a black, plastic, body bag. Alton watched as Willaby clipped one of Black's dog tags in the bag's loop and secured the zipper for the trip home. It would be a long trip and the last one Charlie Black would make. Alton was sad and envious, and sad, again. And he prayed.

Lisa Colodny

****

It was hard to wrap his mind around the fact that Black was gone. It was even harder on his heart when he discovered, Black was scheduled to leave Cu Chi tomorrow and serve the remainder of his time in a cushy office job where his safety was more or less, guaranteed.

Apparently, it was a public service nightmare (especially for an already unpopular war) to have soldiers die within days of their scheduled reprieve from active battle. Therefore, the protocol was such, Black would have spent the last ninety days of his service in the administration office in Japan.

Three days, it was like being stuck in a haunted house with a ghost that could be exorcised. Black would have been escorted back to Cu Chi to pack for a flight out tomorrow, but tomorrow wouldn't come anytime soon for him. It was too sad to continue to think about. Yet, it sat upon Alton's mind like a splinter. Three days, he heard the words echo across the open field. Three days, there it was again on the edge of the breeze that shook the trees. Three more days and Black would be on his way home.

****

There was little time to mourn as the sweep began again on Highway twenty-six. As they grew closer and linked up with two other platoons for the final leg of trip into Truong Mit, the absence of civilians and animals in the village was suspicious.

With the element of surprise no longer an option, the troops flanked the village and brought a heavy firefight up the middle. Alton had been on foot ever since the troop approached the center of the village. He walked steadily, with the butt of the rifle tucked against his shoulder as if it were a living breathing appendage. They were one, he and the gun, in perfect synchrony and cadence. One unable to function without the other.

Alton focused his eyes forward, sweeping the area immediately in front of him for movement. There was no need to sweep left or right,

Wade scoured to his left, while Williams dusted right. Their pace and rhythm were perfect, as if they were in the middle of an elaborate dance.

"We got a bunker," Alton heard the declaration over the radio, recognizing Platt's Bostonian dialect immediately. From his vantage point, the back of Platt's bucket was barely visible through the cluster of trees that partially hid the rest of his form.

"Hold up," Alton directed, as he came to an abrupt stop behind Platt. "Be on the lookout for snipers, Alton advised as another soldier arrived at the scene. "Curtis, with me." Before Curtis could answer, Alton dropped into the bunker and spun around in a full circle, rifle at the ready for any indication he was not alone.

He waited as Curtis dropped down at his side and turned to cover from behind. Together they walked as one through the bunker until they could undoubtedly ascertain it was empty, almost.

They were nearly to the end of the tunnel when something brushed across Alton's arms. It was the gentlest of a touch and for a moment, Alton thought he had imagined the interaction, until he felt it again but on the other arm and closer to his neck.

"What the heck?" He swatted at his neck, surprised when his free hand came into contact with something damp, and slimy. Something that would normally be slithering along the dirt floor or down the wall of the enemy tunnel. Instead, it was tied at its end to one of the thin wooden rafters overhead. The snake twisted and turned to break free of the binding, but it could not. The VC had seen to that.

"A snake," Alton jumped away, out of the snake's reach and took hurried steps back in the direction that he had come. He hated snakes, always had. Even as a kid, he detested them.

"It's just a snake," Curtis fought back a laugh and followed almost giddily behind Alton. "They're everywhere in Arizona."

"I don't plan on going to Arizona anytime soon." Alton explained, climbing up from the tunnel and practically, leaping atop solid ground.

"Approval granted to blow the tunnel," Walter's words crackled over the radio.

"Allow me," Alton pulled a grenade from his pack and motioned for the others to clear.

"Ky don't like snakes," Curtis explained to Wade and Williams as they moved to a safe distance from the blast zone.

"They put snakes down there?" Wade asked, checking the area again for movement.

"Just one," Curtis laughed.

"Fire in the hole," Alton called out before pulling the pin, dropping it into the open hole, and seeking shelter behind one of the tanks where the others were.

It was as if the ground below opened its mouth and vomited from the inside out. Dirt was thrown some hundred feet or more into the air as if propelled from hell and the dust settled upon the ground like rain. For several seconds, all was quiet as if those around the gaping hole were waiting for the other shoe to fall. And fall it did, center bullseye in the midst of where the soldiers, including Alton, were gathered.

The snake, stunned and angry, slithered excitedly, in one direction and then another, its tail still latched to a segment of the wooden rafter. Alton, jumped back, his rifle at the ready, aiming for the longest portion of the slimy, bucking creature. He fired off two shots, both bullets missing its mark, before pointing to the snake and indicating to the driver of the tank. "John," he indicated again at the ground where the snake was trying frantically to get back into the entrance to the tunnel.

The tank moved quickly to where Alton indicated and made a beeline for the retreating snake as it undulated towards another opening. The track engaged the snake in about the midportion of its long, thick body. It struggled at first, as if it thought it might be able to wiggle free and break away. But the weight of the tank was too much as the snake jerked to a halt, its lifeforce expelled onto the ground like blood. No one moved as the tank backed up and came to a stop. There was silence as one and then another encroached upon the lifeless creature.

"Should have just let it go back into the hole, Ky," Curtis' eyes were sad, like a child whose dog had just passed away. "It wasn't bothering anybody."

As Written

"Was bothering me," Alton pulled his rifle over his shoulder and retreated to the cover of the other vehicles. It had been a long day and an even longer engagement in the field. He was tired, body and mind. And he could not get his friend, Charlie Black, off of his mind. How would Black's family react to learn the only thing standing between Black and a reunion with his family had been those three miserable days? Alton closed his eyes and prayed Black's family would find peace and would not learn about the three days. Once they were made aware, it was likely they would never find any peace. And who could blame them. It was three lousy days.

****

April 2, 1969

Dear Sis,

Starting last 6 months today. Glad to get out, had enough of this fire fight. Regardless of how many you kill, they won't quit coming. As soon as you let up, they come again. Hard to know how many people have been killed this dry season and the VC continues to come on strong. Had 5 fire fights last month alone. Crawled into a spider hole and couldn't believe my eyes. It was a snake about 14 feet long. Threw a grenade into the tunnel and got out but the snake crawled from the tunnel anyway. We had to run over it with the track. Will write more soon, Love Alton

****

It had not taken long at all to uncover the bunker. It had become almost routine, as if there was a giant check-off list somewhere buried in the clouds, Bunker-check, tunnel check-check. What was unique to this bunker was the overhead cover and at least ten fighting positions. Alton and Drew had little more than dropped the grenades into them and stepped away for cover when Williams' voice resonated loud and clear on the radio. "Got like ten punji pits over here."

Alton motioned for Drew to stay with the scattered remnants of the bunker and marched cautiously to the coordinates Williams had provided over the radio. The VC were notorious for traps. It would not be surprising at all to find a trip wire or other booby trap somewhere close by especially if the punji pits were out in plain sight, easily viewable from the ground. It defeated the entire purpose of a punji pit and Alton was instantly suspicious.

"They're recent," Williams explained as Alton drew closer. "Within twenty-four hours I'd say by how fresh the sharpened points are." He stretched his neck to get a better look at the second row of pits almost identical to the first set. "Odd, they didn't even try to hide them?"

"What's the order from JC? I'm assuming we're blowing them?" Alton asked, his gaze dropping to the ground in search for anything out of the ordinary. A twig, a rock, it did not matter, he would know when he saw it.

"No response yet," Wade added stepping out from the cluster of soldiers who stood at the perimeter of the pits. "We inquired twice."

"Watch yourselves," Alton reminded them, spinning around in place to assess who was where. Without an acting commander, things had the opportunity to go badly very quickly. It was then he saw, the reflection of the sunlight off the tiny wire that was wrapped from one small tree to another. The toe of his boot was no more than an eighth of an inch from the wire. He was surprised the vibration of the ground around his boot had not set it off.

"Damn," he stepped over the trap and motioned to the others, "Step back." Gently he stepped closer, pulling the limbs away from the tree, to reveal a grenade with the pin already pulled, held in place simply by the thin wire. No doubt, any motion, even a small amount, of the line would have resulted in the grenade dropping to the ground and exploding. "Request orders once more," he barked. "Then blow the pits and the grenade before returning to the extraction site."

"Where you goin', Ky?" Platt stuttered, his words anxious.

"To the radio in the APC, to get new orders." His response was curt, angry almost. He did not want to set up a laager for the night. Not here in the middle of the evacuated village. No doubt the VC would be back at some point. It was a ticking time bomb, waiting here for them to come back.

The troop needed to retreat and wait for reinforcements and give the VC a lesson they would not soon forget when they did return. Problem was, no one in command was around to give that directive. Where the hell had the JC gone? Was he trying to get them all killed?

****

April 20, 1969

Dear Sis,

Haven't written in a while. Writing during chow. Hitting plenty of booby traps lately, almost stepping on a trip wire. There was no one in charge of the troops on the ground. Told them I was going home to Ky and was not getting my head blown off on account of a bunch of idiots. Can't explain to the new guys that you won't make it home unless you have your stuff together. Only 5 months left and still taking JC every 4 nights. Heat is getting really bad, legs are broke out. Friend from the last dry season shared a dream he had. His dream came true. He dreamed he was being carried by 6 guys in a casket. Last firefight, he got it. He was only three days away from R&R and then he was ETS out of Nam. But he didn't make it – he said he wouldn't make it. On May 19th the shit will fly. A new campaign (not TET) will begin and go on much longer. Death toll is high, fighting is everywhere. Hard to determine how many of my troop have turned in. Seen plenty of dead gooks- don't know what they fight for. Close for now, time is running out.

Alton

****

Troop A in conjunction with troop B while performing a reconnaissance mission, located a group of bunker complexes near the Boi Loi Woods and engaged an unknown size enemy force with organic weapons. The NVA soldiers in the bunkers returned fire with small arms, automatic weapons, & RPG's forcing the troops to move the Sheridan tanks forward and pounded the bunkers with machine gun fire.

"Here come the helicopters," Alton yelled above the chaos of gunfire and watched as the gunships pinned the enemy down. "Pull back", he told Kramer, as the APC retreated to allow artillery and air strikes on the well-fortified bunkers.

The backward motion of the APC had just rolled to a stop when it jerked violently to the right, tossing Alton like a rag doll against the metal frame inside.

"Hit a mine," Kramer winced, holding his head where the helmet had cut a six-inch size cut into his forehead. "Vacate," he screamed as smoke rolled from the rear of the vehicle. "Grab a fire extinguisher, before the gas tank blows."

Alton unbuckled from the seat and grabbed a fire extinguisher from the mounted wall bracket and jumped from the vehicle. Almost at his feet, an explosion threw him some thirty feet, behind several rotting tree trunks.

Bullets whizzed by like rain but thankfully, the trunks provided a good shield. "Kramer," he screamed into the mirage of gunfire. "I'm pinned down."

"Me too," he heard Kramer scream.

Alton tried to see if any of the others had been able to get out of the APC, but his station behind the tree trunk did not allow it. His bucket and rifle were trapped on the other side, every time he tried to reach out for it, bullets rained past.

It was useless, he argued with no one. There was no place to go, he was stuck. All he could do was wait and hope someone in his squad got to him before the VC. There was an ache in his arm and another in his leg. God, he thought, had he been hit? Would it be enough to get him home? Or would they patch him up at the hospital in Da Nang and send him back?

He had so little time left to serve in Vietnam, maybe they would simply find him a safe, administrative assignment to serve out his time.

As Written

Maybe he was dying and did not realize it? Would he know the moment before he drew his last breath? Did he really want to know?

****

The ground shook and the sky fell silent as the gunship lit up the area where the enemy had set down roots. Several minutes passed before Alton heard the crackle of the radio, as clear as if it were next to him in the APC, instead of all the way across the field, where it had been abandoned. Smoke trailed in a wavy, circular pattern, disappearing into the clouds. It looked like a staircase, step by a step, ascending into heaven.

God, he prayed. How much more of this could he take? After every firefight, he asked God to let that be the last one. Yet, his prayers went unanswered. There was always another and he was numb to it all, even his own prayers.

****

May 9, 1969

Dear Sis,

Am taking a day pass sometime this month. Am tired of the field. My old JC is on his way home, sure wish I was in his shoes. In a stand down, will leave in the am for the Boi Loi woods, leaving the Ho Bo woods – glad to be away from the mines. The 25th Infantry has the highest body count in Vietnam and the three-four cavalry, the greatest of the 25th Infantry. And I've seen my share. Last fire fight, I walked up on a bunker complex. A 330-caliber machine gun opened up on us. Cut my elbows and knees, tore my pants, crawling on the ground. Dropped my machine gun and lost my steel pot, they were laying on the other side of a log. Every time I tried to reach over to retrieve them, bullets tossed dust up into my face. I ran away anxiously, shot a hole in my steel pot, will probably keep wearing it for the heck of it. I will never come back here for a second, they can have this place. If wet season ever comes, I can stop fighting, it sure is taking its sweet time. Tell Allen and Gail I said hi and I'll see them in Oct.

****

Alton's troop, along with two other troops, were moving northeast of Go Dau, conducting a reconnaissance and search operation when they engaged an enemy company. It was as if he were watching a movie unfold on the big screen at the cinema in town. There were gunships, artillery and airstrikes. One M551 was destroyed, three cavalrymen were wounded, and twenty-five VC were killed.

He was tired of war movies. Next time, maybe he would see a Disney Movie, instead.

****

Ralph Mings looked okay, which was surprising since Momma had mentioned in one of her letters, how he was having a rough time. She had not said what was weighing so heavy upon his mind, but implied it was something he had seen in the field. God, he thought. If Ralphy had seen only half of what he had, Ralph would probably be sent home in a rubber suit.

It was busy at the fire support base as troops reported for duty and others returned to the field to embark upon the next leg of their assignment. Ralph pointed to a table near the mess hall and placed two bottles of Coca Cola upon the laminate surface before sliding into one of the empty chairs.

"You look tired, Alton," Ralph stated, swallowing a big gulp from the bottle before tapping it back against the table. "This war is gonna make you an old man."

Alton rubbed at the sore place along his jaw, aching from where the tooth had been extracted. He considered agreeing and sharing that his immediate prayer was to get out of Vietnam and grow old and fat on Elkhorn Hill. Instead, he nodded and agreed.

"Heard you were sick, spent some time at Cu Chi infirmary?" Ralph took another drink, his eyes roaming across Alton's face as if they were meeting for the first time.

"Spent a few days on my back, stomach flu or something," Alton answered, gulping his bottle in only a few drinks. "Thought I might get to go home for a few days to interview for a job, but my TC would not let me go."

"They're probably afraid you wouldn't come back." Ralph's attempt at humor fell flat and he struggled to regain his footing. "I mean you're so close to being out of here and all."

"If they wouldn't give me leave to go to Aunt Evie's funeral, I didn't really think they'd let me go for an interview," he smiled an anxious smile. "I tried, though."

"Sorry to hear about your Aunt. How's your momma taking it?" Ralph waved to another soldier who wandered by, his arms ladened down with a tray of cocas and slices of pizza. The soldier paused as if to offer Ralph another drink or slice of pizza, but Ralph's attention was focused back upon Alton.

"Momma said she had been sick for a while and it didn't come as a surprise," Alton explained. "Still, I know she will miss her." He thought again of his brother, Garnet, and how neither Momma nor Daddy spoke much about him. Alton knew it was not because they had accepted his death. More than likely, he knew it just hurt too much to talk about it. It was better to keep it between them.

Alton hesitated for a second, unsure if he should off his condolences to Ralph or not. It was well known that a soldier was killed in his sleep when a mortar round hit the camp. Everyone had scrambled for cover, but the soldier did not or could not get out of the kill zone. Maybe he was stunned, maybe he was wounded. No one could really say anything for sure, except he had been killed.

"I was sorry to hear about your friend," Alton whispered. "I heard you guys were friends."

"Adam was a great guy, the kind who would give you the shirt off his back," Ralph explained. "I was able to escort his body home to his family."

"I guess it made the news better, knowing he wasn't alone on the trip home?"

"I don't think anything can make the news any better. They were devastated." Ralph's voice quivered. "It was my honor to see him home." He needed a moment, and he took it before continuing.

"Will you be at Cu Chi for the Fourth of July celebration?" Ralph asked, his eyes wide behind the black, plastic glasses on his face.

"I will be at Cu Chi but packed and ready to get on a plane home." The words sounded foreign, and his body shook at the implication. Home, he would be getting on a plane and going home, very soon.

"Remember that time, Delmore and Wilbur threw our sneakers over the telephone wire then ran from our house to Mr. Benningfield's?" he smiled. "Wasn't that over Fourth of July celebration in like, sixty-four?"

Alton smiled, a genuine smile, for the first time since he and Ralph had sat down. It was an easy weekend to recall, the boys, still in high school had spent most of the day playing baseball in the field behind Daddy's barn. The air had been thick, with a distant odor of tobacco stalks that hung from the rafters. Daddy had started a fire and they enjoyed roasted hot dogs for dinner and marshmallows for dessert. Alton could not recall why he and Ralph hand removed their shoes, but they had. Just in time for Delmore and Wilbur to stroll by, tie them together at the shoelaces and heave both sets over the wire that ran between the houses.

At least one set still hung in place, a monument to a time that was gone and would not come again. Alton wished the same could be said true about his time in Vietnam.

****

May 16, 1969

Dear Momma and Daddy,
Been in base camp for a few days, been sick to stomach. Had a tooth pulled. Saw Ralphy at the fire support base. Looked okay, sure whatever he wrote home was caused by the VC. But he has a good job, wish I could trade with him. Four months left. I had a good job lined up, but my platoon leader wouldn't let me go even for a while. Could have done like a guy who pulled a gun on his first sergeant. They let him go. It's starting to rain so that means rainy season is here.

As Written

I am sick of Vietnam but that doesn't make time go any faster. So I'll just complain about it instead and hang on a while longer. Sorry to hear about Aunt Evie.

Love Alton.

****

May 16, 1969

Dear Sis,

At base camp, had a tooth pulled. Trying to stall as long as I can. Heading to the Boi Loi woods to work with the Rome Plows. Planning to take a 3 day pass if possible but it is hard to get out of the field. Sorry to hear about Aunt Evie but she was old. As for Lackney coming back, guys who was where he was, wouldn't be coming back. I hope I never get shot at again once I leave here so that means never. My teeth are in bad shape, and they won't let us out of the field for dental appointments. Will have to outthink them and have them fixed as soon as I can. Assume Allen and Gail are out of school and looking forward to a nice, long summer. Be glad when I get back from my leave, then I will finish my tour of service and go back to being a civilian.

Love, Alton.

****

May 18, 1969

Dear Delmore,

At base camp on sick call getting a profile on stomach. Have 8 months in and 135 days left. It's a great feeling but am sad I am not leaving sooner. I feel sorry for a guy who has 10 or 11 months left knowing how many firefights, LP, & AP he will be in, but everybody gets a turn. Won't be too long until I can shower and wear clean clothes whenever I want to. Been here 8 months and haven't received a purple heart yet – so that is good. I did get an army accommodation medal. Will send it to Wilbur and he can show it to the outside family. Don't show it to Mom and Dad 'cause it has a lot of wild stuff in it. Looking forward to fixing my car like I want with stuff (stereo, tires, tapes,) from Woolco. I will be 30 years old before I get a car done like I wanted before I left for Vietnam. Tell Curtis to get

Lisa Colodny

those toys off the steps, Robin to get good grades, what is Misty doing for summer vacation?

Chapter Twenty-One

There was something hypnotic about watching the Rome Plows as they yanked the trees from the ground and dropped them effortlessly upon the ground. It was like watching a house of cards fall, only the cards looked more like Lincoln logs. Was that not what Allen and Robin called those wooden blocks they sometimes played with? Perhaps, he should do some shopping and pick up a few gifts for the kids upon his arrival home. No, he considered, it would be too much to pack and travel with. He had already begun sending things home. All he wanted to keep at Cu Chi was what would fit in his large duffel bag. Everything else would be sent ahead and await his return.

Damn, he remembered, a doll. He had yet to pick up a doll for his momma. Although he could not ever remember her having or admiring a doll, she had asked for one in one of her letters. And Sis had mentioned it at least twice. He would need to make a quick trip into town and get something she would like. Lord knows, she asked for so little, he could afford the expense.

Sanford Jarvis was in good form today, his Rome Plow hit every mark. It was like watching Daddy driving his grater. Both men were experts, but it would take more expertise than either man possessed to mitigate the terrain once the incoming rounds, small arms, and RPG fire erupted from the East side of the perimeter.

Three to four incoming mortar rounds found their mark about ten feet in front of Jarvis' plow, it spun and danced like a jumping bean before finally coming to a rest upon its side. It was a familiar sight as two other soldiers were blown from the rig, their bodies twisted and mangled upon contact with the ground. More rounds frosted them as they crawled for cover to the downed plow.

Alton could not see where the enemy had bedded down, but he could pinpoint where he thought the shots were coming from and he peppered the area as heavily as he could, wincing as the hot metal of spent shells, burned his neck and face.

When the firing finally ceased, there were at least fifteen soldiers wounded, the enemy casualties were unknown as the VC had carried the bodies away, and Stanley Jarvis had been killed in action.

Alton could not find the words, he and Farmer, along with Walter had been at Cu Chi upon Alton's arrival. These men had mentored him and taken him under there wing to ensure his safety, sometimes at the risk of their own.

It was the first time Alton cried; heavy, wet tears shed for a fallen brother. Once the tears started it was like opening the flood gates and he could not stop himself. He was an alcoholic, reaching for another drink.

In his mind's eye, he saw their faces and heard their voices. He cried for Waters, Black, Estel,

and Harold. He cried for them all, even Ralph's friend he had not even known. He dropped to his knees and prayed they had found their eternal peace. There were so many lives lost and families who would never stop mourning. He would never forget them and carry a piece of each with him always. It would be his gift and his curse.

****

June 12, 1969

Dear Sis,

Working with Rome plows in the field. Mortaring started about 2 hours after we got there. Shit is getting old, but it can still get you hurt. A guy who came over with Ralph Mings was killed in his sleep by a mortar that hit 2 – 3 feet away from him. No one woke him up. All my friends will be leaving in Aug and I'll be real short. Will be glad when this stuff is over and I can get out of here. Twelve months is too long Just need to hold on a while longer and get home. Tell Allen I will be there in a few months and Gail to get good grades. Heading to chow. Bye for now.

****

June 15, 1969
Trang Bang, Vietnam

The Viet Cong were dug in deep in fortified positions about four miles North of Trang Bang. Troop A was conducting a reconnaissance-in-force to identify enemy weaknesses. During the sweep to the east a firefight broke out as artillery, air strikes, and helicopter gunships were employed to attack the fortified positions.

The engagement lasted several hours with the enemy replenishing its forces just as quickly as the squadron took them out. But eventually, the enemy ceased to return fire and sound of war diminished as air support pulled out and the artillery rounds ceased. All was quiet as Alton, Walter, Wade, and Platt began the tedious task of clearing the many bunkers.

Alton watched as Williams and Curtis helped Willaby get the six wounded soldiers off the field and transported back to Cu Chi. Although, there were numerous VC bodies littering the field, there were no American casualties. Most of the injuries were mild and could be treated at Cu Chi.

The sun was just beginning its descent from the sky, Alton felt the cool breeze against his face and clutched his rifle firmly in his hand, anxious to settle in for the night and grab a bite to eat. They would set a laager at the fire support base for the night. He hoped the kitchen units would wait for the troops to finish before heading back to camp. That way everyone could enjoy a hot meal.

The ground under his boot was soft, mushy from last night's rain, even though the bunker had been drier. The terrain along the ground was mostly flat, like the rest of the terrain in Vietnam, but there was just the slightest of an incline directly in his path.

Alton's boot made contact with the packed dirt, ignorant to the sniper who lay in wait, camouflaged behind a line of trees upon a ridge across the way. The sniper was young, with dark hair, and a scar that ran from the corner of one eye to tip of his mouth. It took up most of his face but affected his aim only minimally. And the enemy's aim was true, it penetrated through back of Alton's helmet. He fell to the ground, unresponsive and unaware of what had just taken place. There was no flash of light or fast forwarding of past events in his recollections. All was still and peaceful, it was quiet as if a Spring rain was about to fall from the sky. It just was.

Walter dropped to his knees and gathered Alton in his arms to offer aid. But there was no need, there was nothing that could be done for him. He was gone.

The shots that echoed from Wade and Platt's AK 47s were loud, angry even. The trail they left in the sky was impatient as they raced across the field to find their own mark within the sniper's brain. He fell face first over the top of his gun, his body limp like a rag doll.

"Ky," Walter cried, holding Alton's body as tightly as he could. "We got him." He rocked Alton like a baby in his arms, tears falling freely from his face. "We got him."

****

Alton took several steps, in one direction and then back tracked to go the other way. What had happened? Where was everyone? At first, he thought, maybe he had fallen into another bunker. But the air was cooler and smelled sweet, like honeysuckle from the woods near home. There were birds nearby too. He recognized their joyful songs as birds near his home not the tropical ones that inhabited the trees in the jungle.

Then it hit him, he knew what had happened. He could make out the faint images of Walter and the others, hovering over something or someone on the ground. He knew without taking a closer look, Walter was holding someone in his arms, someone who had died. And he knew.

"Where are we?" A dazed voice asked as another figure emerged from the mist. He was young, Vietnamese, with a scar on his face. Alton recognized him as the brother to the young girl who had been killed in the tank accident several months ago. He also knew, the young man was the sniper across the way who had taken the kill shot. The young man's hands shook so noticeably, he clasped them together against his belly to conceal his fear. He licked his lips nervously and shrunk away as Alton drew closer.

Alton knew he should be angry at the man, but he was not. In this place, there was no anger and no pain. There was simply peace, and he was comforted by the thought of what he knew was coming. He waited until the young man was closer before throwing his arm over his shoulder. "Come on," he said to the newcomer as he pulled him closer to the light. "It will be okay."

"Where we going?" the young man tried to pull away but Alton held him tightly in a loving embrace.

Alton pointed towards where the light was at its brightest and a golden gate opened slowly. A young man with features similar to Alton, but more closely resembling Delmore, stepped forward. "To meet my brother. He's waiting for me. He'll help you find your sister."

"My sister?" the young man repeated, his pace quickening to keep pace with Alton.

"Yeah," Alton smiled. "We're both home, now."

Lisa Colodny

Dear Family,

If you are reading this, I was not able to keep my promise. I won't be coming home and I'm sorry. I have no way of knowing when it will happen, just that it has. I want you to know that it was all of you that kept me alive this long. You have been my beacon in the night in this horrible place. My motivation to get back home to you all is all I have had. I hope I made you proud and that in the end my death will have meant something. It is not easy to know that over here, there is so much pain and suffering, death is around every corner here. Know that every time I evaded death, I did it for you because I wanted to come home so badly. I know you will be sad at first, 'cause I will be sad, too, knowing everything I will miss. But don't mourn me for too long. Live life like you are living it for me, cause in a way you are now. Know, too, I will look in on you all from time to time and make sure everyone is safe. You can think of me as your very own guardian angel. Sis – don't let Delmore and Wilbur put that old black Chevy in the barn like Garnet's old car. Make them sell it and buy something nice for themselves. Make sure Delmore eats cookies on the porch with Robin (but don't crush them). And Wilbur needs to finish Daddy's old red truck. I know we were going to do it together but that has changed. Finish it for me. And Daddy – hug Momma for me and build her a big front porch to sit on and watch the birds. And Momma – I loved you most and I'm sorry.

Always, Baby

Chapter Twenty-Two

"You missed a spot," Willard Lee pointed to a small place on Delmore's 53 Chevy, the one Alton drove as his own, and stepped back to admire their handiwork. The news of Alton's death had rocked the small town near Elkhorn Hill. Everyone had been by the house to pay their respects and the cousins had gone to work almost immediately cleaning and preparing his old car for the funeral.

"Think he's okay with us driving it in the processional?" Winfrey asked. Dropping an old rag over the front bumper. "I mean the service is at the funeral home but we gotta pass by here to get to the graveyard. Won't it be weird, driving his car past his house to get to the graveyard?"

"I think he would laugh," Willard Lee answered. "You know so hard, his eyes squinted and probably couldn't see one foot in front of the other?" There was a pause before he went on. "I wish Buck could have gotten a leave and be here to say his goodbyes."

"I'm not gonna say goodbye," Winfrey explained. "I think he would want us to tell him we'll see him later." He picked up the rag and went to wiping on the spot Willard Lee indicated.

"I think you're right, little brother." Willard Lee reached inside the cab and flipped the radio on, stepping back as Hank Williams begin to belt out a country song. "Sometime later when all our chapters have been written."

****

"I can't believe you want to drive that old truck to the homecoming dance." Robin moved in and around Allen's legs as he pulled himself from under the truck and wiped his greasy hands upon a worn and stained rag.

"Uncle Wilbur said If I get it to run, he'd help me with the paint." Allen explained. "The dance is still a month away. I have time."

"Do you remember him?" she asked, sliding down to the ground to sit against the back tire of the old red truck her uncles had planned on refurbishing. "I have two memories," her words were strained as if she were pulling them from a tiny place. "I remember he used to tease me with cookies on the front porch when we lived in Louisville. And I remember going to see him once when he was in basic training." She sighed sadly, "That's it." She paused, her face crinkling as if the act might help her recall. "I have visions of him and Uncle Wilbur when they lived with us in Louisville. I know they had the upstairs rooms for a while but I'm not sure for how long."

She paused before adding, "I remember playing out front in your yard when his funeral procession went by." Her words were horse, as she watched the event unfold again like a movie on a big screen. All the grandchildren were there, playing outside. Janet, being the oldest of Alton's cousins, had been tapped to babysit so that everyone else could attend his funeral. She sat on the high porch, perched so that she could monitor everyone's well-being.

"All of us were playing, bouncing balls and riding bikes, oblivious to what his death really meant." Robin went on, "Then we saw the processional coming down the road. Mom and Dad, Wilbur and Jewel, your Mom and Dad, all in their own cars just driving like they were headed to church, all dressed up in their Sunday attire."

There was a moment when Allen thought she was finished but she went on. "The line of cars took forever to pass by but then we saw Ma and Pap driving just in front of the big, black hearse."

"I remember we all stopped what we were doing, quit playing and stood silently until everyone had passed by," Allen added.

"Then we picked up our toys and went on about our play," she said with tears in her eyes.

"I remember he gave me his hat and I remember he used to pull me around in an old red wagon that we had." Allen wiped his eyes, leaned through the open window into the cab, and pulled the ragged army hat from the glove box. "I still have the hat." He slid it on his head and turned to face her. "He said it would fit one day."

"I wish he'd lived long enough to see you wear it," she offered, pulling herself to her feet.

"Mom still has his jacket," Allen confessed. "He sent it home for safe keeping. He was supposed to get her one, but he didn't get a chance. She has his, covered in plastic and hanging in her closet."

"You ever think about how different our lives might have been had he lived?" Robin paced the ground in front of the truck's door. "He would have come home, married and had kids." Her smile took up her entire face, "we'd have had more cousins to grow up with, to love."

"Ma used to say, his job was done." Allen recited as if he had heard his grandmother repeat it often. And he had, in the years after her son's death, it became her mantra. "Jump in and hit the ignition," he waved toward the cab. "See if the ole' girl turns over."

Robin slid into the cab and engaged the clutch before turning the key. The engine rolled to life. It was not the sound of a cat purring, more like one with asthma, as it choked and coughed with smoke rolling from the exhaust.

"Uncle Wilbur said to get it running and he'd help me get it painted," he laughed. "He did not say it had to be pretty." He tapped his wristwatch, "You better go, gonna be late for your date."

She slid out of the cab, slamming the heavy door with a thud. "Get the other parts you need by the weekend. Mike and I will come by and help you fix up the inside." It was no secret the boy she had been dating for the last year was good with cars. If they worked together and Uncle Wilbur helped with the paint job, the truck might be ready for the homecoming dance.

Lisa Colodny

She stole a glance down to her grandfather's house and waved. Even though she could not see him, she knew his was there, seated at the kitchen table, watching through the window as he had nearly every day since Ma had passed. Before her death, they would sit on the big, front porch and listen to the birds sing. But after he lost her, he preferred to sit at the kitchen table and watch out the window.

It would make him happy to see the old truck leaving the house and descending the hill. And she thought, Uncle Alton would be smiling as well. New chapters penned, some chapters closed, and the stories unfolded as they were written.

As Written

In Loving Memory

Alton Ray Philips
September 1948 – June 1969

Lisa Colodny

Acknowledgements

Many thanks to Mr. Warren Yeagley for his advice and support in writing this book. And for caring about my uncle.

As Written

Extras

Written for Memorial Day 2014
By Warren Yeagley, Sargent A Troop 3/4 Cavalry

Things are tense as we pull off the road, as we head towards the wood line, we lock and load.

Then someone spots something that doesn't look right, now we're in the middle of a long firefight.

In the midst of the battle, you don't ask why, you only pray that you will not die.

Hoping your training's been good enough and praying you've learned all the right stuff.

Knowing your buddy has got your back, just trying to get through another attack.

Soon the artillery shells start to fall, but it seems like they're not helping at all.

Then the gunships appear on the scene, with their shark like teeth they really look mean.

With their guns a blazing their rockets they fire, but the battle goes on and we're starting to tire.

We look up and see jets, they're in attack mode, they swoop down and drop, their entire load.

As the napalm hits the black smoke's arising, then we see them head off into the horizon.

We continue to fire as we fight our way through, smoke has now cleared and the sky's blue again.

Then we break through the wood line and into the open, we all made it through is what we are hoping.

But we lost a few men on that terrible day, with their lives, the price they did pay.

As we think of what this day is for, think of the men who have died in war.

Lisa Colodny

Short Story from an Unpublished work *Portraits*

Brothers

I'm not sure why I am so nervous. After all I've rehearsed this meeting in my mind for over twenty years. Finally, I have found the courage to make it a reality. I've never really thought of myself, as brave. Yet, I'm aware that others probably do. Like my Father and Grandfather, I've made my stand on foreign lands in defense of righteousness or injustice.

Every soldier has something to share once he's no longer a soldier; either in a story or a song; or during therapy. I've been very fortunate; so far I've needed none of those to return back to my life. For the longest time, I haven't really wanted to share much of that part of my life, not with my family or friends, or even with the physicians at the Veteran's Administration. I've stolen glances at the notes they've scribbled unto my medical record as I'm assessed at frequent intervals; phrases like 'well adjusted' and 'no presentations of post-traumatic stress', although welcomed by me, may not represent a truly accurate diagnosis. I think a lot about the men and women I served with when I was overseas; I consider those that didn't come home as well as those that did make it home.

Like a walk down a familiar path, I can't help but think of him, my friend, my best friend. I can't think of my time there without thinking of him, how important he was to me, to all of us. Even after all this time, I still miss him.

He talked of his family often especially when we first arrived in Vietnam. I'd pictured them in my mind even before he'd shared the crumpled photograph, he carried with him. His brothers' faces were all very similar, with age being the distinguishing factor and even that was only fractional. By the end of the first few weeks, I knew the names of all the people in his photograph.

Sometimes in the darkness of those pits it was his stories alone that kept me and the others from the edge of insanity. I, like them, hung unto his every word as he spoke of his older brothers, Wayne and David and his sister, Margarite. He read letters from his parents, Ray and Blanche with such tenderness in his voice; it was evident how much he missed them. Even though we were all so far from home hearing his stories made us feel closer to our own families as if he were a testament to life. His eyes lit up and a smile encompassed his entire face. They seemed to be his beacon in the night. And as the months dragged on, they became mine, too.

Going home was something we didn't talk about much. It was easier to survive if our minds were focused on our task. Thoughts of home tend to cloud the mind and judgment. That will get you killed. It was healthier to take it step by step, day by day, and not consider too far ahead. He wasn't like the rest of us; we seldom actually spoke words of home; didn't want to tempt fate. But he didn't seem to be bothered with superstitious tales; there were times he couldn't get his stories out quickly enough. One of the things I remember the most about the long nights after he was killed was how lonely it was without his stories of home. Even with the sound of gunfire and bombs exploding off in the distance, we were deaf without his stories of hope.

I'd always wanted to contact the Brothers after we were discharged home from Vietnam but somehow, I couldn't find the right words after his death. So many times I've written their numbers down on paper, picked up the phone, and dialed. I could never find the words to begin and some twenty years later, I'm still not sure I know where to begin or what to say; my mouth just can't seem to form the words.

He was a good man but, surely, they know that; was he not their brother? He was a good soldier, but do they really want to hear about that? Being a soldier got him killed; I guess they can decide for themselves when the time comes.

It's important to me for them to know that in a way, he was my brother too. Maybe I did not grow up with him as they had, but the short time we were together was burned as deeply in my soul as their time is branded into theirs. I, like them, will never forget him, what he meant to me. I want to resolve the survivor's guilt that haunts me to this day and this meeting is the first step.

The Brothers seemed jumpy, nervous when I arrived and like myself, unsure of the next move; how to proceed. The questions they asked were similar to those asked by my family when I first got back from Vietnam. I tried to remember as accurately as I could but time had blurred my visions and I was sure I was rambling on and on about things they couldn't possibly understand.

I asked about their family and learned that sadness had called many, many times since his death in Vietnam. The two brothers were all that remained of the family in his photograph. They had changed much from the faces I remembered in the picture. Then again time has touched us all in one way or another. Time has a way of changing us all.

They took me out to the house there on the hill. The one he'd grown up in, the one he spoke of so often. It was just as he'd described, and I felt good that at least one of us was able to lay eyes on it again. I asked to see his grave and my heart lifted when I saw the giant oak tree that hovered protectively over him and his family where they'd been laid to rest. I smiled to the brothers, he talked many times about the oak trees here and he hated the napalm that was everywhere there. This was his kind of place and my load seemed lighter.

I motioned for them to sit down near to the trees, close to where his gravestone loomed proudly by as if eager to participate with us. Anxiously they did as I'd instructed; the older one speaking as if he had a question his mouth couldn't bear to ask. I remember how limited information was back then; everything was so secretive. Information was given out on a need-to know basis only. Unfortunately, the military perceived families of the deceased didn't need to know very much. Therefore, I knew their questions were genuine. They wanted to know how their little brother died and for what purpose. I can't help them with the why but I can shed some light on the how. Maybe that would help us all.

I needed them to understand that I am alive today because of him. He saved my life in the time it took to blink an eye and pull a trigger. Yes, he was a good soldier and a very good shot. More importantly, he was a good person. After giving myself a moment to collect my thoughts, I recounted how he was shot by a sniper. He'd sustained a head wound and the bullet had penetrated his helmet. It had been my hope for them to know that he wasn't alone when he died; he died in my arms. Lastly, I shared with them his death was quick and I thanked God he suffered none. It all happened so fast; I doubted he felt anything. Ironically, I always felt as if I let him down. Maybe I wasn't as good a soldier as he'd been; I hadn't covered his back the way he'd covered mine just minutes before. I don't know, maybe it was just his time. I don't have the answers; no one really does. We live from minute to minute by the grace of God.

****

After his death the troops didn't battle very much. The rains came soon after he was shot, and everyone retreated to the trenches to cease fire and wait the storms out. It rained almost nonstop after that, there was hardly any gunfire exchanged between us and the Vietnamese for a really long time; we were in a holding pattern.

By the time the rain ended, the US had negotiated out of the war and those of us that remained in Vietnam went home. I've always thought that if only he'd managed to stay alive a few more hours, the rains would have started and we would have gone home together. But that wasn't the way fate called it. I guess in this life we never really know. I think we all had a job to do and maybe, his job was over.

As I watched their wet, watery eyes dry as they looked longingly to his grave; I realized my job was finished here, too. Yes, I felt younger than I've felt in years, as if my load has been lightened. I regret it took twenty years to finish my task but I'm not sorry for all that I have felt in this time. I mourn their loss; the bond between brothers is unique. There exists nothing else like it. I know they will never truly be free of the emptiness they feel but maybe now they can put it into perspective just as I have.

I still miss him and not a day goes by am I not reminded of him. Now I feel he is at peace, and I think the brothers are more settled than before. I hope we all find the comfort we seek and with God's help it is never out of our reach. Sometimes we just need a push or a shove in the right

Lisa Colodny

direction. I hope the brothers have found the way, I know he has found his, and I'm on the right road. We can all feel better about it and rest assured we can all be at peace. After all, it is a unique bond that brothers of all kinds share.

About the Author

Lisa Robin Phillips Colodny was born and grew up in the rural countryside of Kentucky. She attended the University of Kentucky and Broward College in Fort Lauderdale and graduated with a Doctorate in Pharmacy from Nova Southeastern University.

Her non-fiction publishing history includes numerous publications in the health and science industry. Other titles currently available by this author include an award-winning children's book, Ms. *Abrams' Everything Garden*, and adult fiction, *The Town Time Forgot,* and *Yellow River Pledge*.

Dr. Colodny currently works in the healthcare industry and resides in South Florida with her daughter and their Labrador retriever, Cooper.

Also by the Author
The Town Time Forgot Series
Turbulence

Crossroads

Terminus

Yesterday, Once More

A Rescue Me Series Novel
Chimera

The Coven Queens Series
Wavering Moon

Journeys

Sanctuary Road

Sultana

Yellow River Pledge

As Written

The Place Where Magic Lives
Into the Woods

Walking the Plank

Promise of Wishing Rock

Illustrated Children's Novels
Ms. Abrams' Everything Garden

Jericho Alley

About the Publisher

Kingston Publishing Company, founded by C.K. Green, is dedicated to provide authors an affordable way to turn their dream into a reality. We publish over 100+ titles annually in multiple formats including print and ebook across all major platforms.

We offer every service you will ever need to take an idea and publish a story. We are here to help authors make it in the industry. We want to provide a positive experience that will keep you coming back to us. Whether you want a traditional publisher who offers all the amenities a publishing company should or an author who prefers to self-publish, but needs additional help – we are here for you.

Now Accepting Manuscripts!
Please send query letter and manuscript to:
submissions@kingstonpublishing.com
Visit our website at www.kingstonpublishing.com

Made in the USA
Columbia, SC
10 April 2022